RUNNING WITH HORSES SERIES 2

BREAKING SAM

i

ii

Breaking Sam

Denise Sager

All Scriptures from English Standard Bible

Most grateful to
Gloria Cone Photography
for my portrait photos,
Monica McFadden for her expertise
in helping me navigate formatting issues,
My Arabian horses and Golden Retrievers for showing
me how much they know about everything,
Neil, my husband for giving me the time
I've needed for writing and
Jesus for His inspiration, guidance
and for giving me these stories
in the 'night watches'

"Brothers, I do not consider
that I have made it on my own.
But one thing I do:
forgetting what lies behind
and straining forward
to what lies ahead,
I press on toward the goal
for the prize of
the upward call of God
in Christ Jesus."
Philippians 3:13 & 14

ONE

Sam West shouldered his duffel bag and bolted through the metal security door barring him from freedom. Any longer, he would gnaw his way free from the prison where he'd spent the last two years trapped like a wolf. He deeply inhaled the sharp air, his breath a stream of vapor under a hunkering gray sky. The door clanged behind him.

Shaking to rid himself of the closed-in smell of the facility, Sam swore as he strode forward to never return there. Across the parking lot his father, Tucker West, waited beside his decade old Ford pick-up. Sam reined in an urge to gallop into Tucker's arms as he had as a child. At age twenty-eight, too many regrets gated the way to even a clap on the back. Still, he quickly closed the gap.

"Let's git." Tucker's creased face showed no emotion beneath the brim of his brown Stetson.

Sam clenched his jaw as he threw his bag in the bed of the truck. What could he say? Sam searched for the right words, coming up empty as he slid onto the western styled seat cover. Time spent pacing his cell while he relived all he'd done to earn his sentence left him angry at himself and the one who'd coerced him. Sam vowed he'd make up for it or die from the effort.

His father grasped the wheel, flexing worn fingers as he drove cautiously through the city. When they reached Highway Ninety-Seven, pines and junipers fenced the two-lane road stretching flat lonesome miles under a darkening sky. Tucker adjusted the truck's heater, the warmth filling the cab with the scent of hay and livestock.

Sam didn't blame Tucker for not talking. While he was locked up, his father ran the ranch alone, a job hard enough for two. There were herds of cattle and horses, fields to be hayed, rotting fence posts and leaking roofs that needed mending, not to mention the staggering weight of unpaid bills . . . his stomach squeezed tighter than a lasso around the neck of a rebellious steer.

He cleared his throat. "About the ranch . . ."

Tucker's quiet words raked like spurs through the gloom sharp and hard as his body. "When I'm dead and gone son, you can do whatever you like. Until then, leave everything alone."

Sam pressed on. "I want to run most of my Quarter Horses and cattle through the auction; use the money for payments."

Tucker grunted. "Do with your stock what you want."

Didn't his father care about the ranch? He sure didn't show it. Worrying over it had driven Sam to poison Tucker's Arabian stallion for the insurance money. When the investigation implicated him in the plot, Sam hid in the Wallowa wilderness. He could've frozen up there in the snow. Another stupid move. No matter how desperate he felt in the future, Sam swore to never again bring shame to the Tersis.

The long ride home threatened to suffocate Sam in the same awkward silence he and Tucker had shared on visiting days. Why his father even bothered to come to the prison was beyond figuring. At their last visit, Tucker mentioned going to a Thanksgiving potluck at some church. The prison staff had cooked up turkey and dressing but it was dry and there wasn't enough gravy to add flavor.

BREAKING SAM

Range land slid by as his father drove. A break in the clouds allowed the last rays of sun to blink behind the Cascades. Sam mentally checked his plan to fix up the ranch. First, he'd gather most of his cattle and run them through the auction sale. He hoped his father would be pleased with the money from the auction going for bills. With winter coming, he'd have to wait for spring to do repairs, which was second on his list. Fixing fences wouldn't cost; they had a pile of posts to replace the rotten ones. Without cattle to work, he'd have time to do it. Meanwhile he would check their wood supply for the stove that heated their home and split more if needed.

Finally, his father turned from the highway onto the ranch, the headlights shining through the wooden arch with the metal hanging sign Sam had cut with a torch in high school shop class to spell TERSIS. He stepped from the cab to open the wide metal gate in the darkness and took a deep breath of sagebrush, juniper and pine. Home.

Tucker drove the through the opening, Sam closed the gate behind the truck and stepped back inside for the last mile.

The clock on the dash read nine. His father parked the truck at the barns and climbed stiffly from the cab. The overhead yard light illuminated the way to the house. Sam slid from his seat. Even in the dark he knew how everything would look come dawn. He'd dreamt of it most every night over the past two years.

His father slowly walked to the house. "See 'ya in the morning," Tucker said over his shoulder.

Sam lifted his duffle bag and followed Tucker inside the single level ranch style house with a covered porch the length of the front. Down a short hall his room was exactly how he'd left it. He undressed, thankful to be wearing his familiar snap button plaid western shirt, jeans and boots again instead of the prison uniform.

A few minutes later he slid under the covers on his bed. His muscles ached as if they were tightly stretched barbwire. Slowly he sagged into his favorite dip in the mattress. He reached up and opened the window above his headboard, welcoming the night chill, relishing the fact that he could open the window and enjoyed the faint whiff of skunk.

The yard light clicked off and darkness settled. Sam slept better in the dark. He hated the cell block lights left on all night. He had missed the quiet. So quiet here he could hear his own heartbeat.

Before drifting off to sleep Sam ticked through his plan again to earn Tucker's respect and most important, forgiveness.

Sam awoke before dawn, quietly dressed and stepped softly down the hall, boots in hand. Tucker sat in his favorite brown tweed chair reading a book by lamplight. A fire flickered behind the glass door of the black cast iron woodstove set on a rock hearth warming the living room. The aroma of coffee wafted from the kitchen.

His father glanced at Sam. "You're up early."

Sam bent to pull on his boot. "Yeah. I'm anxious to get the cattle gathered for the auction this week."

"Well, if you're in a rush, help yourself in there. I'll eat later." Tucker turned his attention back to his book.

"Okay." Sam tugged on his other boot, straightened and clomped into the kitchen, flipping on the overhead light. He poured himself a cup of coffee and shoved two slices of bread into the toaster. "Want coffee? It's ready," he called.

"Sure," Tucker answered.

Sam brought his father the steaming mug and set it on the end table. Tucker was reading a Bible. When did he start doing that? Maybe when his favorite horse died and his son went to prison? Sam retreated to the kitchen, slathered peanut butter on his toast and ate standing at the kitchen sink while the ember horizon glowed outside the window.

He gulped the last of his coffee, rinsed his cup, set it on the drain board and wiped the counter, reluctant to cause his father any work on his behalf. Grabbing his Stetson and wool-lined Wrangler jacket from the horseshoe rack by the door, he strode outside.

Usually the saddle horses were kept penned at the barn. Would his Quarter horse be there? Would Tucker keep him close when it'd be easier to let him out on the range with the herd while Sam was gone? He approached the barns, scanning the pens. His father's flea-bitten gray Arab mare stood munching hay alongside Sam's buckskin gelding. Tucker had already been out to feed.

Sam breathed a sigh of relief and made a mental note to thank his father later. He slid a rope halter on the gelding and tugged the lead. The buckskin grabbed another mouthful of hay before following. Sam quickly saddled his horse and smiled as he swung astride. He was whole again. Now if his cattle hadn't changed their habits, he'd be able to find them without too much trouble.

The rising sun cast long shadows ahead of Sam as he rode. He shuddered. Not from the winds icy whip that brought tears to his eyes, but with the memory of being locked inside, stifled in the circulated air and limited space of his cell.

When he'd been sentenced and first arrived at the facility, he'd worked his anger and frustration out on whoever picked a fight with him. It took a while but finally he listened to his cellmate's advice: if you want an early release play by the rules and earn good behavior. If Sam could run from his past, he'd gallop his horse for as long as it took. He spurred the gelding into a gallop anyway, enjoying the speed and power.

Sam reined his buckskin to a stop on top of the ridge to soak in the views of wide-open range below. Situated on the east side of the Cascades in central Oregon, the ranch had been passed down from the Oregon Trail days in the early 1800's through his father's ancestors. Sam couldn't imagine living anywhere else. He could ride all day and not see it all. Named "Tersis" after the nearest towns of Terrebonne and Sisters, everyone including his father would be impressed when he pulled the ranch out of debt and brought it back to its former glory.

Denise Sager

The wind hissed as it snaked through the rocky outcropping, ruffling the gelding's short black mane. Squeezing his horse forward, Sam skidded his biscuit colored Quarter horse down the slope toward a herd of cattle to drive them to the corrals.

A movement in the junipers caught his attention. Tucker's precious Arabian horses. A small herd of bays, a few grays, one black and one the color of a bright copper penny grazed among the brush.

All his father cared about was his stallion and that crazy sport that wasted the ranch's budget. Tucker lived and breathed Endurance racing. Why would anyone want to ride their horse fifty to one hundred miles in one day? So what if it was an International event? Had his father's priorities changed since his top endurance horse died?

Except for their ages, he and Tucker mirrored each other: sandy blond hair, blue eyes and lean build. They both wore the ranch uniform: wrangler jeans, western shirts, cowboy boots and hats. Sam frowned. That's where their similarities ended 'cause they sure didn't think the same.

His buckskin stiffened, sidestepped. Sam swiveled in his saddle from the horses back to the cattle. A black bull pawed, digging a furrow, a cloud of red dirt carried away by the wind. Sam slapped the lariat against his leg and hollered. "Don't even think about it!"

The bull charged. His horse leapt, twisting mid-air. Sam grabbed for the saddle horn. Missed it. The gelding grunted, bucking hard, kicking at the bull. Sam slipped sideways, losing his stirrups. Not much of anything connected between him and his horse. Sam tried to grab the gelding's black mane. The buckskin stuck his head and neck down out of reach. One last smack of his rear in the saddle flung Sam skyward. The ground rose to meet him in slow motion. Sam crashed into sagebrush. Pungent odor filled his nostrils.

Coughing, he raised up on an elbow in time to see his gelding gallop, stirrups flapping as he disappeared over the rocky ridge. Sam took a quick reflexive glance to see if anyone witnessed his fall, then remembered the mountain of beef that caused his wreck.

The bull lowered his head with a snort. His small black eyes, showing white around the edges locked on Sam. Not good. Sweat trickled down Sam's armpits. Those split hooves could pulverize him. Sam scrambled to his feet, caught his spurs in low growing sage and stumbled sideways.

As the bull gathered himself, a copper flash of a horse slammed into its side. Sam blinked and rubbed his eyes. The mare struck with the speed of a cougar. Her hooves pounded against the bull, her bared teeth raked its hide.

Shaking her off like a meddlesome fly, the bull bellowed as he turned toward Sam. The mare cut him off, leaping between them. Dodging the bull's lunges, she worked close to the ground, gathered in a crouch. She danced, her hooves skimming the dirt as she spun from side to side with the grace of a matador, her tail a sweeping cape. Her long mane lifted and fell as she tossed her head teasing the bully.

Sam stood with his mouth half open as the Arab kept the bull's attention for several minutes, pivoting around her hindquarters.

Panting, the bull turned and jogged back to his herd, black hide slick with sweat, his massive neck and chest splattered with white spittle.

The copper mare flipped her tail over her back with a loud snort, hurling a challenge. The bull lowered his head to graze. She spun and stood, gazing at Sam through her veil of forelock. He swore she winked at him before she loped over the rough terrain, her tail a banner billowing behind her as she rejoined the herd of horses standing with heads raised in his direction.

Sam picked his Stetson from the ground, dusted it off and wiped his face on his sleeve before setting it firmly back on his head. This was too much. He'd seen good cutting horses, the very best during his rodeo days. Not one of them could equal the performance he just witnessed. He lifted his lariat from the brush where he'd dropped it, coiling the loops.

His shoulders slumped, his leather chaps flapped as he struggled up the rocky hillside. He hated Arabian horses. They looked ridiculous with their dolphin-shaped profiles, pop-eyes and tails stuck up in the air. Sam and his friends used to snicker whenever someone showed up at a rodeo on one of those crazy Arabs. They had a reputation for endurance; must've been why Tucker raised them.

Sam cussed himself for being out of shape and sat on a rock at the top to catch his breath. If he'd been riding every day as he used to, he wouldn't have been thrown. He replayed the mare's stunt in his mind. She could cut alright.

Cutting: now that was a real sport, the cowboy way of life. He sighed. To own a great cutting horse was his goal; a necessary trait for a horse on a working cattle ranch. Quarter Horses were built for it with their powerful hindquarters bulging with muscle, a true American breed started down in Texas from Spanish Mustangs. Every day for the last two years Sam had anticipated being in the saddle again. He missed the smell and squeak of leather as he rode herd on his gelding. Well, he wasn't riding now. His gelding was nowhere in sight.

He rose from the rock, tugged a round tin of chewing tobacco from his rear pocket and tucked a pinch of chew in his mouth. Slapping his lariat on his thigh, he decided his father probably wasn't going to rescue him.

No sense wasting any more time. Sam trudged the miles back to the barns, his spurs clinking with each step: great, start. Great, start.

Two

Sam's legs wobbled like a newborn calf's by the time he approached the barn, the sun well into the sky. His buckskin gelding stood dozing next to the water trough at the corral gate, reins dangling to the ground, one hind leg cocked, resting on the toe of his hoof. Tucker along with the farm truck was gone, which explained why his father hadn't come looking for him. The buckskin must've been standing there for quite a while. Just as well. No one needed to know he'd been bucked off first day home.

After inspecting his saddle, satisfied that it survived the mad dash home, Sam tugged off his cowhide gloves, turned on the hose, wet his face and quenched his thirst. He had an urge to kick his horse in the belly for dumping him as he mounted and loped the buckskin back to the cattle.

This time he concentrated on the herd, keeping an eye on the bull. His horse worked up a foamy lather on its neck running back and forth after cows trying to turn back to their grazing, holding the cattle tightly bunched and moving in the direction of the corrals. Dust rose as the day warmed without the early morning wind. Thankfully, the bull seemed more anxious about his cows than giving Sam any more trouble.

As he approached the corrals, he pushed the cattle to a jog and ran them through the gate, dismounted and swung it shut. The cattle gathered around the round metal stock water tank, butting each other for a spot to drink.

By the sun's position over the Cascades, Sam figured he had about two hours or so of light. He watered his gelding and tied him to the pen's gate post. Inside the house he wolfed down a slab of beef on bread, slugged a can of beer and rode out again on his buckskin, determined to bring in his horses before dark.

The pasture he kept them in would be pretty grazed down by this time of year so the horses shouldn't give him any trouble herding them to the barns where they knew there would be feed. To add extra incentive, he'd filled the long wooden feed rack with flakes of hay, peeling them from cut bales of hay like slices from a loaf of bread. Sam bumped his tired gelding to a jog.

There was just enough light left of the day to make out the barns as Sam walked his horses to the corral gate. He didn't want any of them spooking. Sure enough, the horses trotted in willingly, lining up side by side at the hay rack. At least one thing had gone right. He unsaddled his gelding and turned him back in the smaller corral with Tucker's mare, then tossed several flakes of hay into the feeder for them.

A light shone in the house. He strode toward it in the evening chill, a hot shower beckoning. Inside, Tucker stood at the stove stirring a pot of chili, the tangy smell of beef and beans a welcome end to his work.

"Long day." His father gazed at him.

Sam glanced down at his dust covered clothes. "It was."

"Did you get done what you wanted?" Tucker spooned chili into a bowl.

"Got 'er done." Sam sniffed. His stomach growled.

"Help yourself. There's plenty," Tucker said. "Since it was getting late, I figured I'd hook the charger on your truck battery. Didn't think you'd mind. You'll probably want to fire it up tomorrow."

"Oh man. I forgot about that. Thanks, Dad." He'd hesitated saying "Dad," but noticed his father's face soften as he said it. "Thanks for taking care of my horse, too. I've fed for the night." How he wished things could go back between them, back to when they could talk and wondered if his father felt the same way.

Refreshed after his shower, he spooned a bowl of chili for himself and sat with his father at the formica table in the kitchen, the Cascades a dark silhouette against the fading sunset outside the picture window. Tucker was finishing his chili, but Sam was glad when he lingered.

"Think I can get some cattle trucks out on short notice?" Sam hoped he could afford the transport.

"Might happen," his father spread butter on a chunk of bread. "You can pay from the ranch account and reimburse it after the auction. What about your horses?"

"I'm selling all of them except my gelding and best mare." He ate a spoonful of chili. "The auction yard is close enough; I figure maybe four trips with the stock trailer." Sam wolfed down his chili, thankful for the loan his father offered.

How could his father be so decent after what he'd done? Sam deserved to be cussed out big time. He hoped the past wouldn't sit between them like a cloud so dark no light could ever shine through.

Sam cracked a half dozen eggs into the hot skillet where he'd just retrieved the same amount of bacon. Biscuits from a tube stayed warm in the oven.

"You hungry?" He yelled out the door to his father. "Come and get it."

Tucker shuffled in with an armload of split wood. "Any more coffee?"

"Yeah." Sam checked the eggs, slid them onto plates with the bacon, and pulled the biscuits from the oven while Tucker fed the woodstove.

Tucker took his plate, filled his mug with coffee, sat and bowed his head.

Sam popped a biscuit into his mouth, pausing mid-bite. Was his father praying? What about? Wondering if he could ever trust his son again? Sam chafed at proving that he had learned his lesson; that he could be counted on.

A moment later, his father spoke. "Any stock you're keeping can run with my herd. It'll make it easier when the snow comes to feed them at the barns."

"Good idea," Sam mumbled. He wolfed breakfast, anxious to get to work.

A short time later he saddled his gelding and rode into the cattle pen. The cows bellowed and dust rose as he eased the mature cattle through a chute into the loading pen, holding back the heifers he'd decided to keep.

Sam rode his horse to the gate, leaned over and slid the latch, bumping his buckskin to side-step it open, step outside the pen while Sam kept his hand on the gate and side-step it shut again.

He repeated the process at the horse corral and rode inside. Working through his herd, Sam shook out his rope and tossed it over the head of his best mare. At the gate, he dismounted and led both horses through. After unsaddling his gelding, he turned both horses in with Tucker's mare.

Taking a pinch of chew, he strode back to the horse pen and watched as the herd settled down. He'd tried hard in the past to build up a good herd of working ranch horses, but it was time to cut losses. Sam turned and gazed at the cattle. Hopefully both herds would bring enough cash to take pressure off the bills for a while.

Sam strode inside, called the auction yard and arranged for the cattle trucks to come that afternoon just in time for the monthly auction the next day, thankful that part of his plan worked out despite the short notice.

Back at the barn, he unclamped the battery charger cable from his truck, fired it up and backed it to the fifth-wheel stock trailer to hitch it, then backed it to the horse corral's loading gate. Sam flapped his lariat and several horses loaded up without too much fuss. The auction yards were thirty minutes away. If he didn't waste time, he could get all the horses moved by lunch.

At the auction yard he filled out the paper work, unloaded his horses into an empty corral and sped home to repeat the process three more times. Finally, all his herd was settled together into a pen to be sold. He slapped his Stetson against his leg to shake off dust and headed home.

Sam had barely finished a bowl of warmed left-over chili when the semi cattle trucks rumbled into the ranch yard, taking turns backing to the wooden chute. The cattle loading went slick as fresh cow pies, cows lowing for the heifers left behind, the heifers replying. He shook hands with the drivers and was left with a
receipt.

The following morning Sam sat near the back entrance to the wooden stands built around the arena as the auctioneer's sing-song chant blared from loud speakers. A bellowing Hereford bull stood in the ring. The huge old barn quickly filled with ranchers as the facility would auction stock from several counties.

Sam glanced around, glad he didn't recognize anyone so he could concentrate on his plan. Time to 'cowboy up,' never mind about anyone's opinion of his past. He studied the program, looking for his lot numbers as the hammer fell, the bull sold and the ring filled with cattle, the pungent smell of manure filling the arena.

By lunch time all the cattle were sold. Most folks headed for the outside concession booths for the break. Sam drifted into line for bar-b-que. Avoiding groups eating at picnic tables, he slipped back to his spot in the stands to chow down his sandwich as individual horses were either led or ridden into the ring and auctioned.

A cowboy on a sorrel reining horse showed off his horse as it spun on its haunches, driving the bids higher as the crowd hooted. The bald-faced gelding worked clean and fast, but much as he hated to admit it, the copper mare's performance would've easily outdone it.

As the bidding on the horse began, Sam caught Russell Miller leaning on the rail, scowling in his direction, Russ's stocky build unmistakable in his trademark black leather vest. They'd grown up together as neighbors but never been friends. Trouble stuck on Russ like a tick on a dog. Sam spit his chew, his mood gone sour.

By late afternoon, all Sam's horses sold. He rose and headed for the auctioneer's booth to collect his earnings. His Quarter Horses brought average money. Their bloodlines were good but none carried enough cow sense to make them great. The cattle sold by weight. He would miss riding out on the ranch looking over his herd but someday he'd build it all back with quality registered stock. As the long shadows slid over the auction yard, he tucked a nice sized check in his wallet. Sam fired up his truck, determined to celebrate and forget about Russell, hoping the bully forgot about him as well.

BREAKING SAM

Sam spat out his chew in the gutter. The neon signs plugging Coors beckoned in the early evening. Familiar smells of stale cigarette smoke, grimy bodies and beer greeted him like old friends at the door of the Brown Bear Bar. He found an empty stool at the far end of the counter and sat as 'Stand by Your Man' played on the jukebox.

"Hey, you got out; huh." Griz plunked a brown bottle of beer on the counter, his huge chest straining against the snaps of his Pendleton. Several customers stared at Sam.

He unclenched his fists. No need to get upset. He ignored them and took a long swallow, relishing the dark brew. "That's right. Keep 'em coming," Sam said, tossing a twenty on the bar. Between sips he glanced around, not seeing anyone from the old bunch in the crowd. Really glad Russell wasn't there. He didn't feel like answering a lot of stupid questions about prison.

Sam swallowed the last gulp from the bottle and nodded as Griz set another beer before him and traced the beads of moisture down the bottle with his finger. While in prison, he passed time studying every Quarter Horse Journal and cutting horse magazine he could subscribe to. The different farms featured listed their stallion's bloodlines, their get and their show records, along with photos showing off their spreads of huge red barns, white board fencing and covered arenas.

Sam planned to breed his mare to a top stud and produce the next world champion. The biggest problem was the amount of time before he'd know if the gamble paid off. A year waiting for the foal, then two years before he could break it to saddle . . . he rubbed his eyes.

How could he make it happen now? The image of the copper mare winking at him came to mind. Whoa; that horse was something. She could win open cutting contests, help build his reputation as a trainer. An Arabian . . . How ironic after what he'd done. Sam cussed under his breath. He would be the laughingstock of all the state. No cowboy in his right mind rode anything but a Quarter Horse.

He swallowed another gulp of beer and asked himself: what was more important; money or pride? Would Tucker even let him use the mare after what he'd done? He considered drowning his past in beer.

A brunette smiled as she sat a few stools down from him at the bar. He couldn't remember the last time he'd gone out. That was something else he wanted. A wife. But who'd be interested in an ex-con? Forget it for now; the ranch had to come first.

His head cloudy and light, he stood as an urge drove him to the men's room where he decided to leave while he still could. Getting drunk wouldn't help him think or plan. He needed to gag down some grub and drink some coffee.

As Sam made his way through the loud music and crowd to the door, Griz shouted. "You got more comin'!"

Sam tipped his Stetson. "I'll be back."

Outside he buttoned his wool lined Wrangler jacket and tugged on leather gloves to scrape the ice forming on the windshield of his battered truck. He stepped inside to the driver's seat, and let the truck idle a minute while he turned the heater-defroster on high.

Somehow in the darkness he got turned around as he drove and ended up on side streets. Sam meant to go out to the main highway to the twenty-four hour restaurant. His headlights lit a familiar sign: High Desert Christian Fellowship. He drove past a packed parking lot in front of the typical white small town church complete with a steeple.

Lights blazed from the windows. Tucker's farm truck sat parked across the street. That's right; Tucker had said something about going to church tonight.

Sam's truck coughed several times and quit. Cursing loudly, he guided it with just enough momentum to the curb. The fuel gage read "E." He thumped his fist on the wheel. Stupid! How'd he forget?

Russ. Sam had got sidetracked after the auction wandering through the stock corrals in order to avoid running into his neighbor who lingered near the auction barn's exit. The only fuel station open now was three miles away. No way would he ask his father for help. Maybe he knew someone else in there.

Sam crept around the cars and trucks in the dimly lit parking lot to the double front doors. One side was propped half open, spilling light. He heard a woman singing. If he could describe the voice of an angel, this would be it. He sidled next to the door as the voice sang, "He has healed the broken hearted, opened wide the prison doors, He is able to deliver evermore."

Shivering, Sam shifted his feet. The tugging on his heart confused him. He wanted to leave but the song held him. Soft, gradually growing stronger, the voice rose to heaven. He slid off his hat and stole a look around the corner.

On the stage sat a vision with a halo of golden curls cascading around a familiar face at the piano. Jessica Rivers. Was she always that talented? He didn't know she could play the piano. They'd played together during recess in grade school. In high school she joined choir, was a cheerleader, while he went for 4H, FFA and junior rodeo. Sam ducked back behind the door. Did she see him?

He jogged back to his truck, bouncing off vehicles in his rush. Just in time. Folks trickled from the church, waving their good-byes and hugging each other. You'd think they were all related, the way they acted. In the cab, Sam slid down on the bench seat and covered his face with his Stetson, hoping to escape notice, especially by his father. He'd hoof it to the station after the place emptied.

Someone tapped on his window. He lifted his hat.

Jessie grinned through the glass. "You plan to sleep here all night?"

17

THREE

Sam groaned. Wished he could disappear and start the whole evening over. Facing Tucker would've been bad, but this was even more embarrassing.

Jessie opened the door, the cab light blinking on as she slid onto the passenger side. "If you wanted to catch your Dad, it's too late. He just pulled out." She shut the door and they sat in the dark.

She smelled like musky baby powder ---fresh and sexy. Whoa; not the way she sang. Passionate, yes; seductive, no. On that stage, she was radiant while he felt lower than dirt.

Jessie punched his arm. "Cat got your tongue? What's the matter?"

"Forgot to get gas after the auction." Sam sighed as he straightened, keeping his eyes forward. "I can't believe the truck quit here! I turned right back there. The Chuckwagon is left; I knew that."

"Mmm. Sounds good; a piece of peach pie would hit the spot right now." Jessie's giggles bubbled into laughter. "Sorry; I'm not laughing at you. It's just that the Lord's got such a great sense of humor." She tugged a tissue from her jeans pocket and dabbed her eyes. "C'mon. I've got a can of gas. We'll get you going, then you can buy me dessert."

He trailed after her in a daze to a vintage green Toyota Land Cruiser, her jeans tucked into knee high leather boots. She unlocked the padlock on the bracket holding a five-gallon can to the rear of her vehicle.

Sam shook his head. Incredible. "Thanks," he mumbled as he lugged it back to his truck. He hoped it wasn't too obvious that he'd been drinking. Coffee would clear his head and allow him to hold a decent conversation.

"The auction? Were you selling or buying?" Jessie asked as he poured the gas into his tank.

"Sold my stock." He glanced at her.

"Oh." Jessie paused. "Remember high school? Boy did we get in trouble the time I stood guard outside the boy's room when you and Matt slimed the toilets."

Sam shook his head. "We did some stupid stuff; but the times camping out as kids were great."

"I always thought we'd all stick together," she said wistfully.

Sam considered Matt Hunter his best friend. They'd been terrors together through high school and later on the rodeo circuit. Sam had lost touch when Matt went pro rodeo. "Wonder what Matt's doing now," Sam mused as the last of the gas ran into his tank.

"Probably locking the church." Jessie spun the cap on the can after Sam set it down.

"What?" Sam sputtered as he carried the can back to her rig.

"'Bout the time you holed up in the Wallowas, Matt enrolled in Bible school." Jessie locked the bracket back in place over the can. "He's the church pastor now."

Sam peered at her in the faint light from the church porch. They were the last ones in the lot. "You're kidding."

"Nope." She swung into her Cruiser, fired the engine and the headlights. "Last one to the Chuckwagon is a rotten egg."

"No fair," Sam yelled. He skittered to his truck. His head spun while following her to the restaurant. Matt a preacher? Couldn't be. Was she dating Matt? A jab of jealousy hit for the first time since word came that Sierra and Ben had married.

Sierra: slim and feisty with her wild mane of auburn hair. He'd been drawn to her from the first day she moved into the mobile home kept for ranch hands on the Tersis. She'd soaked up his father's ways with horses and love of endurance racing like the desert thirsts for rain. She took his place in Tucker's heart. He'd almost killed her along with his father's stallion.

The scene was etched forever in his mind: Tucker parking the empty stock trailer at the barn, Sierra sliding from the cab covered with dirt and blood. Bile rose in his throat at the memory. Tucker relating how Ranger had stumbled and crashed with Sierra while at a full gallop in the endurance race. Right then he knew just how low he'd gone.

Jessie parked in front of the Chuckwagon. Sam pulled in next to her. He opened the door to the restaurant to let her in first to warmth and light. They found an empty booth. Sam set his Stetson on the seat beside him and held out his cup for coffee. "Want some?"

"Please. It's freezing out there." Jessica rubbed her hands.

The waitress hurried over, coffeepot in hand. Sam ordered eggs, potatoes, ham, and biscuits with gravy. Jessie wavered a moment between peach and blackberry pie a-la-mode. Ordered peach.

Sam didn't trust himself until he gulped all of his coffee and signaled for more. "Do you always carry extra gas? How far from town do you live now?"

Jessie shrugged out of her wool coat, the muted greens, golds and purple of the Indian blanket pattern looked great on her. "I need gas for my work. I live in the cabin overlooking the Crooked River on my folk's ranch." She thanked the waitress as their food arrived.

He almost dropped his fork when she reached across, grabbed his hand and said, "Let's pray first." He glanced around; conversations from other tables hummed and silverware clinked.

"Thank You, Jesus, for this food and for bringing us here together this evening. Amen."

His ears burned. Why, she prayed as if Jesus Himself was right there, a person she knew. He cleared his throat as she gave his hand a brief squeeze before letting go. "You think He brought us here?"

"Without a doubt. You think it was a coincidence your truck stopped in front of the church and that I was there with gas?" Jessie tasted her pie. "Anyway, the Lord's been blessing me, allowing me to do what I love, getting recognition as a western artist. Stop by the Great Western Bank sometime. The painting of Smith Rock in the lobby is one of mine."

She paused, tilting her head, staring at him. "You alright? You look a little green. Anyway, I drive in remote mountains a lot, shooting photos of wildlife and ranches. If they turn out they get marketed; otherwise I use them as reference for my artwork."

Sam washed down a bite of biscuit with coffee. He felt better, more alert as his stomach settled. "I'll look for your painting when I stop by the bank," he told her.

Emotions stirred as his arm tingled from her warm gentle touch. He imagined how she might feel in his arms. Whew; where'd that thought come from? All those years in school that he'd known her, he'd only thought of her as a tom-boy that hung around him and Matt.

"Since when did you get so religious?" He blurted. Now why did he say that?

Jessie laughed, a bright happy sound. "Hey, Sam, didn't we sit together in church as kids?"

"Yeah, well. Never meant much to me. After Mom left, Dad and me quit going." He dug into his home fries, trying to think of a way to divert the conversation.

"Your Dad's been at every service since your trouble," she said softly.

"That's Sierra's fault," Sam said. Usually, he made small talk and flirted, keeping his inner thoughts to himself. What was wrong with him?

Jessie must've sensed it. "I met Sierra last fall when she came out to the harvest potluck with Tucker. I like her."

He didn't want to talk about Sierra, either. He watched Jessie nibble her piecrust. Here was his chance to know what others were thinking about him. "Guess everyone knows all the sordid details by now."

Jessie nodded as the waitress stopped by, cleared dishes and refilled coffee. "I know that you wanted to help your Dad. You thought you had a better plan for the ranch. Sierra believes you were conned, just a pawn of her father's partner -what was his name? Robert. He murdered her father; tried to kill her, too, so that he could have the insurance company to himself." Jessie folded her hands on the table. "She knows you didn't intend to harm her. I mean, who'd know the exact moment Tucker's stallion would die?"

Sam interrupted. "She was riding Ranger in that endurance race when he went down. I figured the stud would drop in his pasture. I kept feeding him the stuff. He kept living. Don't know what I'd done if she'd been hurt." Sam shuddered as he recalled the panic that had seized him.

The crazy part was that Sierra was rich. Back then she lived in that dumpy single wide mobile on their ranch and nobody had a clue. Just so she could be around his father and ride the races. Sierra believed his father possessed a rare gift with horses; was a horse whisperer.

"Hey." Jessie tapped his forearm. He met her gaze. "Sierra doesn't hold anything against you. As far as everyone around here is concerned, you've done your time. And if you'd accept it, the Lord has forgiven you. Tucker, as well."

Sam curled his hands around his warm cup. "My Dad? Uh-uh. Did you know he ended up with the insurance money after all? Did he use it on the ranch? I don't think so. We're about to go under, Jessie. Who knows what he did with the payoff." He clenched his jaw.

"I know." She peered at their reflections in the window. "Your Dad hired the best lawyer he could find. It cost him most of it to defend you."

Sam cussed. He looked past their reflections into the darkness, then hung his head, elbow on the table, hand shielding his eyes. He didn't mean to say that word in front of her but this stuff about the lawyer was news to him. Here he was, pouring out his guts again.

What he really wanted was to be able to go back in time and start over. Before he listened to Stevens.

Jessie's gentle voice soothed, as if she was speaking to some wild colt. "Sam. I worry about your Dad. Have you looked at him lately? I mean really looked? Talk to him, get all this resolved. I'm sure he's forgiven you. And you need to forgive yourself so you can get on with your life."

He glanced at her. How did she know so much? "I can't believe he's forgiven me. I want him to, someday. But I'll never forgive myself."

FOUR

As Sam drove home to Tersis, his thoughts lingered on Jessica, the way her hair glowed like sun-ripened wheat around her shoulders framing her ocean colored eyes, her small hand touching his. Gas! He thumped the wheel with his fist. He should've given her money to have her gas can filled. Boy, what a great impression he must've made. Some friend he was when she freely gave her gasoline and time . . . in spite of his past.

He stopped at the front gate, got out and opened it. Drove through, got out again to close it. Because of Tucker's Arabs, they didn't have a cattle guard, the metal grate set in the ground like everyone else around. When his father's stallion, Ranger, was a yearling, he figured out how to walk the edge of the guard and escape. Tucker hooked a wire across the guard to stop the colt. Ranger simply ducked under it and got out anyway. So they yanked out the guard, and put in the gate. What a hassle. Even with Ranger dead, it didn't matter. All Tucker's Arabs learned the trick from the colt. They went wherever they wanted within the ranch, crossing guards from field to field. At least his cattle and Quarter Horses stayed where he put them.

The beer and coffee threatened to leave ready or not so he stood there in the frozen darkness a minute more, listening to a pack of coyotes hollering and yapping off in the distance.

Matt, a pastor? Sam cussed out loud. Well, he'd run into Matt someday and ask him what happened to him. Right now he'd avoid the old bunch. How could he face them? He'd get the ranch going first. He'd show them all how hard he worked to make up for his mistakes.

Sam drove the mile long driveway, his headlights catching a dozen mule deer bedded down under a stand of pine trees. Next fall, one of them would go into the freezer. He stopped at the ranch's fuel tanks near the tall pole with the yard light, stepped out and with the illumination found a five gallon can and set it in the pick-up bed to remind him in the morning that he owed Jessie.

The hay barn loomed over him as he walked past it to the house. With most the stock gone, they had tons more feed than they needed for Tucker's Arabs and his two horses and calves. At the auction he overheard talk of what a poor hay year it'd been. They could sell it now and earn much needed cash.

Tomorrow he'd talk to his father about the hay, the copper mare and what repairs he should start first. Sam loaded an armful of split wood from the front porch and made his way inside to the black wood stove. He'd missed wood heat, the way the warmth penetrated to his bones. The cast iron door creaked as he opened it and sitting on his haunches, shoved the wood in on the coals. Sam closed his eyes as the wood caught fire, the light and warmth comforting him.

Sam woke before dawn and started coffee. He didn't want eggs again. A package of donuts looked better. How could he mention the copper mare? He'd feel like a fool if he told the story.

Tucker shuffled into the kitchen, stuffing his plaid wool shirttails into his jeans, his thin hair sticking out with static. "You look terrible," he told Sam.

Sam glanced down at his favorite worn and stained grey thermal Henley and shrugged. "You should check the mirror."

They sat at the table with their coffee and donuts. Have you looked at your father, Jessie had said. Tucker sat staring out the picture window, hunched over his cup as the first light shimmered on the snowy peaks of the Cascades. He'd always been straight as a T-post. His sandy blond hair was now mostly gray. His hand trembled a bit as he raised his mug to his lips. Tucker had always been lean, but this man looked little more than a skeleton. When did all this happen?

Sam admired his father as a pre-teen. Real close back then, they did everything together. The fact that his father rode his Arabs in one day hundred mile races and could stay in the saddle all those hours awed Sam although he never admitted it. When younger, he'd often crewed for Tucker as they camped in remote locations, fetching water for his father's horse at the vet checks along the trail, watching close to a hundred horses cover various distances at amazing speeds.

What happened? Sam rubbed his face and watched his Dad bite into another donut, followed by a sip of coffee.

Tucker had never been one to talk much. Somehow as Sam grew into his teens, they quit talking at all. In high school Sam and Matt hung out with cowboys and rodeo, adapting the whole lifestyle. His friends made fun of Tucker's dainty dish-faced A-rabs with their long manes and tails. They rode stocky Quarter Horses with wide jowls and bulging muscles, the bigger the hind end, the better. For practical ranch work, working stock and riding fence, one couldn't beat a Quarter Horse.

Sam wished he could talk to Tucker like when he was a kid again. Just do it. He cleared his throat. "You know the first day I went out riding to round up the cattle? I got dumped when that danged bull charged . . ." He went on and told his father how the copper mare jumped between him and the bull and saved him.

Tucker's grin broadened. He laughed and slapped the formica table. "Well now, don't that beat all."

Taking a deep breath, Sam rushed onward. "That mare could win cutting competitions. Do you think I could try her?" He rubbed the silver buckle he'd won long ago at the rodeo as Tucker gazed out the window.

"Sierra started that mare under saddle last spring. She takes after her sire, Nightwind. I know you don't think much of my way of training, but mark my words: with her, you can't demand anything without a fight. You have to ask her, become one with her. Her name is Amberwind." Tucker scraped back his chair and stood. "Let's bring the stock to the pasture behind the barn. It'll make feeding a lot easier for the rest of winter." He glanced out the window again. "Gonna snow soon."

Sam froze in his chair. That'd been the most his father said to him in a long time. "What're you saying?"

"It's up to her. Are you comin'?"

"You bet." Sam jumped, knocked over his chair and tagged after his father like a lost puppy as they reached for their coats hanging on the horseshoe rack by the door.

Out at the barn, Sam cornered his buckskin in the corral, his black mane trimmed short and tail cut at its hocks in the Quarter horse style. Tucker's flea-bitten gray jogged to him the moment he opened the gate, her chestnut freckles splattered all over her white coat. Sam saddled his horse alongside Tucker's. A half-hour later they found all the animals down at the river.

"Let's go, girlies," Tucker hollered. Several heads raised; a few whinnies answered. The copper mare blew loudly.

As the herd jogged up the switchbacks out of the canyon, Sam watched his bay mare and the half dozen heifers he'd saved follow after them. "That's it? You don't have to drive them?" Midway through high school, Sam began taking care of his stock separate from the Arabs; done minimal ranch work with his father. Maybe he should've paid more attention.

Tucker chuckled. "They know where they're going." He turned his horse behind the last calf. "Your stock may not like the pace. We'll just help them along."

"Where're the rest of your horses?" Sam counted sixteen.

"Sold all the youngsters except Amberwind and her black sister. Still have a few geldings for sale. Kept the place from foreclosure." Tucker rubbed his mare's white neck with brown freckles under her white mane.

Sam nodded. His father had given up his years of breeding as well. Maybe Tucker cared more about the ranch than Sam realized, the thought compounding his guilt. He glanced at his father sitting so easy in his saddle like he didn't have a care in the world. How could that be?

Out on the sage brush plain, the Arabs increased their pace to an extended trot. Sam lost sight of the copper mare. His Quarter Horse mare and calves dropped back. He helped Tucker keep them bunched, pushing them at a jog toward the barns where tons of hay was stored. How'd Dad get it all done by himself?

Sam's gelding loped to keep up while Tucker easily posted his mare's extended trot, rising up and down in the saddle like a piston with the motion. "We have more hay than we need since I sold my stock," Sam said. "Heard hay is short this winter. Think we should sell the extra?"

Tucker hooted. "Now, wouldn't that be a fine thing to sell to the good old boys at church that helped me out last summer." He turned back a calf making a break, then rode back alongside Sam. "You take charge of it."

Sam could almost forget what happened, killing his father's prize stud and the time in jail. Except the memory lurked over him like the dark clouds above, threatening to smother this happy morning.

The Arabs had reached the pasture adjoining the stock barn with their heads buried in the feeders Sam had stuffed with hay before they left. Tucker drove Sam's herd in with them while Sam shut the gate.

"Ready to try Amber?" Tucker swung down from his flea-bitten grey, her freckles dotted so close together, she looked rosy. He untied the cinch, pulled off his saddle and turned his mare in with the rest.

"Right now?" Sam stepped down from his buckskin.

"Good time as any," Tucker said as he carried his saddle into the barn.

Sam unsaddled his gelding and slipped off the bridle. The buckskin shook himself, black mane and tail lifting, then settling before joining the others munching hay. He set his saddle down in the barn and picked up a halter and lead.

Tucker sat on the railing as Sam walked toward the copper mare with the halter slung over his shoulder. Amber kept her eye on him as she picked at the hay. When he got within twenty feet, she lifted her head. He stopped; took a couple of steps. She backed a few steps.

He felt clumsy knowing his father watched. He took another step and stopped as she turned away. This wasn't going to work. No way could he corner her in sixty acres. "Aw, c'mon, Amber. Don't play hard to get. I've got to make a good impression here."

Sam thought about roping her, noting her fuzzy winter coat and the tangled knots in her long copper mane. Her short back, muscled quarters and shoulders impressed him with how well-balanced her conformation was, for an Arab, anyway. Her arched neck and dished profile gave away her breed.

Sam half-turned to Tucker, inviting suggestions when the mare slowly ambled toward him.

Tucker called out, "That's good."

Sam knotted the rope halter on Amber's chiseled head. Her huge brown eyes shone, and her small ears pricked forward as she studied him.

Tucker walked beside him and the mare back to the barn. Sam tied her, and after running his hand over her back, reached for his saddle.

"Hey! What do you think you're doin'?" Tucker barked. "How'd you like a perfect stranger to walk up to you without any introduction or explanation as to what they're about?" He grabbed the curry and brush. "Groom her proper so she can learn your smell and touch."

"Okay, okay!" Sam dutifully worked on the copper mare, even brushing off caked mud from her lower legs. When he bent to pick out her hooves, she lifted each one before he touched it.

Tucker stood by her shoulder, picking knots out of her mane that hung down past her neck. "You're a fine girlie," he crooned.

Gee, trying to make me sick, Dad? Sam wouldn't say it aloud. Horses, dogs; all animals on a ranch were either tools or food. Yet Tucker treated them all like family.

Finally, he set his blanket and saddle on her. She slapped him in the head with a swish of her ground touching tail when he pulled on the cinch, knocking off his Stetson.

"Might want to think about that," Tucker warned as he handed Sam a bridle with a snaffle bit.

"What now?" Sam picked up his hat and flopped the stirrup into place.

"Guess some have to learn the hard way, son." Tucker climbed the corral fence and sat, hooking his legs through the rails.

Sam settled his Stetson back on his head, bridled Amber and led her to the center of the corral where he swung onto the saddle. When he nudged her girth with his spurs, she exploded. Bucking, twisting, leaping like a raw bronc. He didn't last eight seconds.

Groaning, he slowly rose from the frozen ground, still grasping the reins. "What'd she do that for? You said she was broke," he gasped. He was losing it, getting bucked off twice in a week.

"You weren't listening." Tucker shook his head. "You can't jerk and kick her around. Ask nice and she'll be your friend. Now loosen that girth and take off your spurs."

Clinching his jaw, Sam dusted off his hat and unbuckled his spurs. When he loosened the girth, she shook herself like a large dog. "Sorry, alright?" Sam mumbled as he stepped up again. Amber cocked an ear and moved off at a sedate walk. Go figure.

Breaking Sam

After twenty minutes of jogging, Sam grudgingly admitted that she impressed him big time. Any subtle shift of weight, she'd turn or stop, each step balanced even over the rough slippery ground. He dismounted and rubbed her forehead beneath her long forelock. Amberwind. Man, what a la-tee-da name. Too bad she wasn't Doc's Brandy or 'Lil Miss Windy.

Tucker climbed down from his perch. "That's more like it. Go ahead and use her. I may hang around when you do; I'd like to see how much 'cow' she's got." He shook his head and grinned. "Now, wouldn't that be somethin'?"

Sam turned to his father, meeting his gaze. "It could be a fluke."

The copper mare rubbed her face against Sam as he took his time to unsaddle her, and let her loose in the pasture. She stood for a moment, watching him, ears pricked forward. Amber rubbed her nose against her knee before ambling toward the herd.

He found Tucker in the kitchen, slicing roast beef for sandwiches. "Hungry? After lunch, how 'bout you load hay while I call Smith's. He told me at church last night that he needed more feed."

"Great." So much for being in charge. Sam spread horseradish sauce on the slices of bread and placed the sandwiches on plates while Tucker brought milk and pickles from the fridge.

They ate in silence. Back to that familiar at odds feeling. According to Jessie, Tucker had forgiven him. This morning they enjoyed their time together. Sam hoped the mare would help draw them closer in the days ahead.

FIVE

Sam woke in the dark and checked his illuminated clock. He could roll over and sleep another forty minutes. Instead, his mind kept circling round thoughts of his father. He deserved his father to blow up over all the trouble he'd caused. He wished Tucker would get it out in the open and over with. Could Jessica be right? Had Tucker forgiven him? But how?

He groaned, tired of wrestling with his past. Lonely nights and days running into years had given him more than enough time to ponder over what he could've or should've done. More than anything he wanted to start over by telling his father how sorry he was, how he'd gotten messed up with Stevens urging him on with visions of easy money during bleary-eyed nights of beer and whiskey at the Brown Bear. Although that was no excuse; if he wanted to really be honest with himself, he'd been brought up knowing right from wrong.

Sam promised himself, as painful as it might be, to watch for the right moment and tell his father how he felt. He had wasted too much of his life. From now on, no more regrets.

He smelled coffee. Tucker had risen earlier than usual. Sam swung out of bed and reached for his jeans.

Tucker was arranging half a package of bacon in a large skillet in the kitchen.

Sam blinked his eyes. "It's not even daylight yet."

Tucker shrugged. "I want to get that post replaced under the barn overhang before church this morning. I'm staying afterwards for the monthly potluck. Those gals are mighty good cooks; you might want to come along."

Sam grimaced. "Being around a bunch of do-gooders doesn't sound fun to me, Dad." He cut a piece of butter and set another cast iron pan on the stove for eggs. "I'll help you, though. The horses have chewed that post 'til there's not much left of it."

While the bacon sizzled, his father poured two cups of coffee and handed one to Sam. A comfortable quiet settled while they each cooked.

Sam filled his plate and joined his father at the table and ate several bites. "What else needs fixing? I think I'll take a look around while you're gone; make a list of repairs."

"You'll see plenty. Take a ride, check the whole ranch while you're at it." Tucker gulped his coffee and rose.

Sam stacked their plates in the sink for later and followed Tucker to the barn.

His father fired up a chain saw to cut out the old post while Sam drug a better one over from their used but still good pile. No wonder Tucker wanted to replace it, the roof sagged overhead. Together, they wrestled the bottom half of the old post from the ground. His father wiped sweat from his forehead with a bandana, out of breath.

"Dad, sit down a minute. I'll finish up." Sam lifted the post and dropped it into the hole. His father obeyed. Sam kept glancing at Tucker as he used a sledge to knock the top of the post under the beam, tamped the dirt around the bottom and nailed the top. His father took some time to recover. What was going on? How old was he now, anyway?

Tucker had always been a work horse, easily outdoing Sam. From now on, he'd take on more of the work to give his father a break.

Soon as Tucker left for church, Sam headed back to the barn. His gelding put his ears back and turned away from him. The copper mare stood with her ears forward.

"Okay, Amber. I'm easy. Guess I'll take you instead." He lifted a halter from a peg and soon had her saddled. He swung astride, deciding to ride the rim of the canyon.

Several miles later he had to admit the mare was not only smart and spook-proof, but was attentive to his subtle shifts in the saddle, anticipating his wants. He laid a leg against her like he would his gelding and she about jumped out from under him. Sam found he needed a much lighter touch with her. He didn't like to admit it, but riding Amber was fun, smooth as a sports car, her hooves lightly skimming the ground, her lope an easy waltzing cadence while his gelding pounded along like a truck without power steering.

At first, Sam paid attention to the fences, noting their condition as Amber loped, her neck arched as she snorted, but soon gave in to the joy the horse obviously felt. The sun warmed his back chasing away the morning chill and glistened off Amber's copper neck. Bright light and shadows defined the canyon walls. The notion of a horse feeling joy had never occurred to him before. His father had a reputation for being a horse whisperer. Was it too late to learn his father's ways? Sam vowed to pay attention from now on.

Sam halted Amber on a rise, gazing at the Cascades in the distance, a long white jawbone on the horizon. The scent of juniper and sagebrush carried on the breeze. He loved this ranch so much his heart ached. And he was still afraid they might lose it.

SIX

Sam filled his pick-up and the five gallon gas can from the ranch fuel tanks, planning to stop by Jessica's that evening. He fired the tractor and drove it to the 'cherry picker' as they called the contraption his father rigged to load a block of hay at a time onto the flatbed. Sam attached the pins to the tractor's hydraulics and soon moved six ton onto the truck. He parked the tractor, jumped off and tied down the load.

Lowering clouds darkened as Sam drove the flatbed down the drive. His father was going to get his wish for snow. Sam drove through the front gate that his father had left open since the horses were shut in the front pasture now.

The miles between ranches gave plenty of time to let thoughts wander. Sam loved the great expanse of land. Few fences, even fewer buildings marred it. Pockets of junipers clothed some rolling hills. Off in the distance, clouds tumbled over the peaks of the Cascades that rose from the pine and fir forest.

Smith's tractor stood ready at the barn when Sam arrived. "Glad to get this feed. Been calling all around," he said, handing Sam a check for nine hundred. "If you've got more, I'll take another load."

"Weather permitting, I'll bring more tomorrow." Sam leapt on the tractor and unloaded the hay. Not everyone had loaders like Tucker and Smith. If he moved the hay by hand, it'd take hours.

Smith thanked him, shook his hand and Sam pulled out onto the road again. Next stop would be the bank to deposit the auction and hay checks. When he returned home, he'd take a look at the books with his father and hopefully, help make decisions on which bills needed to be paid first. He knew it'd be a struggle, but he was determined to make up for lost time.

Not far from Terrebonne, a butterscotch bit of something sat in the road. Sam slowed the flatbed to take a look. A young dog half cringed and gave a tentative wag of its long tail. As he drove on, it ran after him. Sam rolled down his window. The air sharp and cold, smelled of snow. "Go home," Sam yelled.

Sam slowed the truck through the small town, drove by the Brown Bear Bar and the street where Matt's church steeple showed above the rooftops.

A half-hour down the highway he entered Redmond, taking the one way main street to the Great Western Bank and ambled inside. Sam couldn't miss Jessie's painting in the lobby. On a canvas three feet high and four feet wide, Smith Rock looked real, like he could touch the smooth tan rock of the mountain and the blue green river that flowed at its base. He found her signature in the corner. He wondered if she could paint horses that well. The line waiting for the teller moved and he went with it.

From the bank he drove toward Smith Rock, Jessie's inspiration for her painting. He knew where her folks lived –most everyone in their tight knit community knew who and where everyone lived. He'd never seen the ranch's cabin, but he could find it. Her folks raised alfalfa hay. Fields of it bordered both sides of the road with the landmark standing within sight. He turned in at the "Riverside Ranch" sign and drove on past the large Victorian house where Jessie had grown and her parents still lived.

The gravel road meandered between folds of land with junipers and some pine. Jessie's cabin nested within a secluded bend of the river. Her Land Cruiser sat by a nearby shed.

Sam parked beside it, lifted the gas can from the bed of his truck, spun off the cap of her jeep can and filled it. He replaced the can in his truck, then stepped up to her covered front porch and knocked on the door. No answer. He should've called.

He wandered to the river in case she was there. The water flowed peacefully in the bend between the hills. An inviting bench sat between two trees with dormant flower beds around it. Sam imagined sitting with Jessica there, getting caught up on each other's lives. Except she already knew about him. He looked forward to talking to her again. He wondered if his past kept her from considering him anything but a lost friend. Here he was, out of prison, but pacing back and forth within his mind.

Disappointed, he headed back to the Tersis as snowflakes drifted down from gloomy skies. A thin white glaze coated the fields, fences and trees near Terrebonne. Good thing he paid attention or he would've run over the dog still sitting in the middle of the road. He honked, grinding gears as he slowed the flatbed to a stop.

Lifting its front paws like a squirrel, the dog begged. What was it doing there, miles from nowhere? He rolled down his window, blasted by frosty air. "Move it," he shouted.

The dog slowly stepped to Sam's door and stood with its front paws on the running board, gazing at him with golden-brown eyes.

"Oh no. Not me. I'm not your master. You're gonna freeze or get run over out here." At the sound of Sam's voice, the long tail gently wagged. Sam muttered as he opened his door, leaned out and pulled in the shivering honey colored body. "Brother, am I a sucker or what?" It was a male. "Okay little Buddy, this is just until we find out who lost you." The pup curled at his side and laid his head on Sam's lap, his eyebrows lifting back and forth as he watched Sam shift gears.

By the time he pulled in at the ranch, the dog snoozed and snow blanketed the ground as another day closed. Sam parked the truck, scooped up the pup and jogged through the falling snow into the barn. He set the dog down and threw flakes of hay into the wooden feeders that ran down the length of the barn.

The horses waited under the overhang. One by one they shoved their muzzles into the hay. His two Quarter Horses stayed down at the end with the calves. The dog followed at his heels, sniffing everything along the way. From the size, he figured it to be somewhere between four to eight months old.

Sam stood before Amber. She picked through the hay for her favorite grasses. Pressing her nose through the wooden slats, she blew softly on the dog, who returned the gesture with a slow lick on her muzzle. Aw, mush. Maybe he could get Jessie to take the dog. Yeah, he'd call and see if she was home; tell her he'd been by.

He hurried across the space between the barn and house, the dog leaping through the swirling snow behind him, ears flapping. He loved the wood smoke smell in the air; it reminded him of bacon cooking. His stomach growled as he stomped his boots on the porch before going inside.

"Hey, it's getting dark. You should turn on the lights," he called to Tucker.

Sam hesitated. A soft pop came from the woodstove. The old clock ticked on the wall as Sam hung his Stetson and jacket on the horseshoe rack by the door. The pup whimpered. Sam followed as the dog bounded into the living room where Tucker sat in his faded brown easy chair with one boot on and one boot off. Strange he'd fall asleep like that.

The pup sniffed Tucker's hands lying on his lap.

Sam reached the lamp, switching on the light. "I know we need another mouth to feed like a hole in the head, but he's gotta belong to somebody."

Tucker didn't stir. Sam leaned over him and touched his shoulder. "If you're that tired, maybe you should hit the hay." Nothing. "Dad?" Sam's heart weighed sharp and painful like an anvil against his ribs. He felt his father's cool hands. Sam pressed his head to Tucker's chest. No gentle rise and fall of breath, no heartbeat.

Sam's shoulders heaved as he gulped down the sobs that built within his chest, piling up and breaking out of control. No. Not this, not now. There's too much left unsaid, Dad. He sank to the floor next to his father's chair, wishing he had hugged his Dad while he had the chance. Wished he asked for forgiveness, wished for more days out on the ranch together like they'd just had. Finally, the fence between them had been broken by the copper mare of all things . . . why did it have to end this way?

Sam reached up and covered his father's hands with his. "Dad, I love you," he said aloud. The pup wiggled into Sam's lap and licked the tears that leaked through Sam's tightly shut eyes.

SEVEN

Sam didn't know how long he'd sat there with the golden puppy in his lap. The dog had fallen asleep. His father looked peaceful sitting in his chair. Who should he call? The police? Hospital? He rubbed his face and the pup lifted his head, gazing into his eyes. Tucker's church. Ready or not, he would call Matt.

Tucker's Bible sat beside his father's chair on the end table. Sam opened the cover, thankful to find a church bulletin tucked inside. Sam moved stiffly to the house phone mounted on the kitchen wall and dialed the number, the golden at his heels.

On the third ring Matt's voice answered, "High Desert Christian Fellowship, how can I help you?"

"It's Sam. My Dad . . . I came home and found him." He tried to keep his voice steady, not sure what to say.

"I'll be right over," Matt said and hung up.

No questions; just what Matt had always done in the past: being there for his friends. Sam turned on lights in the kitchen, living room and porch, the pup tagging along after him. Sam walked the dog outside, then returned to sit with his father. He relived the last few conversations they'd had together, thought especially about the smile on Tucker's face when he described how Amber saved him. Most of all regret caused a heavy lump in his throat that he couldn't swallow. He'd waited to ask forgiveness and now it was too late.

Sam heard snow crunch as vehicles arrived and opened the door. Matt parked his truck along with an ambulance. "I called 911," Matt said. "It's the right thing to do."

"Thanks." Sam croaked. "Dad's in the living room." He showed the way.

The EMT's quickly checked his vitals. One of them asked, "Does he have a plan?"

"Don't know," Sam picked up the golden who was sniffing everyone.

Matt stood beside him. "Where does he keep important stuff filed?"

"Back here," Sam led Matt to the office, set down the dog and searched through the drawers. The last file with the ranch title deed and insurance had a paper marked 'personal.' He pulled it out and brought it to the EMT's.

They read it. "He has a DNR and a mortuary listed here. You can call them in the morning."

"We need you to fill out some paperwork," the older EMT added. "I'll get the form."

A few minutes later EMT's drove away in the ambulance.

"Are you going to be able to sleep?" Matt closed the outside door after grabbing a few logs for the fire.

"Don't know." Sam returned to the living room, sat on the couch and gazed at Tucker.

Matt stuffed the logs into the wood stove and sat on the other end of the couch. "I didn't know you had a dog." He helped the golden settle between them.

41

"I don't. I almost ran over him on the highway coming home," Sam absently rubbed the pup, who licked his hand. "Hey Bud."

"You named him? He's yours now."

"No; he's got to belong to somebody. Maybe you could ask at church?" Sam didn't want a dog.

"Sure. Hey, I'm glad you called. Should I make some coffee?" He paused. "That pup looks hungry; I'll get him something to eat."

"Thanks, Matt."

Matt rose, headed into the kitchen to return shortly with two steaming mugs and a bowl with leftovers for the pup. "I'm going to miss Tucker. The whole church will want to attend his memorial. Would you mind if I had Jessica take care of that part? She told me she talked to you after church the other night."

Sam slowly nodded, inhaled the fresh coffee steam and sipped, watching the pup gobble chopped potatoes and meat. "It'd be a relief to have her do it. She knows everyone; I don't and I wouldn't know what to do or say anyway." He gazed at his father, loads of regrets pressing onto his shoulders, adding to the lump in his throat.

He rested his coffee cup on his thigh as tears blurred his vision. "I don't even know when to have a memorial or how long it takes for arrangements. I know Dad wouldn't want a big fuss or for it to be drug out too long."

Matt set his mug on the coffee table. "Well, it's too soon for this Saturday; how about the following one? We'll let the mortuary know when they come in the morning. We can talk about details later." He helped the pup back onto the couch as it struggled. "Do you have Sierra's number? She'll want to know and she can pass the word to Tucker's endurance friends."

Sam nodded, thankful for Matt keeping calm and remembering details to line up.

Sam stood next to the front pew of the church, amazed by all the people that overflowed the small building taking turns to squeeze their way up the aisle to shake his hand and offer condolences. The sanctuary hummed with quiet conversation.

He assumed that his father didn't have much in common with the ranchers and farmers in the area since Tucker raised Arabian horses and wasn't what Sam considered a 'real cowboy.' But the fact that they loved Tucker West was evident.

Some of the older folks belonged to families that went 'way back' to the Oregon Trail days, people whose grandparents settled there long ago, passing their land down through the generations, like the Tersis. As Sam caught snatches of conversation, he realized that what most of these people had in common with his father was their faith.

From Sam's reckoning, just about every endurance rider in the Pacific Northwest mixed throughout the crowd as well. Sierra cried when he called her to tell of Tucker's passing. He'd wiped tears from his eyes and felt awkward asking her to help pass the word.

"Thank you for letting me know," Sierra sniffed. "The Endurance world has lost a great friend; a real legend."

A legend? Sam had hardly thought of Tucker in that sense, but before service a woman with cropped gray hair gushed about how proud he must be that Tucker had been one of the first to ride the same horse over one thousand miles in endurance races. Sam hadn't known. How many other things about his father didn't he know?

He ran his hand across the polished surface of the best coffin he could afford with his father's small VA benefit, sorry for not spending more time with his father through the years; for all the opportunities he'd passed by to talk and share moments like they'd had since he'd been home.

Jessica stood nearby. She appeared at the ranch the day after his father died to help him make the arrangements, writing a list that made his head ache. There was so much involved. He would've forgotten the obituary for the newspaper. She even took charge of making the painful phone calls to everyone in Tucker's address book. After Tucker's memorial and gathering at the house he'd tell her how much he appreciated her support.

The crowd rippled. Sam turned. Sierra and Ben stood at the door. She wore a black dress of some kind of fabric that floated above her black boots. Her hair waved like a flame shawl clear down past her hips. They made their way forward, greeting friends.

Sierra gently hugged him. "Sam, I'm so sorry. Tucker will be missed by all of us. He was family to me." She met his gaze. When he faltered, she whispered, "You have to move on now. We'll be praying for you."

Ben shook his hand, looking sharp in his black western-styled suit. "If there's anything we can do, anyway we can help, let us know."

Sam nodded and offered them a seat in the pew with him as Matt made his way to the pulpit to start the service. He still couldn't imagine his old friend being a preacher after all the hell they raised together while in school and rodeo.

He didn't remember much what they'd talked about the night his father died. Matt helped him plan the funeral after the mortuary came for Tucker's body. That day had passed quickly with visits from both Matt and Jessica, but the rest of the time he'd been on automatic, taking care of horses, heifers and the dog that no one seemed to know anything about. Most of all, missing his father each moment more than he thought possible.

Matt's brown hair was still unruly as if that part of him refused to be tamed, in contrast to his very proper dark grey suit. The rustlings and low conversations stilled as Matt spoke. "This is a day of sorrow, for we all will greatly miss Tucker West. He was quick to give of his time and substance, slow to anger. Tough as nails. His ways with horses are legendary. I'd bet each one of you here could tell a story about him. I think Tucker would be honored if you did so at the reception later." Matt paused.

Jessie sat to Sam's right. The warmth of her hand on his arm convinced him that this wasn't a bad dream, although his only suit was old and it could qualify.

Matt continued. "This is also a day of joy for we have that blessed assurance that even now Tucker is with our Lord. The Bible says that whosoever believes in God's Son shall not perish but have everlasting life." He lifted his Bible, eyes shining. "By grace are we saved not by works lest any man should boast. How thankful I am for that. Most of you know where I came from."

Laughter erupted from the crowd. Sam smiled, thankful that Matt was keeping the service real, not the stiff formal thing he'd been dreading.

Matt set his Bible before him on the pulpit. "When Jesus hung on the cross, the thief hanging next to Him said, 'Lord, remember me when You come into Your kingdom.' And what did Jesus say? 'Take a hike? I'll think about it?' No! He said, 'this day you will be with Me in paradise!'"

The congregation shouted "Amen!" Matt signaled for quiet. "Tucker wasn't one to pray in public. He attended church whenever ranching and riding allowed. Last time we spoke, he told me how close he'd drawn to the Lord. And most of us know his favorite song. Jessica?"

She rose, gracefully stepped onto the stage and sat at the piano. The melody softly lifted over them, Jessie's voice like water in a stream. "Amazing grace, how sweet the sound . . ." Her voice wrapped each word soulfully "-that saved a wretch like me! I once was lost" she soared "-but now am found; was blind but now I see."

As Jessie played the choruses, Sam wiped his eyes along with everyone else. Again, she reminded him of an angel with her voice that gave wings to the song. She looked like one too, in her lace topped velvet dress that brought out the blue in her eyes.

Like a sleepwalker, he helped carry his father to the hearse and rode with Matt to the cemetery, a few acres of ground surrounded by ranches where Matt spoke the final words under a frozen sky.

Sam stood for a long time as the crowd dwindled, the cold piercing his dark blue western suit to the marrow of his bones. Snow covered the mound of dirt beside the coffin. Memories played like a video in his mind. Sierra, twisting out of his grasp, calling him a jerk . . . His father, down in the grave with his stallion, Ranger, cutting a hunk of mane to keep. "You just don't understand," Tucker had said. What did his father mean by not understanding? Horsewhisper stuff?

His chest ached for all the things he wished he'd said to his father, over things he wished he hadn't done. And he wished he would've had time to make his father proud. Sam choked out a whisper, "Dad, how can I earn your forgiveness now?"

Embarrassed by his tears, he wiped his eyes and nodded to Matt, who drove him silently home to the Tersis. Cars and trucks were parked in front of the house and barn. "I don't want to do this." Sam glanced at Matt.

"They won't bite you. Just do it. You'll feel better afterwards." Matt slid from his truck as Sam slowly stepped down from the cab. "My folks sent you a card; they're out of town since Dad's buying stock for a cattle company. Anyway, don't be a stranger. We have some catching up to do."

Sam opened his kitchen door, gazing in amazement at all the food the ladies from the church brought crammed onto his table. Smells of fried chicken, coffee and apple pies tempted him. He hesitated. Matt shoved him into the warmth, shutting the door against the cold behind them.

Jessie chatted with folks as she organized food and poured coffee. Someone had stoked the fire and set out folding chairs. The house was stuffed with people eating and talking. Overwhelmed, Sam rubbed his eyes. Of course they were there for Tucker; not him, but still . . .

Sam startled as Jessie handed him a paper plate filled with food. "Where'd that cute Golden Retriever come from? I put him in your bedroom for now."

"What Golden Retriever?" Was he missing something here?

"The yellow pup that looked so lonesome on your doorstep when I got here." She filled a cup for him. "I meant to ask you when I came over the other day. He was sleeping in the living room."

"A Retriever? Is that what he is?" Sam groaned. What a cowboy he'd turned out to be. Instead of a Quarter Horse, he'd ride an Arab; instead of a ranch dog like a Border Collie, or Heeler, he was adopted by a Golden Retriever. What next?

EIGHT

Jessica lingered, tossing paper plates into a garbage sack and spooning leftovers into plastic containers for him to warm up later as the last of the funeral crowd packed up folding chairs and coffee makers and drove away.

"I don't know how to thank you." Sam leaned against the kitchen counter. "You've been great. I couldn't have gotten through this day without your help." Bud sat at his feet and pawed his leg. "Maybe you need a dog for protection out there all alone."

Jess crouched down and ruffled the pup's ears. "He's darling, Sam. But it wouldn't be fair to him. I'm not home much. He needs companionship." She rose, still fresh and beautiful after the long day. "I think the Lord sent him to you. Don't you think it's quite a coincidence and meaningful that you rescued him when you lost your Dad?"

"Not really," Sam scraped left-overs into a bowl for the Buddy pup, whose hind end swung side to side with his tail as he eagerly licked up the scraps. "You sure no one's missing a dog around here?"

"Several folks noticed him today. Nobody mentioned seeing him before." Jessie offered the pup a piece of chicken, smiling as he carefully took it from her hand. "Most everyone I know already has a dog or two, so I can't think of anyone else who'd want him."

She walked around the kitchen and living room. "I think that does it; everything is back in place. Will you be alright?"

Sam sighed. "I'm missing Dad more than I thought possible. I mean, in prison I knew he was here and he visited, but I still can't believe he's gone for good."

Jessica hugged him and he gently returned her embrace, soaking in her warmth and fresh scent for a life time, a sweet salve to his wretched heart as she withdrew and waved goodbye from the door.

"Well, Buddy, we're stuck with each other, I guess." Bud sat next to him in the truck like a human, watching the scenery. Sam rubbed Bud's ears. The dog leaned into Sam's hand, his eyes half closed. Sam never felt such silky soft hair on an animal. The longer hairs behind the Retriever's ears curled like a girl's perm. Some macho dog.

"How many loads of hay have we delivered since the funeral?" Sam spoke his thoughts out loud, amused by the way Bud's eyebrows would lift at the sound of his voice. "I'll have to make another deposit soon." Sam was thankful for the all the calls for hay diverting him from the emptiness at home. Bud glued to his side helped, although he'd never admit to anyone he talked to his dog.

Every time he opened the truck door, the young golden would try his best to jump inside. Sam lifted the furry blonde onto the seat. At least Bud never pooped in the house since it was hard to ignore the dog when he stood at the door and whined. The golden never chewed on anything although he stole boots and laid on them. Bud's constant presence grew on him. Sam had to admit they needed each other and hoped Buddy's real owner would never claim the dog who appeared out of nowhere.

Tired from another long day, he stopped the truck near the barns. Soon the huge hay barn would have enough room in it to work the copper mare since the corrals would be a mucky mess from snow until late spring. He wouldn't go public until their first competition. Sam cringed as he imagined the crowd's conversation: "Look who's riding an Arab now, ha-ha."

Evenings were the hardest. Evidence of his father lay in every room, painful reminders of Tucker's absence. Memories he'd forgotten surfaced and surprised him, like the conversation they'd had about breaking horses. His father stood in the middle of the round pen, walking a small circle in the center even with a brown colt as it loped the perimeter. "Why don't you throw a saddle on him and get it done?" Sam asked impatiently as he leaned against the wood fence.

"We're having a conversation, son. This colt isn't ready yet," Tucker replied.

So many regrets, so many things he wished he'd done and said while his father was alive. He'd round up his father's boots, jackets and clothing and give them away. Maybe someone at the church needed some clothes.

The golden followed with Tucker's glove in his mouth as Sam went from room to room, throwing clothes in the washer; socks from under Tucker's chair, long underwear hanging behind the bathroom door.

Sam called Jessie and asked her about the clothes.

Her voice reminded him how much he wanted to see her again. "Oh boy, we can use men's clothes at the Warm Springs reservation and at the downtown mission. How about you bring the clothes to church tomorrow? After service, I'll fix you lunch. No excuses –be there."

Yeah, he owed Matt a visit for the funeral and all. He'd just let it be known that he wasn't about to make a habit out of going to church.

Finally, he put the last of Tucker's clothes from his dresser and closet into large plastic bags. A framed photo stood on the nightstand of Tucker, Sierra and Ranger. Sierra might like to have it. He'd save it for her.

The only thing of value his father owned was a wrist cuff made of thick twisted strands of silver wire braided together. Sam had no idea where it'd come from. The silver cuff must have been meaningful in some way; Tucker had worn it as long as he could remember. Sam slipped it on. "Dad, I know I disappointed you," he said aloud. What an understatement. "I hurt and embarrassed you. I wanted to make it up to you, cause you to be proud." He sighed. "We ran out of time. I hope you don't mind me wearing this. Every time I see it, I'll be reminded of you, to try harder. Maybe you'll know somehow."

Back in the kitchen, he heated a large can of baked beans. He'd put off going through the files and bills in the office. It was time to find out exactly where he stood. He carried the pan of beans with him and ate using the wooden stir-spoon.

Between bites, he opened newly arrived bills, sorted through old and checked out the latest bank statement. His auction money brought the mortgage up-to-date but with another payment due soon along with hefty balances owed to the vet, farrier and the Grange feed and farm store, he needed more money.

Bud pawed Sam's thigh. His eyebrows lifted with each bite of beans. "You have your own food." The dog swept the floor with his tail, stirring dust. "Okay. Just don't drool and don't embarrass me in front of company. And don't pass gas."

Money. He needed to sell Tucker's Arabs. He wasn't sure how or where to do it. Certainly not in the Western Horseman magazine; not on the bulletin board at the feed store. Sierra would know. He pulled the address book from the drawer and reached for the phone as Bud licked the pot, scooting it noisily across the floor.

"Sierra? It's Sam." He tapped his pencil on the balance sheet.

"How're you doing?" She sounded surprised.

"Okay. I'm calling because I need to sell Tucker's horses. I don't have a clue about where to advertise them." Sam leaned back in the chair, balancing on two legs.

She didn't hesitate. "Leave it to me. I'll get the word out to the endurance people. You've already got three sold."

The chair banged as he leaned forward. Bud jumped. "What do you mean? How?"

Sierra laughed. "No way would we let anyone else get their hands on Nightwind's babies, Ebonywind and Amberwind. We want their dam, too. How 'bout five grand for the broodmare and twenty each for the daughters?"

He choked. "You're kidding me, right?"

"I think that's pretty fair, Sam."

He paused. "Sure. Except Amberwind. She isn't for sale. Dad sort of gave her to me."

"I thought you didn't like Arabs."

"I don't- didn't. But the copper mare saved my life," Sam said and winced.

"Really? I'd like to hear about that. Would it work to come for them on Monday?"

"Sure." He hung up, dazed. He would've never guessed how much those Arabs were worth. He could pay off bills and have a little cushion left over.

"Come on, Bud, let's celebrate." The dog's ears lifted as he followed Sam to the kitchen. Sam opened the fridge. "What happened to all of my beer for crying out loud?" He searched the cupboards and found leftover oatmeal cookies from the funeral. "Guess these will have to do. Here." He bit into one, gave one to the golden and carried the paper plate with the cookies to sit in front of the woodstove with

Bud at his feet, tilting his head at each bite Sam took and leaning forward to gently take each piece Sam offered.

Cookies gone, Sam headed to bed, cracking the window over the headboard for fresh air, cold from the snow covering the ground. He burrowed under his blankets. To show on the cutting circuit would take a lot of money. Between hay and selling the rest of the horses maybe, just maybe it'd all work out.

A gentle thump bumped against the bed and hit the floor. Bud's warm wet tongue wrapped Sam's hand dangling over the edge of the bed. Sam rubbed the dog's ears.

NINE

As Sam slid into the back pew, several heads turned briefly in his direction. Jessie smiled at him from her seat at the piano, looking country in her skirt, tall cowgirl boots and a sweater. Matt and two other men strummed guitars. The whole congregation sang, "White as snow, white as snow, though my sins be as scarlet, Lord, I know I'm clean and forgiven . . ."

Did any of these songs have a country beat? When did Matt learn guitar? Back in prison, Sam taught himself the harmonica to pass the time. Don't go there now. He shifted, trying to relax. Somehow he could relate to a calf all trussed with the branding iron headed his way.

At least this morning Matt was dressed in wranglers, cowboy boots, and a navy wool henley. Sam still had trouble with Matt holding a Bible instead of a beer. The verses he read sounded familiar. Oh yeah; the prodigal son story. He'd heard that one as a kid in Sunday school. He frowned. Did Jess tell Matt he was coming? Was that the reason to have this sermon -for him, the wanton son returning home? It was worth sitting through as Jessica picked up a violin for the last song, her fingers and bow causing a sweet melody to flow along with the guitars; a song about hope, peace and redemption . . . things he felt were out of reach for himself but longed for.

After service, Matt stood at the door in the weak sunlight, shaking hands as everyone filed outside. Sam strode through, went to the truck and brought the clothing bags around the side, storing them in a room marked 'Helps Ministry.' There. He'd done his good deed for the day.

Sam leaned against his father's truck, the sun's reflection on the metal warmed him in the cold breeze. He reached in his back pocket for the round tin of chew. He'd left his truck at home. Tucker's Ford needed to be run once in a while to keep the battery from dying. Bud stuck his head out the half open window and nosed the back of his head.

Matt spent time with each person, which made for slow going. Sam recognized several of them from his father's funeral. Matt held Jessie's hand longer than anyone else's. Could he be interested in her? Sam played with the tin.

Finally Matt eased on over and joined him while Jessie visited with a young couple. "You know, I was feeling a bit put out that Jessie invited you to lunch. I'll rest easy now knowing she'll never let you kiss her as long as you're spittin' that stuff."

"You're one to talk." Sam pinched a bit of tobacco in his fingers. "You're the one who got me started. What happened to you anyhow?" Resentment burned his neck.

Matt grinned. "One Sunday on the rodeo circuit I wandered over to the 'cowboy church.' I was sitting on top, winning like crazy but I'd begun to feel empty and lonely –if you can believe that with all those cowgirls hanging around." He raked a hand through his unruly hair. "Some cowhand talked about the Lord being 'the God of the second chance.' Well, here she comes. You stop on by sometime." He walked back to the church, waving as folks drove away.

Sam slipped the tin back in his pocket as Matt paused beside Jessica. "See you tonight?"

"You bet!" Jessie sure looked classy, like one of those models from a western wear catalog in her brown corduroy skirt, boots and her colorful blanket patterned coat. He figured she could wear a feed sack and still look amazing.

Sam lifted an eyebrow as she approached. "You going out with him later?"

Jessie looked over her shoulder at Matt. "Would you care?" She turned, gazing into his eyes. "Tonight's evening worship service and Communion; you're invited."

You bet he'd care. He wondered what she thought of him. Was he just a childhood friend, a lost soul or possibly something more? "Where's your Land Cruiser?"

"I rode in with my folks."

"Okay." He opened the door of the truck for her.

"What's this?" She squealed as she stepped inside. "Oh, Buddy! Boy, are you growing!"

Sam rushed around the front of the truck and sprang into the driver's seat. Bud rose from his blanket nest and licked Jessie's face as she giggled and hugged him. Lucky dog. "Don't let him pester you. Bud, that's enough."

Buddy glanced at Sam, sat between him and Jessica and yawned.

Jessie directed him to an alternate route to her home surrounded by alfalfa fields and rocky hills bordering the Smith Rock recreational area. "Sorry I wasn't here when you brought the gas," she said as he parked. Buddy jumped from the cab and bounded through the snow, running crazy circles with his tongue hanging out and ears flopping.

Sam called his dog and climbed the steps onto the veranda that surrounded her house. She let Bud in with him. A tantalizing aroma of simmering stew caused his stomach to growl. Did Matt visit here often?

"Have a seat. It's almost ready," Jessie slipped off her coat and plopped dumplings into the kettle, covered it and grabbed a couple of logs to stoke her woodstove.

Her home defined mellow. Old hardwood floors gleamed. Butter colored walls reminded him of warm sunshine. White cabinets. Bud lay under the table. Good dog. What made her place different?

Sam rose, wandering into the living room and dropped his coat on the couch next to hers. Her artwork and photos covered the walls. She knew how to paint horses all right.

"Come and get it," she called.

He returned and sat across from her at the table. A sunbeam from the window lighted her pale curls framing her face as she prayed. She opened her eyes.

Sam tasted a bite "This is great! My mother always made dumplings." He shoveled in several bites, savoring the flavors until curiosity won over. "How'd you get those photos of the bear and antelope?"

Jessica made a face. "Hours of patience."

"Could I tag along sometime?" With his work load he'd have to work like crazy to catch up, but it'd be worth it.

"Maybe." She went on to tell him about her latest assignment for a client, a painting of coyotes. She rose and hefted the coffee pot; Sam nodded.

"Thanks for all the clothes. I hear you're selling tons of hay," Jessie said while pouring coffee into his mug.

Sam tasted her coffee. Good and strong. "I guess I'm competing with your folks. The hay barn is about empty and the phone is still ringing with requests."

"No problem; hay is in demand this year. My folks are doing fine." She sat across from him as they sipped coffee, laughing together as Bud snored under the table.

Sam followed her to the kitchen and helped her wash dishes in her farm sink, regretting the passing of time as they talked about the weather, memories; nothing too personal. He wondered if she felt as comfortable with him as he did with her.

"Time to feed at home." He hung her dishtowel. "Thanks for the great grub."

Jessica walked him out in the cold snow to his truck, where he helped Bud half jump and scramble onto the seat. "Don't be a stranger. Call me," she told him.

Near home he realized what it was about her place. Not just cozy. Peaceful. He'd been rested there and quiet within for the first time in years. He hoped she wasn't just being polite asking him to call.

The ranch house at Tersis bordered on being a dump, needing TLC long before he went to prison; his scheme to get the money needed only brought shame. He'd begun repairing the barns and fences, but the ranch house's peeling faded paint surrounded by barren ground was embarrassing. Tucker must've been pressed just to take care of the stock the last couple years. Overwhelmed, he couldn't imagine where to start.

His stomach lurched as he turned onto the gravel drive. A column of black smoke rose in the distance. Sam stomped the accelerator, holding the wheel tight as the pick-up fishtailed around a curve in the road.

Ten

Sam roared to a stop at the barn. He cussed; Bud barked. Flames licked through his pick-up, the acrid smell of burning plastic and oil filling the air. The flatbed's windshield was shattered, the tires slashed and 'ex-con' was spray-painted in red on the doors of both trucks.

He leapt from his seat with Bud right behind him. His dog ran back and forth sniffing the ground. The hood of the flatbed gaped a toothless grin.

Who did this? Why? He clinched his fists. The cowards; he'd rip their heads off. He ran to the barn to check the horses. Churned snow with yellowed tufts of grass covered the expansive pasture. Hopefully, they'd be in the ravine. He opened the gate. Bud raced through.

Sam yelled, "Buddy, no!" as his dog kept going, leaping through patches of snow and disappeared.

Sam hesitated; started after him. Dumb dog would probably get kicked or spook the herd. He took several deep breaths to calm himself, looking to the mountains and hoped whoever did this left a clue to track them down. Sam dreaded what may have happened to the horses. The malicious attack on his vehicles caught him off guard.

Sam winced. What a fine greeting for Sierra and Ben tomorrow. He wouldn't be able to relax until he'd sold all Tucker's horses. All but the copper mare.

At Bud's barking, he turned. The dog ran with his tail a feathered plume, ears flapping. The horses loped a few strides behind him. Beyond, the cows ambled toward the barn. He'd never seen anything like it. Best of all, they were okay.

"Good boy! How'd you do that?" Bud wiggled to him and jumped, paws reaching Sam's waist. He scratched the dog's ears. Buddy really was growing; his belly and legs sprouted fringes of long hair. Sam tossed hay to the stock and headed to the house to call the Sheriff, Bud trotting beside him past the burning truck.

The charred truck barely smoked by the time the Sheriff arrived. He took Sam's statement, then looked around in the snow at the tracks. "I'll take photos of the evidence." The Deputy turned to Sam. "Have any idea who would've done this? Got any enemies?"

"None living that I know of." Sam turned up the collar of his wool lined Wrangler jacket and shoved his hands into his pockets. That slick con, Stevens, had played him good; preyed on his need in order to get him to do Robert's dirty work. How could he have been so stupid, so wrong?

The Deputy shook his head, dug a camera from a case in his vehicle and snapped photos of the wrecks and ground around them.

If Sierra had died when Tucker's stallion collapsed under her, he would've been an accomplice to murder. As Sierra had told Jess, he'd been but a pawn in the plot to kill her. Sam regretted that both Stevens and Robert Lane had died before he could pound them to death himself.

Sam shook his head. He'd been such a fool. The Deputy asked questions and filled out the report form on his clipboard before he drove away.

From the leather case on his belt, Sam dug out his harmonica, rubbed it between the palms of his hands and blew some mournful tunes into the cold wind as he sat on the porch watching the fire burn down. Buddy lay beside him, tilting his head one way, then the other. Even if Sam could forget his time in the slammer, he bet there'd always be someone out there to remind him.

Sam cupped his hands around the harmonica and blew some more, thankful his father wasn't there to see the charred wrecks.

Bud's barking announced the arrival of Sierra and Ben. Sam flipped the coffee maker on to brew and noticed his breakfast mess. Too late to clean it now. As the green and gold diesel crew-cab truck and matching trailer slowed to a stop, he stepped out on the porch.

Sierra slid from the cab, staring at the vandalism. Ben came around to her side and reached for her hand. "Are you okay?" She asked as they approached the house.

"Yeah. I wasn't here when it happened. Coffee's ready." Sam avoided her gaze, ashamed to have played a part in the attempt on her life. This was nothing compared to what she went through.

Other than Tucker's funeral, Sam hadn't seen either of them since his court hearings over two years ago, where he learned Stevens had been stabbed by Robert in Sierra's cabin and died. Robert then set the cabin on fire and Sierra barely saved her life by jumping out the second story window.

Ben furrowed his brow. "Bunch of cowards."

They followed him to the office where Sam laid out the registration papers for the horses. While he poured coffee, Ben and Sierra looked over the pedigrees and made notes. The two of them looked good together wearing dark green jackets with the Valley View Farms logo.

Jealousy mixed with shame. He'd been such a jerk around her. Although Sierra had never showed any interest in him, Sam had spent many a night dreaming of her back then. And he'd been just a pawn in the plot . . . He scraped out a chair and joined them at the desk.

Sierra removed a bill of sale and a check from her briefcase. "If this looks right to you, we have a deal. I wrote down some notes on the other horses for you. I remember them well; I'll make sure the right people find out about your sale."

Sam checked the paper work. "Looks good to me. Where do I sign?"

She pointed out the line and he noticed the large diamond ring. What a fool he'd been, again. He grudgingly admired Ben; he must be a really nice guy. Sam signed off on the Arabian horse registration certificates and the bill of sale.

Ben finished his coffee. "We should get the horses loaded. It's six hours back to Williams. I'd rather not cross the Cascades this time of year in the dark. Thanks, Sam, for calling us first."

Buddy was still checking out the truck's tires as they headed toward the barn. Sam whistled him to come. The retriever bounced over and sniffed Sierra.

Sam opened the gate and whispered to Bud. "Where's the horses? Whatever you did yesterday, I hope you'll do it again!"

As the dog bounded off, Ben put both hands on his hips. "This I've got to see."

A few minutes later, Bud ran back, tongue hanging from his grin with the horses following, cows trailing behind. "Good dog!" Sam grabbed Bud's ruff and gently shook him.

The horses pranced through the churned mud and snow, tails raised like flags waving as they snorted, their heads high, several of them bucking and rearing.

Sierra calmly walked out with a halter into the center of the herd. Sam couldn't hear what she said; didn't even seem like she was doing anything. The dark bay brood mare Sierra bought strolled over and stood while she buckled the halter on the mare's head. Sierra handed the lead rope to Ben, who held the mare while Sierra turned to the herd with another halter.

"This gift of hers never ceases to amaze me," Ben confided to Sam. "She's coached me but my timing stinks."

Sierra stayed near the mare while poking around in the snow with her boot. After whirling and dancing around, Ebonywind took a few hesitant steps to Sierra. They stood nose to nose as Sierra stroked the black filly's neck.

Sam found it hard to believe when Sierra left the filly and headed toward Ben and the mare. Ebonywind followed close behind her.

"There's no magic," Sierra explained. "The filly naturally wants to stay near her dam. And she's curious. She wanted to see if I'd found something good to eat." Sierra took time haltering the black filly. "All this happened without a fight. The filly thinks it was her idea. When she sees her mother lead into the trailer, she'll follow."

The rest of the horses settled down, some looking for hay in the feeders under the overhang. Amberwind nickered softly, her eye on her dam.

Sam rubbed the copper mare's neck and opened the metal gate for Ben and the mare.

Ben hesitated beside him. "That's a really nice horse. Sure you won't change your mind about her?"

"Nope."

Sierra followed with the filly, facing him as he shut the gate behind her. "What're you going to do with Amberwind?"

He slid the bar home on the gate. "I think she'll make a good cutting horse."

"Sam! You of all people should know what you're up against," Sierra sputtered as she brushed her flame colored braid over her shoulder.

"Yeah; I can imagine." Sam rubbed Bud's shoulders as the golden sat beside him. "Someday I'll tell you about it."

ELEVEN

Sam lifted his hand as Sierra and Ben drove away. "C'mon, Bud, let's get warm by the stove." His dog took a last look at the retreating rig before following him inside. He would've liked to have seen Sierra's face when she found the photo of herself, Tucker and Ranger. Sam slipped it into their cab while she and Ben loaded the horses. Neither of them tried to talk him out of using the copper mare. He'd take it as a good sign.

Amber needed more workouts. To do that, he needed more space in the barn. He still received calls for hay. But with the flatbed truck trashed, he couldn't deliver. If the flatbed could be fixed, he needed to tow it into town. It'd be nice to get another opinion and some help towing the truck to a repair shop. He shoved a pinch of chew in his mouth.

Help. He could go back to the bar; maybe some of the guys there that he used to hang out with would give a hand. Sam imagined going in there after all this time and saying, "Yeah, I'm back and I need help." No way.

His father's friends might give him a hand, but he didn't want to owe anyone. Sam's pride and goal of saving the ranch wouldn't allow him to ask for help.

Matt. For some reason every time he thought of the guy, he got angry, like Matt betrayed the cause or something. He knew Matt would want to come and see the damage. Maybe he'd offer to help. Sam wouldn't ask him. Help offered wasn't the same as help begged for. He spit chew into his coffee cup and grabbed the phone.

"Oh, man, look at this!" Matt leaned over the grill of the flatbed. "Brake line is cut, too. You want my advice? Total it."

Sam slammed the hood shut. He'd pretty much decided the same thing, especially when he noticed the fuel cap missing. No telling what'd been poured in there. Just wait 'till he caught those jerks. He'd make them pay. "I'll be lucky if the insurance gives me enough to have them towed away. Now I'm stuck with Tucker's gas hog."

"Look around, maybe you can trade it in. Hungry? I didn't figure you'd have dinner ready so I brought a pizza." Matt grabbed a box from his truck.

"Giant size?" Sam led the way inside, Buddy sniffing at the box in Matt's hands.

"Yeah. I suppose you want some of this too," Matt spoke to the dog.

Sam opened the fridge and pulled out a couple of beers.

Matt opened the box releasing smells of cheese, pepperoni and sauce and swung onto a chair. "You got anything else besides beer?"

"Coffee?"

"I'll have water." Matt bowed his head, asked blessing on the food, then snagged the first piece of the rancher's special loaded with every kind of meat possible.

Sam dove in. Several bites later, he reached for his beer. "I suppose you're just itchin' to tell me to stop drinkin' and chewin'."

Matt laughed. "Doesn't work that way. You gotta catch fish before you clean them."

Heat climbed Sam's neck. What was it about his old friend, anyway? Matt came, helped and brought food. Just let it go, don't get hotheaded over stupid words you don't understand.

Matt reached for another slice of pizza, the cheese stretching from pan to plate. "We've gone down different trails."

Sam met Matt's gaze. "Yeah; you were sure pointing it out last Sunday."

"That was not directed at you. My sermons come from where we as a church are reading through the Bible." Matt chewed a bite of pizza and swallowed. "If it hit home, that wasn't me, it was the Spirit talking to you."

Sam slowly shook his head. Bud rested his chin on Sam's leg.

"Doesn't mean we can't still be best friends. I'm glad you called. I've missed you." Matt flicked a pepperoni. It bounced off Sam's shirt and fell to the floor to be licked up by Bud.

Sam swigged his beer. "Me too."

"Seriously, Sam. Whoever trashed your trucks has it out for you. Call me if you need help anytime or just want to talk about anything. That's what friends are for," Matt leaned forward and cut the last piece of pizza in half.

"Thanks." Sam bit into his slice.

Matt wiped his hands on a paper towel that Sam used for napkins. "Remember how we used to go in the woods and chop our Christmas trees? I bet Jessie would like to do that again. I'm planning on getting one for the church with Christmas almost here."

Sam blinked. Christmas here already? Tucker loved Christmas. A wave of nostalgia choked him. "I don't know if I'm ready for the holidays," Sam muttered.

"I get it," Matt said. "Think about it and let me know, okay?"

After Matt drove away, Sam sat on the old leather couch with Bud lying at his feet. The local news reporter gave the weather report on the TV, but Sam wasn't listening. Hanging out with Matt felt like old times and suggesting Jessie come along for a tree cutting was natural. But he didn't want to talk about his feelings with anyone, especially when he wasn't even sure of them himself.

What he needed was a new life. Sam looked around the room. The old ranch house smelled musty and looked tired. It was depressing. He wanted the house to be bright and fresh, like Jessie's. That's it. He'd clean the house up next. The fences couldn't be repaired until spring anyway.

By the time the wrecker made two trips to haul away the trucks the following morning, Sam yanked all the faded and thread-bare curtains from the windows and ripped out the stained carpets. He'd guessed right, the old floors were hardwood.

Light reflecting off the snow outside almost blinded him through dirty windowpanes. He'd deal with washing windows this summer. The cluttered rooms held all the junk Tucker had accumulated through a lifetime. Most of it didn't hold any sentimental value to him.

Buddy lay near the wood stove. Sam chuckled. The dog followed him with his gaze, eyebrows lifting one at a time as he gathered what was good but didn't want and stored it in his old room since deciding to move into Tucker's larger bedroom.

Sam dragged Tucker's worn recliner chair outside to the heap with the curtains and carpet. Back in the living room he lifted the end table to add it to the pile outside when a black leather book fell out from the shelf. His father's Bible.

He picked it up and opened the front cover. The page read: "This Bible presented to Tucker West by Earl West, Christmas 1942." Earl. Sam barely remembered his grandfather, who wore a handle bar mustache. Below that, written in his father's familiar scrawl, was "for Sam West, love Dad." When did he write that? Did he sense his time was near, or did he do it a while back? Sam stood there several minutes, holding the Bible, feeling connected to family, his heritage. He brought it into the bedroom and placed it on his father's dresser, now his.

Striding back to the living room he carried out the end table and threw it on the heap, added another chair and torched the whole pile, flames soaring with a little help from diesel fuel, melting a ring around the fire in the snow.

The hen and rooster wallpaper in the kitchen and tiny flower print wallpaper in the bathroom had been there for as long as he could remember, back to grade school, even. Out in the barn, he found a scraper. Buddy ran the length of the building as the horses gathered. He tossed flakes of hay into the feeders. With the mare and filly gone, the pecking order changed. The two oldest mares led the way with Amber right behind them. He reached over the rail and stroked her face. Loose hairs stuck to his hand and jacket. How he hated shedding time. Horsehair would stick to everything as the days gradually warmed. He picked up the scraper and went back inside.

Hours passed to the beat of the country western radio station. Large strips mingled with flakes of old wallpaper littered the floors. Memories drifted by with the peelings of his mother frying ham, eggs and potatoes before dawn as Tucker listened to the weather report on the radio; the smell of warm apple pies when he got home from elementary school.

"Sammy, I hope you won't hate me," his mother had said as he ran inside one day after the school bus let him off. "But I can't live here anymore. I'm dying of loneliness; I need a job where I can be around people and go places." She hugged him tight. "I want you to stay here with your Dad. I know you, Sam. You wouldn't be happy away from the ranch."

"Please, Mom, don't leave!" Sam rubbed his face. He had clung to her as she loaded suitcases in her car and drove away while

Tucker was busy with the cattle. He cried for days. Even now, he wondered why she never called or returned to visit.

Sam stretched his aching shoulders and shoved a frozen potpie in the microwave. Tucker had never talked about Mother leaving. When he came inside at dinnertime from working, he'd looked around and patted Sam on the back. "Guess it's up to us to make dinner now," Tucker told him.

Thinking back, that was when his father began riding Endurance; spending long hours in the saddle conditioning horses out on the ranch and breeding Arabian horses.

The microwave's bell dinged. Sam placed his potpie on the table and sat. He watched the burn pile glow in the darkness outside the window. He didn't blame Tucker. His father had encouraged him to ride with him, spend time together. They all made their choices.

Sam rubbed away tears. In a way, he was no better, ditching his Dad for the rodeo. His heart heaved . . . so many regrets.

Bud's tail wagged as he scarfed kibble from his bowl, a furry comfort he never expected.

Sam ate, forcing the past from his mind, satisfied with the progress he'd made prepping the house. He decided he could get by with one truck for now. By trading in Tucker's, he wouldn't have to spend much of his horse money. Tomorrow he'd check car lots for a flatbed and buy paint for the walls.

"One step forward; two back. That's how it's been for us, huh, Dad. But I'm determined to keep trying." Seemed like every time his life headed in the right direction, another cloud stormed his way. The silver cuff on his wrist gleamed.

He washed his plate after Bud licked it, thinking about what Matt said about going together to cut Christmas trees. He'd missed the last two Christmas holidays already. Tucker had been alone, except for coming and visiting him at the facility. Maybe Matt thought it was time for Sam to get on with his life. Was he?

BREAKING SAM

Sam huffed as he dumped the trash. Hard to get on with life when someone out there seemed determined to remind him of his past. Once he knew who vandalized the trucks he'd beat the snot out of them, then put the past behind.

TWELVE

Sam drove south on Highway Ninety-Seven to the larger city of Bend. While driving between used car dealerships, he passed a couple of Christmas tree lots reminding him of the upcoming holiday. He stopped at the third used car lot of the day, hoping to find a good deal and stepped from the cab of his father's truck. "Wait here, Buddy." The golden stood on the seat, sniffing the air through the open passenger side window.

A salesman at the end of a row of trucks walked toward Sam. "Can I help you find a truck? What are you looking for?" He tugged a sheaf of paperwork from his coat pocket.

Sam patted Bud. "I hope so; need a Ford one ton flatbed, not too many miles on it, four by four diesel."

"I'm Charlie," the salesman tapped the hood of a nearby truck. "Yep; you want the rancher's classic. I could sell trucks like that all day long around here." He flipped through the pages listing inventory and smiled. "Looks like you're in luck. We just took one in; let's go check it out."

The truck could've been flashier, but white was okay. Tucker would have given it a 'thumbs-up.' Sam wrangled a deal which included his father's truck, shook hands with Charlie and happily transferred Bud.

He cruised his newer used truck to a Burger King drive through, ordered hamburgers and fries and parked. Buddy poked the bag of food with his nose. "Just hold on a sec, Bud-boy." Sam reached inside a fed the golden a couple fries. "We'll share."

Between bites of burger, he fed Bud. On the bright side, after he adjusted the truck insurance, taking off his father's truck along with his old truck and flatbed, he might save money. New truck; now paint for his house. Another step forward.

The sun shone in a clear cold sky as Sam put the truck in gear, heading north. In Redmond he stopped at the building supply, the glass front doors painted with wreaths and 'Merry Christmas.' "Bah, humbug," he mumbled under his breath.

His eyes glazed in front of the paint display. Time for a new color, something other than off-white. Jessie's place was pale yellow, which suited her but he wanted an earthy color. There were so many to choose from, he didn't have a clue which would look best in his home.

"What're you thinking?" Jessie stood right beside him, her hair tumbling over her shoulders in pale curls, like Bud's hair behind his ears. On her it looked great. Below a chunky turtleneck sweater, she wore jeans.

"Can't decide what color to paint the inside of my house. What brings you here?"

"Buying a tarp. I heard about your trucks. I can't imagine why anyone would do that."

Sam hooked a thumb in his pocket. "Well, on the bright side, I sold a couple of horses and now have another truck."

"That's great." She shook her hair back and ran a finger over paint samples. "So what's your favorite time of day?"

"Why?" He stared; he couldn't help it. Did she have any idea of how beautiful she looked?

"I'm trying to help you find the right color."

"Sunrise and sunset. Colors are intense at that time. It's the start of plans and plans realized and the feeling that comes with both. Anticipation and satisfaction."

"Wow. That's pretty deep." Jessie studied him a moment before turning back to the charts. "Okay; what do you like best at that time?"

"Guess I like the way the sage brush looks."

"I know what you mean, the way it's all lit against the deep blue-gray of the Cascades. Let's see," Jessie picked a few strips of color and sorted through them. "I think I've got it. What about this?" She handed him a strip of gray-green in a warm tone. "Try to imagine your rooms this color."

The color was perfect; not too pale or dark. "Yeah. I'm impressed. Hope you don't charge consulting fees; I'd have to give you an IOU."

She laughed. "Seems to me it's your turn to invite me over for dinner. Call me when you're done painting."

"Sure. Sounds good." Sam hoped by then he'd think of something worthy to cook for her. She waved goodbye. He purchased several cans of the paint.

Back on the road, Bud laid his hairy paw on Sam's arm. "Okay, I know it's been a long day. Just got to get some groceries before home."

He looked forward to dinner with Jessie. Chef Boyardee wouldn't do. He compared Jessie and Sierra. Sierra: earthy, fiery, and strong. Jessie: warm sunlight on water; yet she flowed with an inner strength to go tramping all over the boonies alone.

At the ranch, a message on the machine inquired about the Arabians for sale. Whew, Sierra worked fast. He returned the call. Could they come out tomorrow? You bet.

"Well, Bud, I'll be up late. I'm going to paint the office so we can make a good impression." Sam gathered the supplies, brought them into the room and lit a small fire in the pot-bellied stove. Folding a piece of sandpaper, he went to work on all the wood moldings around the doors and windows. Bud sneezed and lay in the hall.

Shortly after midnight, he finished. Jessie had given him good advice. A warm sage colored the walls. The ceiling he painted what Jessie called cream, the woodwork stained a honey-maple. The hardwood floors, desk and chairs he cleaned with oil soap.

He'd do the whole house the same. Yawning, he unplugged the coffeepot and headed to bed.

At daybreak, he revved the tractor and used the blade implement to scrape out the overhang, hoping the smell of urine and fresh manure would dissipate before his company arrived as he spread the mess off to the side of the still snowy pasture. While he tossed flakes of hay into the feeders, Bud went after the horses at the far end of the pasture. When the last one jogged in for breakfast, Sam shut the gate so they couldn't leave the shelter corral and tackled them one by one with the currycomb and brush. The shedding hadn't even really begun. He wasn't looking forward to March, when there'd be gobs of hair everywhere.

Two hours later, spitting horsehair and slapping smelly dust from his coat, he headed for a hot shower. Long ago, after a rodeo, he'd gone with Matt to a Quarter Horse farm to see a popular stallion. The owner had chewed out his trainer for being sloppy. "What we do here, breeding horses and selling them is a professional occupation. That means I want this stable to look professional. Hire help if you have to."

The concept made sense to Sam even if he didn't have much stock. Someday, he would. He'd gradually build back with only the best. He could afford to breed his Quarter Horse mare now. He'd improve the ranch with an eye toward a professional image, all part of the new life he was making for himself.

Sam reached for the folder of pedigrees as a truck and four horse slant load trailer stopped at the barn. "Bud, try to be a bit more professional, okay?" He looked his dog in the eye as he opened the door. Buddy slowly wagged twice and followed Sam to their company.

Two tall women stood at the gate, staring at the horses. The one with short gray hair did the introductions.

"I'm Liz. You must be Sam. Sierra told us about your father. I'm sorry we missed his memorial. I rode with him a few times and always liked his horses. This is my daughter, Jackie."

"I'm glad to meet you both. My Dad has ride records and info inside, if you'd like to see them. Or, I can take you on a ride if you want to try any of the horses." Sam glanced at the small herd, wondering how they looked to the women. They were ranch bred, not stalled like show horses.

Liz's daughter slipped through the metal gate. "Could we just hang out here with them for a while?" Liz paused.

Sam shifted his weight from foot to foot. He couldn't tell them anything about the horses. "Go ahead. They're all for sale except the two Quarter horses, the flea-bitten grey and the copper mare." He headed for the house. "It's pretty cold. I'll brew some coffee. When you're ready, we'll meet in the office over there."

Sam looked through Tucker's files while the coffee dripped, filling the pot. The office would smell good; it looked fresh with the new paint. Yep; Tucker had logged each horse's accomplishments as dams and endurance horses. That should help the sale along with the pedigrees and photos identifying each animal along with Sierra's notes on pricing.

A half hour later the women entered the office, sat in wooden chairs at the pot-bellied stove and thanked him for the mugs of coffee he offered. Sam showed them the papers he'd found. After tossing numbers back and forth, they agreed on thirty-five thousand for a mare and three geldings.

He helped load the horses into Jackie's slant load trailer. As the women drove away, he stared at the check. Tucker's Arabs brought in more than he ever would've guessed. They must've been good ones. Sierra had told him how much they were worth. He didn't actually believe it 'til now. His Quarter horses had brought good prices, but not this much. Nine left to sell. Dad, I had no idea.

He gave Bud a rub and walked back to the office where he called the farm owning the stud he'd researched for his Quarter horse mare. Early spring they'd ship semen. Next, he wrote checks to pay off the vet, farrier, and farm equipment company. A new metal roof on the barn, more gravel for the road, and other repairs would drain the rest of the money. At least he'd be caught up, the ranch would look better and his mare would soon be bred. Another step closer to realizing some goals.

Out at the barn, Sam loaded the truck with hay to make a delivery on the way to the bank. Bud leaped into the cab all by himself. Gee, the golden was grown up now. "When we get to town, we'll get burgers to celebrate. You like burgers?" He gently thumped his dog on the ribs as he headed the truck down the drive. What a great day.

Two teenage boys stood ready at their barn as he maneuvered his truck at the ranch to deliver the hay. They heaved the bales one by one onto a narrow chain driven metal hay elevator that nosily deposited them into the barn loft. Sam pulled on leather gloves and showed them mercy, slapping dust and hay from his jacket and jeans when finished.

In town, he made it to the bank right before it closed. As promised, Sam drove to the burger place take out window and bought food to go for himself and Bud, who sniffed the warm delicious smelling bag.

Sam hesitated as he drove past the Brown Bear. He made a quick decision, turned the corner and parked. "Wait here, boy. I'm gonna see if anyone I know is hanging out. I won't be long." He rubbed Bud's head as the golden whined.

The bar wasn't as crowded as last time. Griz slid a bottle across the polished counter. "I still owe you. Took you long enough to collect."

"I've been busy." Sam took a slug and looked around in the dim light. "Doesn't Bill or Redfeather hang out here anymore?"

"Crowds turned over while you were gone. Some old timers come once in a while. Redfeather is at Ka-Nee-Ta working at the Indian Head Casino." Griz poured a drink for a customer to Sam's right. "Bill got work in Bend as a laborer. Bend is booming, contractors buying ranches and subdividing, selling houses like hotcakes." Griz wiped down the bar, poured more beer.

Sam listened to some honky-tonk tune. The bunch next to him horsed around, jabbing each other in the ribs. He got bumped; the cowboy turned. "Sorry; no offense."

"No problem," Sam smiled. The cowboy nodded, got back to his friends. In prison, he would've had to stomp the guy for that or appear weak. He drained the last of his beer. Bud was waiting; time to leave.

Long purple gray shadows dimmed the front of the bar as Sam stepped outside on the sidewalk.

"Hey, it's the con!" Someone jerked his elbow from behind, spinning him around. He caught a glimpse of some guy near his age before a fist smashed into his face. He staggered back, caught his balance and took a swing. Before it could connect, something heavy struck the back of his head and he went down.

THIRTEEN

Somebody viciously kicked Sam in the ribs as he laid on the sidewalk, sending a jab of hurt to his lungs. "Didn't you get our message? Get lost!"

He groaned; saw several pairs of cowboy boots before pain blurred his vision and everything faded.

Sam blinked. In the dim neon lights above the bar, he could make out a figure bending over him. He swung at it as he fought to raise himself.

"Easy, son. I'm here to help." The man offered a hand and helped Sam stand. His badge reflected the bar lights. "First your trucks, now this. You're on somebody's list."

The back of Sam's head hammered out each heartbeat. He winced and gingerly touched it. A few customers from the bar gathered round, including Griz.

"Think you need a doctor? I can call for help. Judging by the obvious bruises, you're going to be one sore cowboy." The Deputy reached for his radio.

Sam swayed slightly as he lifted his hand. "No, I'll be okay in a minute. I've done worse riding bulls."

"Lucky for you, I happened to be patrolling here; noticed those punks working you over. They scattered when I flashed my lights and siren." The Deputy scanned the crowd. "Anyone see anything? Recognize those guys?"

Griz's customers shook their heads. "We came out when we heard your siren," a young woman said.

"How 'bout some ice for that egg? I'll be right back." Griz headed back inside the door.

Everyone drifted away as the Deputy filled out a report. Sam flexed his arms and legs. He trembled, clenched his teeth and took several shallow painful breaths of cold air. He vowed to get even. In a fair fight, they wouldn't stand a chance. Griz returned with a zip lock baggie full of crushed ice and handed it to Sam.

The Deputy walked Sam to his truck. "Take care now," he said.

Sam opened the door, his cab light exposing Bud licking his lips, burger wrappers shredded all over the seat. "Didn't you save me any fries?" Sam bit back the urge to laugh as Bud hung his head and burped. How could he stay mad with that guilty face sitting next to him?

He put the baggie in the crown of his Stetson and carefully placed the hat on his head, started the flatbed and nodded as the Deputy advised him to get medical help if he felt nauseous or sleepy. He couldn't tell if the ice helped or not. One step forward and two back.

Sam's body ached. The next day he lay low, moving slowly to feed the animals and the woodstove, stewing over the guys that jumped him, restless staring at the unpainted walls. A day later, he sanded and painted in spite of a splitting headache.

BREAKING SAM

Riding Amber in the huge near-empty hay barn brightened every other day as he healed. Since Amber lived with cows all her life, riding her around the calves, following them and moving slow through his small herd was just part of the game. The copper mare quickly learned to read his body language. She taught him by swishing her tail if he used too much leg or pinning her ears if his hands held her too tight.

Sam had never ridden a horse that responded so easily. He paid attention to small things he noticed about the mare. Like how she'd keep one ear tuned back to him when he asked for something new and pointed both ears forward as she figured it out.

He had set a goal: to prep and paint a room a day, spurring him on as the house slowly transformed by the fresh color lifted his mood. Project done, body strong again, he celebrated by spending the morning loping Amber in figure eights, changing leads in the center.

She caught on quickly as he worked her in circles, jogging through the middle, using the corner to help her pick up the lope on the correct lead as she curved through the turn. The quiet inside the barn broken only by Amber's occasional snort and muffled hoofbeats in the soft dirt. Sam sat back and the copper mare slid to a smooth stop.

"I thought you wouldn't be caught dead riding an Arab."

Both Amber and Sam jumped at the voice. Matt casually leaned against the doorway post, looking like his old self wearing Wranglers and a Carhartt coat. Bud raised his head from his nest in the hay and yawned.

Sam frowned, stepped down from the saddle and led the mare to Matt. "I know what I said. It still goes for all of them except her."

Matt shrugged. "What's so special about this horse? Besides pretty?"

Sam led his horse back to the stock barn and pulled off the saddle, debating whether or not to tell Matt his plan and why he rode the mare.

"Glad to see you're all right. Heard you got pounded in front of the Brown Bear," Matt said following behind him.

"Oh, great. Seems like everybody knows everything around here." Sam turned the copper mare out with the other horses. "Can you keep a secret?"

"I always have," Matt said seriously.

"Alright; come on inside for a bit." He decided to run his plan by Matt. His old friend used to do all kinds of crazy stuff and make it work. Besides, who else could he confide in?

"Hey, you've been working hard!" Matt whistled as he wandered through the freshly painted house. "This looks great. And what's that awesome smell?"

Sam quickly shut the oven door on the roast he'd just checked. "None of your business. I've got company coming soon so shut up while I talk fast." He poured two cups of coffee and put them on the table with a package of old fashioned donuts. Matt bit into one.

"You would've been blown away if you saw how she played that bull on her own." Sam described how he'd been bucked off, how Amber blocked the bull, most likely saving his life. "She could win cutting competitions; what do you think?"

Matt reached for another donut. "Oh boy; you know the way folks feel about Quarter Horses, especially at cutting. Hope you're not thinking that the prize money will make you rich, even if she is as good as you say."

"I'm having my Quarter mare bred. In the meantime, at least I'll get a name for myself, get started." Sam shared his donut with Bud, who sat with a paw on Sam's boot.

Matt shook his head as he held out his cup for more coffee. "I don't mean to be a bucket of cold water. Besides the commitment involved with training and showing, cutting is an expensive sport. You have to pay thirty-five dollars a practice for the cattle; two hundred plus for a class at the shows." He sighed, looking Sam in the eye. "I'm saying this as your old sidekick: after what you did, killing Tucker's

Arabian for the insurance; suggesting he get a Quarter Horse stallion . . . you'll be eating humble pie my friend."

"I know. Believe me, I can hear the jeers already. Amberwind is a fluke." He shrugged. "I know Arabs under normal circumstances can't compete with top Quarter cutters. The two breeds have different muscle structure. And Quarter Horses have 'cow' sense bred into them." Sam swallowed the last of his coffee. "Anyway, that copper mare is going to make them sit up and notice, just you wait and see."

Matt stood to leave. "You know what? I hope you win big-time. You've got guts." He looked around the room as he sauntered to the door. "Jessie's gonna be impressed."

Sam shook his head. Nothing, absolutely nothing was secret in a small town.

Sam lathered his face as Bud watched. The dog's waving tail kept pulling out the toilet paper into a messy pile on the floor. He chuckled while re-rolling the paper and rubbing Bud's shoulders. Sam checked his reflection in the mirror with a critical eye. What did Jessica see? Did she like his blue eyes, sandy blond hair, square jaw? An old scar above his eyebrow, faint crow's feet and slightly crooked nose might not be considered handsome. At least his bruises had healed.

Picking up the razor, he scratched at his face, puffing out his cheek, the fresh light scent of cream on his face felt clean. He wanted to look good when Jessie arrived any time now.

The roast and potatoes stayed warm in the oven, the meaty smell causing his stomach to rumble. The only other things he could cook were bar-b-que and eggs; someday he'd cook those for her, too.

Another thing Matt said while walking out to his truck was "don't live your life in other people's minds. They don't think of you that often." Where did Matt get this stuff?

Sam rinsed his face and dried it with the towel he'd wrapped around his waist. He dressed in Wranglers and a chamois shirt, reaching for his tin of chew from the dresser top. Sam hesitated before slipping it into his back pocket. A faded circle branded the left rear pocket of all his jeans; part of the cowboy image. He thought about Matt's remark that Jessie wouldn't want to kiss a chewer and dumped the tin in the trash. He better remember to buy chewing gum.

Bud ran to the door barking, his tail whacking his sides. Sam let Jessie in and hung her coat on the horseshoe rack by the door.

She had a bundle wrapped under her arm and handed it to him. "This is an early Christmas present for Buddy."

"Really? Hey, Bud. Look what Jess brought you." At the mention of his name, the golden jumped up and down in place. Sam set the gift on the floor. "Open it, Bud."

Bud sniffed, then carefully bit the corner of the paper and pulled, tearing open the wrapping, exposing a thick fleecy dog bed. Bud drug it near the table and curled up on it.

"We both thank you. That's really thoughtful." Sam gathered up the red and green wrapping paper, wondering why he hadn't bought his dog a bed himself. Guess he was learning about pets, including Amber.

"This is even better than I imagined," Jessie said as she looked around. "Show me the rest!"

Sam led her through the house and office. She noticed and approved of the photos of Tucker riding his endurance horses on the office walls. Back in the living room, he liked her suggestion of moving the old leather couch to face the woodstove. She helped him rearrange the room, which made it romantic and cozy like the photos in the ranch magazines.

"Now you have the perfect corner to decorate your Christmas tree," she said, pointing out the spot.

"Yeah, Matt brought up that subject." Sam gazed at the empty corner.

Jessica touched his arm and he turned to her. "Matt mentioned after church recently how he missed cutting Christmas trees together with our families. I miss those times, too."

"I wasn't planning on much for the holidays," Sam looked down. "Hard to get in the spirit this year, you know?" He gazed at her face. Her eyes glistened. "Maybe it'd be fun to start up the old tradition again?" By her smile, he knew it'd make her happy.

Since he didn't have candles, he lit an old oil lamp on the table and served dinner. Bud sat with his head on Sam's lap. If Jessica heard about the bar incident, she didn't mention it. Her prayer at the table was sweet, asking a special blessing on his "new" home. She shoved her sweater sleeves up to her elbows, the slate blue color the same as her eyes, and helped herself to a slice of roast.

"Did you get the picture of the coyotes?" Sam drizzled ranch dressing on his salad and passed her the rolls.

"No. They're really smart. I think I've located a den. Hopefully this spring I'll get some shots of the pups. I'll have to spend hours waiting and watching. If you're not too busy planting hay fields, you can keep me company." She smiled. Lamp light glinted off her curls.

"I'll be cutting hay this summer for sure. But why would I be planting?" Raised as a farm girl, she knew about hay. He filled her glass with ginger ale.

"You have rich bottom land along the river. With the demand for hay, you should think about expanding your business. It's good money." Jessie paused as she cut her meat.

"You have a point. Except I don't want to be a farmer; I'm a rancher, a cowboy." Sam slid Bud a piece of fat.

Jessie nodded. "I know that. But as you gradually increase your herds, won't you need more hay?"

"I'll have to think about that," he mumbled.

"So what are you going to do with all that stuff crammed in your spare bedroom?" Jessie helped clear the table. "I have a friend at church who lives off garage sales. She's in Terrebonne; she'll take your stuff on consignment."

"Sounds good to me; I'll even deliver it to her. Ready for dessert?" He'd bought mocha flavored ice cream dotted with chocolate covered coffee beans. Sam led the way to the leather couch, sinking into it beside Jessica as they watched the fire in the wood stove through the glass door.

Jessie spooned the ice cream and closed her eyes. "This is the best."

Bud tugged his bed over and sacked out at their feet. Sam edged closer to Jessie, putting his arm around her, enjoying the way she fit against his side. He touched her silky hair and wondered how her lips would taste.

She gently leaned apart. "Let's go slow, Sam. I really want to get to know you. I want you to know who I am, too."

He angled away to get a better view of her. What a switch. Most girls he'd been with in the past practically tore his clothes off. None ever tried to get to know him. Jessica was different. He liked the thought of getting to know her.

"Okay; what do I need to know about you?" Sam rubbed his thumb over her hand.

Jessie smiled, her face shining. "If you ever run out of this ice cream, I'll really be disappointed!"

He joined her laughter. He wanted her in his life. The thought scared him. Sure, she was here now and wanted to see more of him. But he knew her parents. He'd bet his silver buckle they wouldn't want their only daughter hanging around an ex-con.

She touched his cheek. "I can pretty much guess what you're thinking right now with that serious face. Sam, remember when I told you that I always thought we'd be together? I've dreamed of you since I was ten. What's happened in the past is past; what matters now is what you're going to do with the future."

Fourteen

Sam carried in an armful of firewood and set it down on the rock hearth beside the woodstove. Another storm dumped several inches on top of a foot of snow overnight. Buddy shook beside him, snow flying from his coat. "Could you do that outside next time?"

He grabbed a towel he kept by the door and wiped up the mess. The quiet morning reminded him how empty the house felt without Tucker as he rubbed the silver cuff on his wrist.

The phone ringing broke his mood.

"Hey, Sam. I helped my folks cut a Christmas tree off their ranch yesterday. There's got to be a dozen perfect trees in that one spot. Think you could pick up Jessica and meet me at their place? We could cut trees for each of us." Matt paused. "Don't make excuses. Call Jess, then let me know so I can meet you there."

Sam hung his head. He was getting roped into the holiday whether he wanted to or not. But what else would he do today? Spending time with Jessie would be great.

"Okay, Matt. I'll call and let you know." Buddy lifted his head from his bed and gazed at Sam as he hung up the phone. "I suppose you're invited, too," Sam told his golden.

Sam glanced at Jessica as he drove to Matt's family ranch at the base of the Cascades, memories of their childhood excursions with their parents drifting back after years forgotten. Again, she reminded him of a model in her teal colored snow coat and tall insulated boots. He wore tall waterproof Muck boots with his jeans tucked in, standard footwear for barn chores in snow and mud.

"I'm so glad Matt invited us to come up here," Jessica said as she snuggled Bud sitting between them. "I used to love riding up on the buckboard to get our trees." She caught his glance. "I don't know why the folks quit doing it."

"Might be because you, Matt and me grew up and went different directions for a while." Sam stopped at an intersection and looked both ways before crossing.

Jessica sighed. "Yep; you're probably right."

Sam rubbed the golden's ears. "Well, this ought to be fun; what perfect weather, right?" The Cascade Range with the Three Sisters peaked above them, brilliant snow white against a deep blue sky.

"That's for sure. Glad I brought my camera," Jessie said.

A large black wrought iron gate with silhouetted conifer trees marked the entrance to the Hunter Ranch. Sam turned at the gate, reached out and pressed the key pad numbers.

"I'm guessing the code hasn't changed," Sam closed his window against the chill.

"You're right." Jessica tugged her camera back pack from the floor to her lap.

The gate automatically swung open and he drove on through, snow banked along the plowed road as it wound through tall conifers to a log two story ranch house. Sam passed it by and parked at the large barn and equipment shed.

Matt stood next to the buckboard and tractor and waved. "Hurry up before I drink all the hot chocolate Mom made for us."

Jessica smiled as they all joined Matt, who handed them steaming cups. Buddy raced around in snow, tongue hanging from the side of his mouth. Sam patted the buckboard and the golden jumped up onto it.

"This is good," Jess said between sips. "Thank your Mom for us."

Matt climbed up on the tractor and fired it up as Sam helped Jess climb up to sit with her back against a wooden equipment box holding the chainsaw and settled beside her.

The tractor's chain wrapped tires dug in on the climb, the loud engine chugging breaking the silence as Matt guided it up the snow packed road. Jessie snapped pictures of Matt's profile as he drove, Bud hunkered down to keep his balance, nose taking inventory of the woods and leaned in close to Sam to take their photo, holding the camera at arm's length away.

Where the road leveled at a wide spot, Matt stopped the tractor. Sam inhaled the sharp cold air, his breath a vapor as he gazed at the thick forest. "These firs are way too tall," he said after helping Jessica down.

Matt lifted the chainsaw from the box. "Follow me; there's some young trees not far from here." He balanced the saw over his shoulder on the flat of the blade and broke trail through knee high snow.

Buddy leapt through the snow alternately burrowing into it and rolling.

Jessica laughed. "What a sweet boy; what joy." She followed after Matt, using his tracks for easier going.

Sam stepped close behind her as she paused often to snap photos of the scenery, his dog, Matt and himself. It was as if time went back to their high school days. It felt good.

Matt stopped and faced them. "Some things don't change. Feels like we never parted, doesn't it?" His smile was huge.

Jessie danced where she stood. "Yeah; like déjà vu! Let's stick together from now on, okay?" She faced Sam.

"I'd like that," he said, happy that their feelings were mutual. Bud raced by, spun and jumped on Sam. He bent to rub his squirming dog, wondering how often his recent past would spoil it for him. He straightened, missing his Dad, knowing how much he enjoyed Christmas.

A snowball smacked his shoulder. Jessica dodged the one Matt threw. Sam scooped a handful of snow, packed it and repaid Matt, the golden leaping between them, snapping at the snowballs.

"Time out!" Jessie yelled. "Where's those trees, Matt? We've got to cut them and get me home. My folks are expecting me for dinner."

Matt picked up the saw. "Really? Right over there." Jessie hit him in the back with one last snowball as he turned.

Sam followed behind, wishing Tucker was home, picturing his face lighting up with the tree.

FIFTEEN

Sam set the tree in the corner of the living room, its fresh forest scent filling the room. He found the box of ornaments Tucker had stored and rummaged through them. A new string of tiny white seed lights replaced the old colored bulbs; he set the lights aside and decided most of the ornaments were old and held no meaning for him except for the antique harness bells at the bottom. He found brown twine and hung them from the branches along with the lights.

Bud sniffed the Christmas tree, yawned and laid near the woodstove. Sam sat on the couch and gazed at the scene. He blinked a tear, wiped it; his heart heavier than a bucket of iron horseshoes missing Tucker. He'd just had a great day with his closest friends. One he didn't deserve.

Sam worked hard the next two weeks, cleaning out the barn organizing tack and tools, often riding Amber in the near empty hay barn, breaking only to play with Buddy, who was hard to ignore. The phone rang several times but he ignored it.

Christmas eve, Bud went into a barking frenzy as Matt drove up to the house. Sam opened the door so the golden could greet their friend, running circles around him up to the front porch.

"That's enough, Bud," Sam said as he let them in the house.

Matt slapped the powdery snow from his coat and hung it by the door. "I had to check and see if your phone is working. I've tried calling you; so has Jess."

"Phone works okay." Sam turned away. "I've been busy."

"We've missed you." Matt said.

Sam felt Matt's hand on his shoulder. "Want some coffee?"

"That sounds good." Matt scraped a chair back from the table and sat.

Sam poured in water, added coffee in the filter and turned on the pot. "It's not about you or Jessie, I'm just working through some stuff."

"Holidays are hard," Matt nodded. "What you're feeling is normal, missing Tucker."

"It hurts; I miss him so much," Sam admitted. "I don't deserve Christmas. I can't imagine how hard it was for Dad last year."

Matt clasped his hands on the tabletop. "You're not alone, Sam. None of us deserve it. But Jesus' birth came so that His Light can shine in the darkness, even this dark time of the year . . . especially for you."

Sam shook his head. "I'm not ready to face the church crowd either."

Matt tugged an envelope from his pocket and laid it on the table. "Jessica understands. She wanted me to give you this."

The coffee smelled comforting as Sam filled a couple of cups and sat at the table across from Matt.

After a few quiet moments sipping coffee, Matt cleared his throat. "About that church crowd. They rallied around Tucker last year, made sure he had plenty of pie and cookies. They picked him up for the church Christmas potluck, too."

Sam rubbed his face. "If I could have one wish, I'd turn back time." He reached down and scratched Bud's head laying on his boot. "I appreciate you coming by, but I don't want to spoil Christmas for you or Jessie. I feel like a cold wet dog that rolled in the muck to make it better."

After Matt left, Sam opened Jessie's Christmas card. A snowy evening scene with a cabin and a star shaped like a cross shimmered on the front. Inside she'd written in her graceful script: 'Merry Christmas Sam. Think on these gifts Jesus offers to us: Mercy is not getting what you do deserve. Grace is getting what you don't deserve. Always, Jessica.'

He read it over several times, trying to make sense of it. So how did you get this mercy and grace? Don't you have to earn it? He left the card on the table and took his golden outside one last time before going to bed.

Sixteen

Sam wrestled with his sheets and blankets. His mind wouldn't shut down. He kept going through different scenarios of how to work Amber on a calf. He didn't have to try hard to imagine the response he'd get taking the Arab horse to a practice. Finally he drifted to sleep.

Jessie returned and snuggled close, planting hot sexy kisses all over his face. Her hair was so silky soft, her warm body . . . smelled like a dog. He opened his eyes and gazed into Buddy's golden brown ones. Sam yelled. Bud cringed and leapt off the bed.

Sam rubbed his face hard. He slid from the covers and crouched beside Bud, scratching the dog's head. "I'm sorry, boy. You're my Buddy, alright." The golden thumped his tail on the floor and laid his paw on Sam's arm. It'd be really lonesome around the house without his dog.

BREAKING SAM

The copper mare perked her ears as Sam rode her slowly to the calves that munched hay in the corner of the overhang. A few more steps and one calf panicked as Amber stood between it and the others. The calf bolted. Amber spun on her haunches and blocked the way. Each time the calf ducked around, Amber crouched low, nose to nose with the calf, dancing side to side with her front legs. After a minute, Sam picked up the reins and patted the mare as the bawling calf rejoined the herd. Amber snorted and tossed her head. In spite of the cold, sweat dampened Sam's armpits as he thought about going 'public.'

He turned the mare loose. A chunk of snow slid off the metal overhang and splatted in the mud. The day warmed. Bud barked as an old pick-up rolled into the yard. He recognized the couple as long-time friends of Tucker's.

"Hello, Sam." Mr. Miller's coat didn't quite close in front of his overalls. He moved stiffly as he stepped from the cab.

Sam knew the man as a hard worker. He'd raised a large family and ran a dairy on land adjoining his. Sam wouldn't hold a bully of a son like Russell against him. "What can I do for you?"

"Well, Pastor Matt mentioned you selling off the A-rabs. Me and the missus," he turned toward his wife; she rolled down her window and waved. "We're retiring. Going let the kids run the dairy; they're bringing in a brand new doublewide mobile home. Anyway, we can't be without animals, they're such a part of us so-"

Mrs. Miller interrupted. "Just spit it out, Ralph! Tucker used to worry about Ranger's dam and grand-dam. They're getting old. He talked about retiring them."

"Yeah," Mr. Miller rubbed the stubble on his chin. "What'd you say they retire with us? Those old mares would get all the hay and pasture they'd want and shelter, too. We've always enjoyed watching the horses whenever they've grazed near our fence line."

Sam looked from one to the other.

"'Course we can't afford to pay much," Mrs. Miller added.

Sam didn't take long to decide. Sierra mentioned the two aged mares with valuable bloodlines. They might not carry a foal after being open for several years. "If you go get your stock trailer and come back today, I'll give you the two horses free." By the smiles on their faces, he knew he'd made the right choice; knew his father would approve.

By the end of the week a fresh warm wind blew. Snow dripped off the roofs and green grass grew as the rest of the snow melted into puddles. Sam bought a truckload of posts and two-by-sixes to repair the corrals at the barn from the feed and farm store, pausing at the bulletin board. A regional cutting association notice gave schedules for cutting practice at a ranch arena in Madras, a town north on the main highway. Sam wrote down the dates, winching at the thought of all the work ahead of him. He made time to ride the copper mare every day, teaching her cues for spins and rollbacks in the empty hay barn. No more hay deliveries meant more time freed up . . .

Who was he kidding, telling himself he needed to get the place in shape first. The problem was simple: showing at the arena to practice cutting with an Arab went against his pride.

He drove home and parked beside the corrals with his load of lumber. Bud leaped from the cab and chased quail from the yard. That afternoon, he tore out the old corrals at the barns, cutting and splitting up the old wood for next year's kindling.

SEVENTEEN

Sam hooked a chain around the rotten field post, climbed on the tractor and pulled it out of the ground. After dragging it to the burn pile, he chained a new pressure treated post to the tractor and drug it to the fence line. He drilled a new hole in the ground with the auger. Next, he wrapped his arms around the post and lifted it above the hole and dropped it in. Satisfied it was level, he tamped the dirt tight around it with a heavy metal pole. Finally he stretched the top strand of barbwire to the post, tacking it in place with a U-shaped nail. Four more strands spaced below it finished that post.

He walked the fence line checking the posts for the next rotten one, knowing that with the size of the ranch, this chore would take all year, fitting it in as time allowed.

One by one Sam whittled down his list of projects timing each with the weather conditions, like the barn corrals. The ground dried out enough the next day for him to finished replacing the posts and boards for the last corral; this one connected to the horse stalls where he'd keep his Quarter Horse mare with her colt within the secure fencing come spring next year.

The shipped semen arrived. Sam needed to call the vet; his mare came into heat and needed to be artificially inseminated. Dr. Mitch Fisher was the best; Tucker had counted on him for years. Dr. Fisher had done Ranger's autopsy; knew Sam's past along with everyone else around. Would Mitch hold it against him?

Only one way to find out. Sam settled in the office chair and tapped the vet's number on the ranch phone's speed dial.

"Dr. Fisher."

"This is Sam West; I've got a mare that needs artificial insemination." He held his breath.

"Alright. I can be there tomorrow morning. These things need to be timed right. She's in strong heat?" The vet's voice sounded all business.

"Yes sir. Tomorrow morning would be great," Sam leaned forward, marking the desk calendar. Another step forward.

Sam had his Quarter horse mare haltered, groomed and tied to the hitching rail ready for the vet's arrival. The rest of the horses stood at the gate, curious to see what was going on with her. He gave her a pat and headed inside for another cup of coffee, the golden at his heels.

Bud stood at the kitchen door and barked. "Someone here? Let's go see." Sam set his cup on the counter and opened the door as the vet parked his rig at the barn.

Dr. Fisher opened the custom refrigerated compartment that filled the bed of his truck, then looked around at the mare and barns as Sam strode to his side.

"This is quite the improvement to the ranch since I was here last at Tucker's memorial." He held out his hand. "You've been working hard."

Sam grasped his hand, glad the vet noticed the changes. "Thank you, Dr. Fisher." The vet had been at the memorial? Sam didn't remember seeing him. But then, other than Matt and Jessica, he couldn't say who'd been there, he'd been so full of loss.

"Call me 'Doc.' Who's this?" Doc reached down to scratch the golden's ear.

"That's my Buddy." Sam explained how he'd rescued the dog the day his father died. "I've never wanted a dog before, but this guy is hard to ignore. We keep each other company."

Doc laughed. "Yep, I can see that." He straightened. "You have the container? Tell me about the mare."

Sam stepped into the tack room and grabbed the semen container, handed it to Doc, sharing his hopes for a champion colt out of the mare as the vet donned elbow length surgical gloves and checked his mare.

"She seems ready so I'll go ahead with the insemination," Doc said as he inserted a long tube.

Sam stood at his mare's head, holding the lead rope for the next several minutes as the sun warmed his back.

Doc collected his instruments and tube. "That should 'take.' I'll come back in a month and check if she's in foal."

"I'll mark the calendar," Sam said as he turned the mare out back with the herd, the golden at his heels.

Doc joined him at the gate. "I heard you sold off most your stock and Tucker's." He pulled his ball cap from his overalls pocket and settled it on his head. "I was at Miller's dairy the other day; they sure enjoy watching the horses you gave them."

Sam shook Doc's hand. "I'm glad they got a good home."

He stood watching as the vet drove away, grateful that the vet treated the farm call same as any client. Sam hoped his past would be forgotten by the locals and fade away with time, even if he couldn't.

By the time he finished this stretch of fence, the bottomland would be ready to plow. Sam lifted his Stetson and wiped his face, the warm sunshine reminding him of Jessie's smile. Her suggestion made sense; he'd be a fool not to plant alfalfa.

Reaching with the wire-stretcher, he grabbed another strand of barbwire and tacked it a foot below the top strand. The purebred cattle he planned to raise needed a good fence. It wouldn't happen overnight; he'd invest in the best stock and go from there. Three more strands of barbwire tacked; Sam rose and stretched his back. He'd worked on the perimeter fence line all week.

The next post in line stood sound in the ground. Sam pulled the barbwire tight, hammering more U nails for extra strength.

Another post pulled to the burn pile. He released the chain and heaved the rotting post into the flaming ten foot circle of old posts. Sparks and smoke billowed skyward as he wiped his brow with the back of his gloved hand, gazing over the open rangeland. Bud stood and stretched when Sam trudged to the truck.

"Workin' hard, aren't you?" Sam rubbed the dog's ears and reached for his small ice chest. He sat against a tire in the sun. Although the day barely reached sixty degrees, he could feel the warmth of the sun through his plaid flannel shirt, warmth that kept his sweat from chilling. He poured water for Bud, popped open a beer and unwrapped a cheese sandwich. Bud lay at his side, watching each bite.

Since the bar incident, he'd become cautious, keeping the gate to the ranch locked and watching his rear view mirror for anyone following him. How he itched for a chance to teach those losers a lesson. No doubt they'd be back. Bud carefully took the corner of sandwich from his fingers, gulped it down and sniffed as Sam opened a bag of potato chips.

The white jawbone peaks of the Cascades rose on the horizon. Would Jessica share this life with him someday? He'd been so busy. Didn't help that he'd never been one for telephone conversations. Just to see her again would be worth it. Her words stayed with him -"I thought we'd be together . . . the past is past." He needed to prove himself first. To be good enough for her. In the meantime, remembering the way Jessie looked at him when she came for dinner; standing together at the sink washing the dishes afterwards . . .

Bud put a paw on his arm. Sam fed him a chip. Tuesday night was the cutting practice. No more putting it off. He and Amber needed the experience.

EIGHTEEN

Sam shifted gears as he turned the flatbed onto the highway. Amber stood in the gooseneck stock trailer hitched to the truck. "You're going to have to wait in the cab during practice." He headed off Bud's attempt to give him a wet ear with his shoulder. "Think you could pretend to be a guard-dog?" Bud panted as he paced the seat. Sam checked his watch and slowed down. He didn't want to arrive at the arena too early.

High clouds broke at the Cascades, allowing a glimpse of the last golden highlights of the day. One more week to spring, the best time of year. Sam stifled a yawn. He'd worked hard on the fence again today.

For several minutes he hummed a tune before he realized it was a song Jessie sang. Her voice had transported him into a quiet place. "Spirit, fall on us like the rain; Spirit, blow on us like the wind; Holy Spirit, shine on us like the sun, like the sun . . ."

His lips twitched. He imagined her in the rain, her hair blowing in the wind and the sun breaking through the clouds, beaming on her, like the sun was doing at this minute. There was something special about her. Whatever it was radiated from her.

Sam braked at a stop light in town. A truck towing a stock trailer in front of him turned and he followed it to the ranch arena. He parked off to the side of the lot away from the line of rigs, grateful as dusk settled. No one would notice Amber 'til he led her into the arena. He'd go sign in first.

Inside, he waited his turn at the folding table that stood in front of the bleachers. A dozen cowboys warmed their horses by loping circles in the well-lit covered arena. Sam gave his name and money and headed back to the copper mare.

Before leaving Tersis, he groomed her 'til his arms ached and the dirt around her was covered with shed hair. Her long mane and tail flowed. She looked good as he saddled her; the only fault was not being the right breed. He closed Bud in the cab. "You be good and wait."

Unsnapping the lead rope, he took a deep breath and swung into the saddle. "Make me proud, Amber," he whispered, guiding her to the light spilling through the wide doors of the arena.

Other than the muffled hoofbeats and snorts of the horses being ridden, the covered arena was quiet. Sam knew that afterwards the cutters would hang around, swap stories and visit. Right now though, even at a practice, they rode focused. He slid from the saddle and opened the side gate to lead Amber into the ring.

Besides the group jogging and loping counter-clock wise around the arena, several horses stood tied to the railings on the perimeter. Four "turn-back" riders kept a herd of a dozen calves bunched up at the far end.

Amber's eyes glowed in the lights as she lifted her head high, pricked her ears forward 'til the tips almost touched together. Sam tightened his hold on the reins. "Easy, girl." She flipped her tail over her back and half blew, half whistled loudly.

Three horses shied. One cowboy lost his hat. Everyone looked at Sam and the copper mare. Sam wanted to disappear, kissing his hopes for slipping in and avoiding notice until his time to work cattle goodbye.

Acting as if it were the most natural thing to do, Sam mounted Amber, her neck arched and tail high. He held her to a prancing walk until she settled. Jogging around the arena, he couldn't miss the stares or the mutters.

"Dingie Arab."

"Is that some kind of joke?"

A list posted on the gate let the riders know when their turn came. Sam stopped Amber beside it and leaning from his saddle, found his name near the end. Everyone took turns going one at a time, picking calves from the herd with two and a half minutes to practice. A frail old man with thick glasses called the first rider.

Sam halted Amber along the rail where she could watch; the quiet broken by hushed conversations in the stands, an occasional snort and call from a calf. The faint smell of cow manure wafted from the pens behind the arena.

He recognized the name of a well-known trainer. The man rode his experienced blue roan gelding deep into the herd and eased three calves away as the turn-back riders kept the rest of the herd against the back wall. The trainer let two calves return to the herd, blocking the calf he wanted. Gripping the saddle horn with his free hand, the trainer lowered his rein hand, giving his horse loose rein to work on its own. The blue roan ran back and forth, spinning, sliding and leaping to keep between the calf and the herd. A couple of cowboys, turn back riders on their horses, kept the calf from running away down the opposite half of the arena. The timer called out and the trainer raised his rein hand, stopping his dark grey-flecked horse with black mane and tail.

Sam shifted in his saddle. Another name was called and rider rode forward for his turn. The other cowboys kept busy moving their horses or watching the action and ignored Amber. The copper mare stayed quietly alert. When he figured his name would be called soon, he asked her to jog and lope circles with the few still waiting.

"Sam West is next," the timer announced.

As he rode Amber even with the timer's table, Sam heard some snickers along with loud laughter. Forget them, just concentrate and make the most of this practice.

Amber coiled like a spring beneath him as he guided her into the herd at a slow walk. He kept his eye on a black calf that no one had used. The others bolted back to the herd. Amber's ears locked on the black calf and Sam gave her rein. She sat down and spun as he gripped his saddle horn. The copper mare dug in deep and leapt sideways as the calf changed directions.

The calf doggedly tried to return to the herd. Amber crouched low and went into her dance, Sam hanging on and bracing himself in the stirrups. Amber was incredible for her first time. She never quit. The tired calf gave up. Sam lifted his rein hand and stopped his horse. "Time!" The old man called.

Amber puffed from her exertion, her nostrils flared. Sam rubbed the copper mare's damp neck, wiped his hand on his chaps and glanced around. Everyone gawked as he rode to the gate and swung from the saddle. He could've heard a mouse squeak.

Sam self-consciously touched the rim of his hat as everyone stared. Outside in the dark, he kept a straight face although he wanted to raise his fist and shout, "Yes!" He led the copper mare to his rig, her horseshoes clomping on the parking area pavement, tied her to the side and pulled off his saddle, storing it in the tack room in front of the trailer.

Two cowboys wandered along behind him and stood frowning at his horse. Sam reached for his chew that wasn't there and instead swung open the back of the trailer and turned on the lights.

"Heard the timer call your name." The cowboy wore a baseball style jacket with an Indian design across the front. 'Two thousand one

National Cutting Horse Championship' was embroidered across the left shoulder. "You the Sam West that served time?"

"Reckon so." Sam bent to run his hands down Amber's legs, checking her joints for signs of swelling.

"That one of your father's Arabs?"

"Yep." Sam straightened and glanced at the other cowboy who stood, slapping a lariat against his thigh.

"Don't know what you're trying to prove, boy. But she won't make the cut." They swaggered away, spurs clinking.

Sam untied Amber. Bud stuck his head out the open window of the cab and barked as a truck drove beside them and stopped. The headlights went off as the window slipped down.

"If I hadn't seen it, I wouldn't have believed it." Matt hung his elbow out the window. "Good thing I don't have to see the Lord. Seriously, Sam. That mare is special. You should've heard them cutters; they swore she had to be part Quarter. You're going to stir things alright."

"Yeah. Think I should get a bumper sticker that says 'my other horse is a Quarter Horse?'" Sam leaned against Matt's fender. Amber stepped close and snuffed Matt.

"Hey, she's sensitive. Don't hurt her feelings." Matt rubbed her between the eyes.

"Right. How'd you know I'd be here?" Sam toyed with the end of the lead rope.

"I had a feeling. You want company, let me know."

"Okay." Sam tugged on the rope as Matt slowly drove away. "What's with all this 'feelings' stuff?" He stepped the copper mare into the trailer and tied her to the sidewall.

Amberwind turned her head. In the faint overhead light, a slow tear dampened her face. Horses didn't cry. Did they? He rested his hand on the crest of her neck. "You're a really good horse. Just hang in there with me a while. Someday I'll call Sierra. She'll give you a good home and love on you."

The copper mare pressed her head against him. Sam was suddenly ashamed for using her, surprised by the choked up sadness in his chest.

NINETEEN

Sam dropped everything he knew he should be doing, like plowing fields when Jessica invited him along to photograph the coyotes. She even invited Buddy, as long as the golden stayed quiet.

Jessie waited for him at her cabin. She fired up her green Land Cruiser. Sam felt like a kid again, bracing his knee against the dash and rolled down the window, the air almost too warm for the long sleeve henley he wore. Bud stood behind Sam's seat with his head over Sam's shoulder, his nose twitching in the wind while Sam played his harmonica.

Twenty minutes later, he wiped the harmonica on his jeans and slid it into the leather case on his belt. "Are we there yet?"

Jessie laughed and shook her head. "Don't you dare complain about being thirsty or needing a bathroom." She paused. "I didn't know you played the harmonica; I like it. You're very good."

"Thanks; it helps me think and feel sometimes," Sam quietly shared with her.

"I know what you mean." She gave him a quick look and smiled.

Jessica pointed to a sagebrush flat below. "Pronghorn. They're spooked. By the time I got my camera out, they'd be gone."

Jessie parked in the shade of a pine near the top of the mountain by a rocky overlook and slung a backpack over her shoulders. "If you'll take the cooler and the blanket, I'll carry my tripod."

Sam stuffed Bud's leash into his back pocket. "How do you manage all alone?"

"I don't bother with any extras; just a water bottle and energy bars in my pack." She plopped a wide brimmed canvas hat over her curls and hoisted the tripod. "Let's go."

Bud waved his tail and stayed on her heels. Sam gathered the small cooler and blanket, following along a narrow deer trail that hugged the mountain, the sun warming his back, the air smelling like herbs as their legs rubbed through the brush.

Jessie checked her watch and the sun. She stopped a few times to scope the mountainside across the drainage that separated them through field glasses hung around her neck.

He liked being behind where he could watch her. She moved with the grace of a cat. Her sand colored jeans blended in with the landscape along with her tiny flower print shirt. She wore lace-up Durango boots, same as his. She stopped in a brushy clump of junipers and set down her camera backpack.

"The breeze is cooperating. We can talk quietly. Our noise and scent will move upslope behind us." Jessie set up the tripod while Sam laid out the blanket.

"How can I help?" He motioned for Bud to lie down next to the cooler.

She handed him the glasses. "Keep an eye on the mountainside over there, especially near that spring. Mama usually gets a drink there before going to her den."

Jessie lifted a camera dwarfed by its huge lens from her pack and attached it to the tri-pod. "In about an hour, the light will be perfect as the sun lowers. Ready for food?" She handed him an egg salad sandwich and opened a bag of chips. She even packed a bone for Bud.

Sam held her hand as she prayed over the meal. He almost chuckled when she added that she'd like the pups to show themselves. He kept a watch through the glasses between bites. Bud lay content to gnaw the bone.

Jessie asked about the copper mare. Sam told her about Matt showing up at the fairgrounds. "Matt said he 'had a feeling' -that's how he knew I'd be there." He helped himself to a banana and eyed the package of pecan cookies.

"That's Matt, alright. He has lots of what he calls 'divine appointments.'" She peered through the camera lens and adjusted the F-stop. "I wish I was more that way," Jessie said and hummed a song.

"Isn't that the one about prison doors?" Sam looked through the glasses and pointed. "What prison doors are you singing about?"

"There's all kinds of prisons," she whispered as she squinted through her lens. "Thank You, Lord." She clicked the shutter. "What do you mean?" Sam scoped the spring area and caught a glimpse of tan hide in the brush.

"We all want to be free." Jessica adjusted her lens. " Jesus said that if we'd learn of Him, we'd know the truth and the truth would set us free."

Sam poured water in a cup for Bud. "That's pretty radical."

She held his gaze. "Yes it is. Jesus said He is Truth and the Word. I can't explain like Matt."

He raised the glasses. The lone coyote moved slowly through the rocks, nose testing the air. Sam reached down and petted Bud, his dog more interested in his bone than the wildlife. The coyote paused in front of a small hole between two boulders. Two fuzzy pups tumbled forth and weaved through their mother's legs. After sniffing and licking her pups, she regurgitated a meal for them.

Jessie's camera clicked continuously as mama coyote lay in front of the den, the pups pouncing on her neck, playfully biting her face and each other. Finally tired from mock battles, the pups snuggled their mother's belly to fall asleep nursing.

Sam lowered the glasses. A shadow fell across the den as the last of the sunlight moved up the mountain, lowering the temperature.

Jessie straightened and turned to him with a wide smile. "Wasn't that great? I got some really good shots."

"Do you always have such luck?" Sam bit into a cookie as he put away the food and lifted drinks from the cooler.

She carefully packed her camera. "No. Sometimes it's pretty boring, sitting all day, seeing nothing. Although if I look hard enough, there's usually something; a plant, a rock or interesting scene." She glanced up at him. "So how'd you know Amber could cut cattle? Isn't that unusual for an Arab?"

He grinned. "Matt didn't tell you?" He helped her with her backpack.

Jessie shook her head. "What?"

"You'll hear about it anyway; may as well get the whole story." Sam followed her back toward her Toyota. "My first day back on the ranch, I rode out to drive in my cattle for the auction . . ."

Jessie turned to him as he finished his story at her Cruiser. "Wow, Sam. When can I meet Amber? Can I watch? I'd love to take photos." She laughed. "This is another 'God thing' you know."

"Really?" Sam stowed her gear, and patted the back seat for Bud to jump inside. "I don't know if I believe that, but sure –you can come see Amber."

The drive back to Jessie's cabin flew by way too fast for Sam. Talking to her came naturally, like he could tell her anything.

Besides everything about her interested him like her work and how thoughtfully she'd planned the day. Well, everything except for church, which definitely was a huge part of her.

TWENTY

As Sam drove home with Bud in the flatbed, memories of Jessie's hug goodbye along with her wide smile brought him contentment, something he hadn't felt for a long time. He switched on the headlights and rubbed his dog's ears. Amber's story delighted Jessie and she wanted to see the mare. He tapped his fingers on the wheel, wondering when to invite her again; to the ranch or cutting practice, or both?

A truck passed him and then slowed down in front of him. Irritated, Sam braked. He looked ahead; no traffic in sight so he shifted down and pulled out to pass. The truck in front of him sped up. Sam eased over, back into his lane behind the truck. He couldn't make out the dirty license.

A few minutes later, the truck braked again. What was going on with that jerk? After the next rise in the road, Sam tried to pass again. He'd almost made it when the truck accelerated, keeping pace with him.

Sam braked hard. So did the truck beside him. The glow of oncoming headlights silhouetted a sharp curve ahead. No matter what Sam did, speed up or slow down, that truck wouldn't let him over. In the dark, all he knew about the truck beside him was that it ran duallies and was deep blue with orange clearance lights across the top of the cab.

The oncoming lights brightened. A log truck loomed into view of his lights; no way could either of them stop in time. Sam punched the throttle, veering left. His flatbed flew as the road shoulder abruptly dropped. His bumper met with the top two strands of a barbwire fence. The wires screeched as they stretched, then snapped.

Sam's flatbed landed hard in a newly plowed field, coming to a sudden stop as the front wheels dropped into a narrow irrigation ditch. He slowly loosened his hold on the wheel. He opened his mouth to curse. Bud whined, cringing on the floorboards of the cab. "Hey, Bud. You okay? Come here." Sam patted his leg.

Buddy crawled onto the seat and buried his head in Sam's lap. His hands shook as he examined the Retriever. They both bounced hard when the truck landed. Satisfied that Bud was more scared than injured, Sam stepped from his flatbed.

The log truck stopped a ways down the road, loudly idling on the shoulder. A beam of light lit the break in the fence and bobbed toward Sam.

"You okay? I radioed for help." The driver lurched across the deep furrows.

"Thanks. Did you get a look at that truck? He deliberately tried to run me into you!" Sam clenched his fists. He knew this wasn't an accident or coincidence.

"Nope; happened too fast. It was too dark." The burly man wore a baseball cap. He flashed his light over Sam's truck. "Looks like your rig survived."

"Can you shine your light up front? I'm wondering if I can drive it home," Sam ran his hand over the hood. Bud jumped from the cab as the truck driver moved forward.

"You may be able to back it out of this ditch and over the furrows, but the road shoulder is too steep." The driver bent over,

114

shining his light under the front end. "I'd take it in and check for sheared bolts or anything else that might've come loose."

Sam wiggled the front tire. "No doubt probably need to be realigned." He inhaled the scent of freshly plowed earth, trying to calm his jangling nerves.

The sheriff car arrived, lights flashing. Sam, Buddy and the driver trudged to the break in the fence. When the Deputy shone his light on Sam, he shook his head. "What happened this time?"

Sam gave his story along with the driver. The Deputy wrote down their names and filled out his report. "Neither of you can identify the truck? Get a license?"

They both shook their heads. The log truck driver was free to go.

Sam shook hands with him. "Hey; thanks again for your help."

"No problem; I'm sure you'd do the same for me." The driver climbed into his cab. The brakes hissed, and he slowly drove away.

"Okay, Sam, let's take a look at your truck." With the help of the Deputy's spotlight, they made their way back across the field, Bud leading the way. "Somehow, I think we're going to be seeing a lot of each other. You may as well call me BJ."

Sam strode over the furrows. "Hope not, BJ. I can't think of anyone that has a truck like the one that ran me off the road." Heat crept up his neck. Someone had him targeted; for what? And for crying out loud, why? Sam couldn't wait to confront this jerk on even terms. He clenched his fists.

After noting the flatbed's position and condition, BJ radioed for a wrecker. "One of these days, you might run into these boys with the odds in your favor." BJ tapped his finger on Sam's chest. "Call me. Don't try to get even. Unless you like spending time behind bars, in the hospital, or possibly the morgue."

TWENTY-ONE

Sam walked alongside BJ as the deputy's flashlight highlighted the top edges of furrows in the field back to the fence, where they both noted the bent t-posts and broken barbwire. Bud sniffed around while Sam helped BJ pull the wire off to the side so the wrecker could reach the truck.

As they waited BJ said, "I'll notify the property owner what happened here." His radio squawked; he strode a few paces away to answer the call. Sam climbed the embankment and stood with arms crossed next to the sheriff's car with Bud pressed against his leg.

The sheriff scrambled up and opened the passenger door. "The wrecker can't make it until morning. It'll be better pulling your truck out in daylight anyway. Get in, I'll give you a lift home."

Sam blew out a sigh. "Why am I not surprised." He ducked onto the seat, and patted his lap for Bud. The golden dog jumped in, sat and laid his head on Sam's shoulder as BJ shut the door.

BJ walked around the front of the car, the headlight beams glinting off his badge. He slid inside, put the cruiser in gear, and turned up the heat. "Temps dropping out there," he said. "Let me know if your dog gets too hot."

"Thanks for the ride. I'm on the other side of the river." Sam rearranged Bud on his lap.

"I know where your ranch is. I knew your father." BJ grunted. "Listen up, okay? And don't take it wrong, what I'm telling you. I know your story. I know you're trying to do right now, but don't go looking for trouble. That's my job."

Sam glanced at BJ, met his gaze in the light off the dash. "Don't I have a right to defend myself?"

"You do. But no vigilante stuff." BJ turned off the main highway. "I know most everyone around here. We both know someone is out to get you. I'll be poking around, looking for a pattern. You just keep watch and try to avoid stirring it up." He reached inside his uniform pocket and handed Sam a card. "Anything comes up, even if it seems small, call me."

BJ turned beneath the ranch sign and drove up the long driveway.

Sam opened his door and let Bud off his lap. In the overhead light, he took a good look at BJ. Close cropped dark hair and eyes . . . the face of a friend.

The same wrecker who'd hauled off his vandalized trucks called that morning to let Sam know he'd retrieved his truck from the field and wanted to know which place to leave it for repair. Sam told him, then called Matt.

"Hey. You got time to give me a ride?"

Sam loaded firewood on the porch and hauled hay from the horse barn on the tractor to the stock shed, Bud trotting alongside with an old glove of Tucker's in his mouth. Ready for town, Sam sat on the porch, and waited for Matt.

He bowed his head, clasping his hands behind his neck, then rubbed his face hard. He'd tossed and turned all night, wishing he could really have a fair fight with whoever was picking on him. What'd he do to anyone around here? He wasn't even around for the last couple years to cross anyone he could think of.

His father had been in his dreams. Sam missed their morning banter, the relationship they'd been building. Wondered what Tucker would say about everything he'd been doing on the ranch and all the attacks. He rubbed the silver cuff and rose as Matt arrived in his pickup.

Sam opened the door, let Bud jump in, and followed.

Matt put the truck in gear, and headed down the driveway. "What happened to your truck?"

On the way to town, Sam vented. "I'm sure it's the same guys who trashed the farm trucks, same ones who jumped me at the Brown Bear-"

"You think it's all connected?" Matt raised his eyebrow.

"Yeah, what else could it be?" Sam sputtered as he rubbed Bud's shoulders.

"You've never gotten a good look at any of them?" Matt reached across and punched Sam's arm. "Well, start from the beginning, then. I gotta hear it all."

By the time Matt parked in front of the repair shop, Sam even mentioned spending the day with Jessica.

"Boy, my life seems pretty boring right at the moment." Matt turned to Sam. "I'm here for you, anytime. Don't hesitate, alright?"

Sam nodded, surprised at the way his eyes teared. He opened the door and stepped out so Matt wouldn't see. "Stay, Bud. We'll be right back."

Inside the shop, which smelled of motor oil, the repairman showed them how he'd repaired a hole in the radiator, where he'd tightened bolts, and the fresh scratches from the wire. Sam thanked him and paid the bill, thankful it wasn't too expensive.

As he opened Matt's door to let Bud out, Matt asked, "What are you going to do now?"

"Take Jessica's advice and buy alfalfa seed."

Denise Sager

TWENTY-TWO

The river bottomland fluffed the color of rich tobacco beneath the wheels of Sam's tractor. He'd broke the fallow ground with a plow first, then worked over the fields several days with discs until they lay level, smooth and ready for the alfalfa seed being broadcast by the seeder attached behind the harrow.

Late afternoon sun slanted across the neat patterns the discs made in the soft dirt and sparkled off the blue green of the river bordering the fields. Although he knew the crop would do well, Sam would rather be separating calves, branding and inoculating cattle instead.

If he did his homework and put the hay money into the best cattle he could buy, he could use his inferior heifers as surrogate mothers by inseminating them with embryos from registered cows and increase his herd faster. He needed something a bit different to create a market. Would Santa Gertrudis work? The red cattle would be beautiful on his ranch.

Across the field, Buddy barked from his lookout on the bed of the truck. Sam couldn't hear him over the noise of the John Deere motor, but he noticed Matt's pickup crossing the cattle guard. He finished seeding the section, stopped beside the trucks and turned off the tractor.

Matt hopped on the flatbed, sitting on the edge next to Bud. "Don't you ever check your answering machine? I've been trying to reach you all week."

Sam pulled himself up on Bud's other side and scratched the dog's ears. "Been too busy."

"I guess so. How many acres did you plant?" Matt gazed across the fields.

"Hundred. Probably be sorry come haying time. What brings you out?" He set his hat aside, bent over and poured water from a jug over his head, the cool water washing off his sweat.

"I brought you a copy of the Cascade Horseman; there's an open cutting show week after Easter in Klamath Falls." Matt swung his feet, hooking his boot heels on the top edge of a tire.

Sam mopped his face with his bandana and looked Matt in the eye. "You miss riding, don't you."

"Yeah. Always loved the smell of horses, everything about them. Don't get me wrong, though. The Lord's given me a heart for people; I love the ministry and its challenges. But watching you with that Arab just tickles me. I'd like to tag along."

Sam smiled at the plea. "How about a quick trail ride down to the river? My buckskin hasn't been ridden for a while; think you could handle him?"

Matt leaped down and headed for his truck. "If that means he'll buck, let's go!"

Sam slid down and opened the door to the cab. "Meet 'ya at the barn," he yelled.

Minutes later, he stopped at the barn with Matt right behind him. Together they grabbed halters and ropes and with Bud at their heels, entered the pasture. The horses stood nearby.

Amberwind strolled to Sam and stuck her head into the halter. He buckled it on and rubbed her between her eyes.

Matt chased the buckskin around a couple of times. He left for the tack room, returning with a lariat. "Enough of that game," he said, shaking out a loop. The rope snaked out and settled over the gelding's neck. "Yee-haw; I haven't lost my touch," Matt sang out.

Sam grinned and turned his attention to the copper mare, grooming her with the shedding blade. Large scoops of loose hair fell to the ground. As he scratched the metal blade over her withers, she stuck out her upper lip and wiggled it with her eyes half-closed.

Next, he smoothed a Navajo blanket over her back and lifted the flat-seated cutting saddle on top.

Matt chose a heavy roping saddle and took the curb bit Sam handed him.

Slipping a hackamore over Amber's head, Sam turned to watch Matt mount. Matt barely got his feet in the stirrups when the buckskin cut loose. Buddy leapt about barking which didn't help. Sam couldn't stop laughing as Matt stuck one hand in the air, kicking the gelding shoulder to flank in rhythm to his bucks; a real bronc rider. The horse quit and shook himself like a large dog.

"That's enough, Buddy." The Retriever settled as Sam stepped into his stirrup and swung a leg over the mare. They headed to the river. Sam laughed as Matt resettled his hat. "Been a while since the rodeo; but I bet you could still stick on anything that came through the chute."

Matt grinned. "Aw, this pony hardly bucked. Sure was fun, though." They jogged the horses a while before he spoke again. "I read the police report in the paper about you getting run off the road. Your truck's still running, I see."

"I had it realigned on the way home. Bottom of the radiator's holding. One of these times, those boys are gonna slip and I'll get my hands on them," Sam growled.

Buddy chased quail running through the sagebrush, wings whirling through the air. Sam smiled at the sight, momentarily diverted.

The buckskin pulled for more rein, trying to snatch bites of spring grass. "You have any idea yet who it could be?" Matt asked.

"Figure it's gotta be someone local. Someone that knows my habits. Someone with yellow clearance lights across the top of their cab."

"I've been praying about the situation." Matt reined the gelding back, letting Sam and Amber take the lead.

The copper mare tucked her hind end under her as she slid down the steep trail. Sam gave her rein, trusting her judgement in negotiating the narrow switchbacks.

Bud shot past at the bottom to wade in the river. Both horses drank deeply. Matt hooked a leg over the saddle horn. "Jessie's been trying to reach you. We're invited to her folks' for Easter dinner."

"How's that?" Sam let the horsehair reins of the hackamore slide through his fingers as Amber reached for the grass growing along the bank.

The buckskin pawed the water, splashing and Bud leaped to catch the droplets in his mouth. Matt laughed at the antics. "Her folks always invite all the singles, especially those without families. They put out quite a spread."

Sam started back on the trail. "Sounds okay." Any excuse to spend time with Jess sounded great, actually.

Near the top, both horses dug in and scrambled up the trail, breaking into a lope at the top. Bud's tongue hung out the side of his mouth but he kept up with the horses on the way back to the barn.

The mountains rose dark against a red sky and the horse's manes whipped back and forth with their strides; the tips highlighted like flames in the sunset. Sam locked gazes with Matt as they both raised their fists and whooped like old times.

Sam rose before light Easter morning, pulled on a clean pair of wranglers, a denim shirt and sheepskin vest. Going outside, he tossed hay into the feeders for the animals and checked the water level in the stock tank. Hurried back inside for some coffee and shared a donut with Bud.

By six-twenty, he arrived at Smith Rock and found a place to park in the crowded lot. He left Bud curled up in the truck and followed the crowd to the river. The cloudy dawn nipped as everyone huddled around Matt and the musicians. Sam worked his way near Jessie.

Matt started with a song; it sounded like one of the gospels. Guitars and Jessie's violin filled the air. Matt sang about how Peter denied he knew Jesus at the Lord's trial, how he wept and ran as the rooster crowed and Jesus looked at him; of the crucifixion and how Peter was with John on the third day; the women coming with news of the empty tomb.

As Matt got to the chorus, Jessie and the other musicians joined in, their voices ringing as they sang, "He's alive!" At that moment, golden sunlight burst upon the tops of the rocks towering above the crowd, the clouds glowing like embers.

Sam blinked his eyes. Everyone broke into applause.

Matt set his guitar in the stand and reached for his Bible. "What do you suppose was the first thing Jesus said to His followers after His resurrection? They'd all deserted Him; none had figured it out when He plainly told them what was going to happen. 'Fear not,' He said." Matt stretched out his arms. "Because Jesus died for my sins and yours, we fear not. We're forgiven. He has risen! Fear not dying, for heaven is waiting. Fear not the future or your present problems for He is with us."

Breaking Sam

Sam rubbed his eyes while concentrating on the light moving down the face of the rock cliffs. Tears threatened. All this talk of death and heaven when he'd lost his father was a bit much. He rubbed the silver wrist-cuff. That must be it. He folded his arms against his chest. Matt ended his message. Jessie closed her eyes as if praying.

The crowd broke into small groups. Jessie rushed to his side. "Could I ride with you?" She wore another angel dress, some filmy cream layered thing that ended in points about her calves.

"Sure," Sam told her. "But Bud's with me. He might mess up your outfit." He'd been holding his Stetson. He settled it on his head.

"I'm not worried. Let's go!" A light breeze lifted her hair, spinning her curls, wafting a fresh flowery scent his way. "Isn't it a glorious day?"

"Sure is." Sam reached for Jessica's hand, pleased as she squeezed his.

Bud licked her cheek as she settled in the truck for the short ride to her parent's ranch. Sam parked in front of the Victorian home behind several other vehicles in the circular driveway.

Like Matt said, her folks put on a spread. After Matt gave the blessing, Sam heaped his plate with ham, ambrosia, asparagus and yams. There was more; he'd have to make several trips to the buffet.

The only problem was Jessica's mother, who paired everyone at the table. A name card marked each of the twelve places. Jessie sat next to Matt. Sam found his name across from Matt and eased into a seat next to a tall young woman with long straight black hair.

She held out her hand. "Dawn Stillwater. You don't remember me, do you?"

Sam shook her hand. "Sorry."

"I'm Jessie's friend that took all your stuff for my sale." She raised her fork.

"Yeah. Sure. I wasn't paying much attention to anything back then. You saved me a bunch of hassle." Sam reached for his coffee. "Jessie said that's what you do, garage sales."

Dawn laughed. "It gets me by. Sounds terrible, though. Doesn't it? Like I'm a bag lady or something. At least I'm free all week long to volunteer at the reservation."

Sam glanced at Jessie. A couple of times she looked his way with a smile, but someone always claimed her attention. He grew uncomfortable as he realized that most the conversation centered on Jesus. Like he'd noticed about Jessie, they all related to Jesus like He was their personal friend.

He helped clear the table. In the kitchen, he snagged a piece of ham for Bud and slipped out the back door. Bud rose from the porch, stretched and nosed the napkin Sam held. "C'mon boy. You can eat it in the truck. I've got to get out of here."

Sam sat in the cab of his flatbed feeding Bud ham. The screen door slammed as Jessie ran across the yard to him.

"You're not sneaking off, are you?" She stood on the running board, hooking her elbows through his open window.

"Jess, I don't belong here. I'm not a Christian; being with you all makes me a hypocrite. Sorry; but don't expect me to be a regular at church, either." His heart constricted as her ocean colored eyes pooled with tears just inches from his.

"Don't you remember your Sunday school lessons?" Her voice broke. "We're all hypocrites. Christians aren't perfect, just perfectly forgiven because of Jesus dying on the cross. You can't work your way to heaven. You just have to make a choice to believe."

"That simple, huh?" Sam held her hand, rubbing the back of it with his thumb. "This religion thing has nothing to do with the way I feel about you. I want you to know that."

Her tears wet her cheeks as she cupped her hand around the back of his neck, drawing him closer. She kissed him, her lips soft, yet salty, a sweet lingering kiss that left him reeling.

Jessie drew back as Bud wiped her tears with his tongue. "You too, Buddy." She stepped down and walked to the house without looking back.

1

TWENTY-THREE

Sam slid the last sheet of rusted corrugated tin roofing onto the pile stacked on his flatbed. He'd spent a couple of days pulling the old roof off the barn. Just a few more sheets to load. Earlier, he roped himself off to the tractor, climbed the steep slope to the opposite side of the roof and let the old tin slide off once he yanked the nails. After the second piece rattled down, Bud retreated to the front porch, laying his chin between his front paws.

While Sam worked, he thought about Jessie's kiss. Did she imagine how it affected him? Did she have any idea how much he wanted to wrap his arms around her and never let her go? Would she ever want to see him again?

He positioned his truck next to the pile, loaded the old sheets of roofing on the flatbed and tied the load down, planning to drop it by the salvage yard on his way to buy new roofing at the building supply. "Buddy, go for a ride?" His dog bounded from the porch and leapt into the cab. Sam jumped in after him and rubbed Bud's ears. "Good boy." He chuckled as Bud sat next to the window, looking straight ahead. The dog seemed almost human.

He started the flatbed and drove the road out to the front gate, stopped to get out and pull it shut, locking it with a padlock on a chain. What a hassle. A pick-up drove by; Sam checked for running lights. None.

The country western song on the radio cried of broken dreams as he drove to town. He shut it off, glancing at Bud. The golden coated Retriever lifted his eyebrows as their eyes met. "Sure wish you could talk." Buddy's tail thumped the seat.

Sam stood leaning against the door of his truck at the salvage yard, watching traffic while the yardmen stacked the old roofing on their forklift. Bud stood inside the cab, his head out the window next to Sam's.

A dark blue pick-up cruised by. Sam stared hard at the yellow clearance lights over the cab. Two guys inside looked his way, their faces shielded by the brims of their cowboy hats. Sam spun around. His truck sat half-loaded. He clenched his fists as the pick-up moved on down the road. Guts churning, he asked the men, "Can you guys hurry?"

Minutes later, Sam sped down the highway. He searched the streets of town for the blue pick-up. Where'd it go? Giving up, he drove to the building supply and loaded new metal roofing. On the way home he bought burgers and fries for himself and Bud, keeping an eye out for the blue truck. Someone had to know who owned it.

Back at Tersis, Sam parked alongside of the barn. He buckled nail pouches around his hips and tugged on his leather gloves. The first row he worked off the bed of the truck, sliding a twelve-foot sheet onto the rafters into place. Standing on the stack of tin, he reached to pound two nails with washers into the bottom of the sheet, the banging off the metal sending Bud back to the porch to watch. He climbed next to it and drove two more nails in the middle. Sam stretched to reach the top edge and nailed it down, straddling the rafters.

Each two foot wide sheet needed to overlap the previous sheet by two ridges in the metal or else they'd leak in the next rain. The second row was harder. He pounded some nails part way into the rafters so he could shove several sheets sideways on the level he worked.

After Sam finished the second row, he took a break. Buddy brought him a stick as he rested on a hay bale. "Hey Bud, sorry for all the racket." The golden sat with his front paws resting on Sam's knees. "Okay! Don't get started now; I've got work." He took the stick and tossed it. The Retriever bounced after it. Ranch dogs weren't supposed to be cute!

To finish this side of the barn, he needed to cover two more rows to the ridge, plus the overhang for the animals. He parked the tractor on the opposite side of the barn and tossed two ropes tied to it clear over the ridge to hang down on his working side. Sam tied one rope to the sheeting, the other around his waist. When he pulled himself to where he left off, he hitched the rope around a rafter to hold him. Sam pulled up the next metal sheet. At least it didn't weigh much. Wrestling the sheet into place, he nailed it and slowly let himself down to tie on another sheet.

He pulled and struggled to place it and reached across with hammer and nail to secure it. His boot slipped. He grabbed for a rafter and missed, his hammer falling to the ground inside the barn. He hit the end of his rope and clamped his teeth as it cut into his waist. He dangled four feet under the rafter; all he had to do was reach.

Suddenly, his hitch gave way. He fell almost ten feet, stopping hard as the rope caught on the ridge. Gasping for air, he swung back and forth, yet another twenty feet from the ground. Fighting to stay conscious, he saw his Stetson below. Bud stood next to it and barked.

TWENTY-FOUR

Sam thought about cutting himself loose as he dangled above the ground inside the barn. If he didn't break a leg, he could fall onto the double set of knife-edged discs that he'd brought into the barn for repair and end up as sliced deli-meat.

He grabbed the rope holding him with both hands and pulled himself upright. Could he climb the rope to the rafter? He spit on the palm of his glove and reached as high as he could and gripped the rope. Letting go with the other hand, he spit on that glove and pulled. His shoulders burned and arms ached. He'd gained three feet.

Reaching upwards, he doubted that he'd make it. He strained to pull himself up, wrapping a leg around the rope. Sweat trickled down his face. He half-smiled and almost lost his grip, thinking of what Matt would say if he could see him. Something like "Someone hung for you."

He gritted his teeth and concentrated on his next move. Buddy barked again, racing back and forth beneath him as somebody drove toward the barn. Matt's pick-up stopped at the doorway. Doubling his efforts to reach the top, he trembled with pain. Now that help arrived, he really wanted to make it on his own.

Matt's door slammed. He ran to the tractor. "I'll lower you down. Unless you're trying to prove something."

Sam laughed and coughed. "Yeah, right. How much you wanna bet I would've made it?"

Matt loosened the hitch and slowly fed out the rope. "If I hadn't come along, you might have. Seriously, didn't anyone ever tell you that in order to hang yourself properly you're supposed to tie the rope around your neck, not your waist?"

Sam allowed the rope to slip through his hands, giving up the feet he'd gained and hoped Matt had a good hold on the rope as he eyed the discs. "Funny you showed; I was just thinking about you. Is this another divine appointment?"

Matt braced a boot against the tractor tire and leaned away from the rope. "Thought I'd come by and see what time you're leaving for the cutting show on Saturday since you're still not checking your messages."

There was a reason Sam didn't play back the machine. Jessie might've left a message he didn't want to hear. He'd hurt her. He could still see her tears glistening on the edge of her eyelashes and taste her lips as they melted on his.

"Hey, anybody home?" Matt's hand waved in front of his face.

Sam fumbled with the knotted rope around his waist while Buddy danced around him. "What show?"

Matt coiled the rope. "I told you about it two weeks ago. It's a big one. Top horses. I thought it could be like old times: you and me on the road."

Sam unhooked his nail pouches, dropped them and tugged his tee loose from the waistband of his jeans.

Matt whistled. "Ouch. Got some Corona ointment in the tack room? That's quite a rope burn."

They walked without talking to the room at the end of the stock barn. Sam gingerly dabbed the buttery stuff on his burn. He looked Matt in the eye. "We did some real hell-raising, you and me. I can see it now; you'll be trying to convert me on the drive to Klamath and back."

Sam wiped his hands on a rag, following Matt to the fence. He leaned against the boards and patted Bud. The horses grazed in the pasture beyond, swishing their tails to ward off freshly hatched flies.

Matt tipped back his hat and lifted his boot onto the bottom rail. "Guess I can't help it. Like an artesian well, the good news just keeps bubbling out."

Sam shook his head. "Could you put a cap on it for me?" Bud nudged his hand. "Go fetch my hat, Buddy!"

The golden retriever shot into the barn and soon returned, tossing the hat into the air and leaping after it.

"I hope that wasn't a good hat." Matt rubbed his nose, hiding a grin.

Buddy clamped the rim in his mouth, shaking his head furiously before trotting over to Sam. "It isn't now." Sam grabbed his Stetson. "I'll probably regret this. Bring some Kentucky Fried Chicken Friday night; we'll be heading out before dawn."

In the dim light of the cab, Matt maneuvered the flatbed and stock trailer through Redmond. Bend would follow several miles down the road in central Oregon. From there to Klamath Falls at the southern end of the state on Highway Ninety-Seven would be almost four hours of sparse population, pines and views of the Cascades on their right. Bud sprawled on the seat between them, his head on Sam's thigh, snoring.

Matt broke the comfortable silence. "Don't know about you, but I'm excited. Sure feels good to drive a rig again." He shifted into neutral, coasting as he waited for the signal ahead to turn green. "That dog has mellowed you out. I never would've imagined you'd have a Golden Retriever or an Arab."

Sam rested his hand on Bud's shoulder. "Tell me about it. I'm gonna get laughed at for sure at the show." He shrugged. "The way I ended up with Amber and Bud is hard to figure. I guess we're stuck with each other."

"Sam, why can't you admit you love them? I suspect you're in love with Jessica Rivers, too." Matt grinned and shifted back into gear.

"You ever love a critter?" Sam rubbed the sleep from his eye, refusing to talk about Jessie.

"Remember the Australian Shepherd I had as a kid? Him and my roping horse." Matt started to say something else but stopped and covered his mouth, eyes on the highway in front of them.

"Capping it?" Sam grinned and settled deeper in his seat. He closed his eyes. Yesterday evening it hit him as they bathed Amberwind, cleaned tack and packed the trailer how much he had missed Matt. He appreciated Matt coming along and helping with the drive and just being around. They'd all be tired later; it'd be after midnight by the time they returned home.

Sam tried not to think about the cutting contest. Somehow, besides being an Arabian in a Quarter Horse dominated sport, he couldn't shake the feeling that Amber would find a way to attract attention.

TWENTY-FIVE

The saddle creaked as Sam leaned forward and rubbed Amber's shoulder. The copper mare glistened in the early morning sun. All that currying after the mare's bath yesterday paid off. Matt pinned the stiff paper with the entry numbers from the underside so the safety pins wouldn't show on the back corners of the Navajo blanket that Sam used beneath his saddle.

Sponsored by the Northwest Cutting Horse Association, this was an 'open' show, meaning any breed of horse could enter as long as the owner was a member. Amber turned her head and touched Sam's boot with her nose as he sat in the saddle.

Matt finished pinning the numbers. "Okay, you're set. I've got you entered in the Novice Horse Class." He turned and scrutinized the rigs parked in the lot. "We could've entered the Amateur or Non-Pro classes but you're right; let's start her off slow and see what happens."

Sam checked out the contestants preparing their horses. Farm logos and trainer's names emblazoned over half the trailers. Some of the rigs held a dozen horses pulled by huge tractor trucks. The 'big boys' were here for sure. He grimaced and reaching his rear pocket, missed his chew. "All Quarter Horses. We're not too obvious, are we?"

The horses around them wore short manes and tails tapered off about hock length compared to Amber's mane hanging past her neck and forelock that half hid her eyes. She carried her tail high, a thick cloak that touched the ground, growing steadily even though Sam cut four to six inches off of it regularly. Sam had considered cutting her hair more the Quarter Horse style but anyone taking a look couldn't mistake her arched neck or her huge eyes in the dished face to know she was an imposter.

"Ready or not, we better get warmed up." Sam straightened in the saddle. The copper mare tossed her head. There would be three sets to determine the winner.

Matt tied Bud to the trailer. "I'll be close by."

Amber walked like a queen to the arena entrance. Sam compared his outfit to the other riders. Show rules required chaps, a long-sleeved shirt and a hat. His earthy colors complemented the copper mare. He rode tall, confident that he and Amber looked good.

A large outdoor arena held the classes. He joined the crowd of horses and riders jogging and loping in circles, conscious of startled glances and stares. Amber felt alert yet steady under him as she broke into a slow lope.

Down at the far end of the arena, turn-back riders settled the first bunch of cattle. Sam paused at the side gate to check the posted numbers. He would be the fourth go. The day promised to be perfect, not too hot or cool as huge billowy clouds hung in a deep blue sky.

The official timer tapped the mike, checking the loudspeaker system. "Folks, we'd like to acknowledge all the sponsors helping us out today: the Big R Store, Grange Farm and Feed, Sundowner Trailers and the Mac Phearson Farm. Next time you use their services or shop their stores, be sure to tell them you appreciate them." He unbuttoned his leather vest and covered the mike with his hand as he spoke to an older woman on his right. Probably the scorekeeper. "Our judge is Dustin 'Dusty' Taylor," the announcer said.

The judge rose from his chair and tipped his Stetson from the bed of a new pick-up parked in the center of the large arena separating the warm-up and cutting areas.

The timer announced the class and called the first number.

Sam kept Amber walking and paid attention to the cows being used ahead of him. When his turn came, he'd know which animal to cut. Remembering his rodeo days, he flexed his muscles and relaxed. If he tensed, Amber would sense it. He tuned everything out but his horse and the job at hand, the familiar scents of manure and stock settling him.

The announcer called his name and number. Sam worked Amber deep into the herd and separated the brown speckled steer. Amber coiled beneath him as he lowered his rein hand.

Bawling, the steer spun back toward the herd. Amber hunkered down, her hind legs well under her body, hocks near the ground. Nose to nose, she stuck to the steer. When she spun, she dug so low that Sam's stirrup almost touched the dirt. The speckled one quit. Sam raised his hand and turned the copper mare back to the herd.

Matt yelled "Fifty!" Sam knew fifty seconds remained of his two and a half-minute total. He cut a white face from the herd along with two others. Amber locked on to the white face he wanted and he lowered the reins again, turning control over to his mare.

Amber dove after the cow. Sam tightened his grip on the saddle horn, holding his balance as her front end dipped before him and launched sideways. She twirled, her front legs spraddled and danced, her mane and tail flying.

"Time," the loudspeakers blared. Sam raised his hand. Amber stopped, sides heaving as the whiteface scampered back to the safety of the herd.

Squeezing the copper mare into a walk, Sam headed back to the warm-up area. All eyes focused on the judge as he cleared his throat. "Seventy-three," he said gruffly. Only one horse had even come close so far.

Sam rode to the rail where Matt waited and stepped down from the saddle.

As he loosened Amber's cinch, Matt whispered, "If looks could kill, you'd be dead meat by now."

Sam rubbed the mare between her eyes, a lump of admiration for her stuck in his throat. He glanced about as a murmuring swept from one end of the arena to the other.

"They're probably wondering who you are. Amber is awesome," Matt added as he sat on the top rail of the arena. Sam joined him and they watched the rest of his class work the cattle. Amber relaxed with one hind hoof cocked.

Every eight cutters, the turn-back riders changed the herd of thirty cattle for fresh ones so it took a couple of hours for the class to finish.

Sam self-consciously went forward, leading Amber when he heard his number called for first place. The woman scorekeeper handed him a fine rawhide braided bridle with different colored patterns on the buttons. The others that placed came forward and stood apart from him. Well, he couldn't blame them. In the past, he would have done the same. He actually felt apologetic for beating those Quarter Horses.

Matt accompanied him and Amber back to the trailer where Bud pulled on his leash, tail wagging hard. His next class was half a day away. Sam pulled the saddle and bridle off, slipped a halter on the mare and tied her to the side of the trailer next to a hay net while Matt filled a bucket of water. Amber sucked down half of it.

Bud jumped onto the flatbed and stretched out in the shade of the gooseneck, his nose close to Sam and Matt as they sat on the edge of the flatbed, eating burgers from the concession stand and watched horses and riders coming and going from the arena.

Matt took the sweet-iron snaffle bit and reins off Amber's old bridle and attached them to the one she'd won. "Judging from the remarks I heard back there, no one's about to let an Arab best their horses no matter how good it is."

Sam lay back against his saddle, pulling his hat low over his face. "Amber doesn't get left alone for a second. Have any idea what they might pull?" He reached over and rubbed Bud's ear.

Matt lifted his Stetson and ran his hand through his hair. "Nope. Better be ready for anything. It'll be underhanded but subtle."

Twenty-Six

Sam decided not to take any chances getting bumped against a rail or caught in the warm-up pack so after mounting Amber for their next set, he headed for the cattle pens. The heat of the afternoon ripened the stench of manure and urine as the cattle crowded in the pipe corrals behind the arena. He found a round pen. Sam guided the copper mare inside and jogged circles for several minutes, then rode back to his rig.

Matt tied Bud's leash as they headed back to the arena. "Glad you came back; after the dun, it's your turn. Go for the solid brown; no one's used her yet."

Sam rode Amber through the gate. Matt headed for the bleachers. The stands had filled since morning. Every time a horse really got down while cutting, the crowd yelled and whistled.

A tractor had raked the arena during lunch followed by a water truck that sprayed down the dust. Perfect footing. Sam rode past the judge as the timer called his number. Amber cocked an ear toward

Sam as he slowly eased her into the herd. Both ears pricked forward as Sam pointed her at the brown cow.

Now. He lowered his rein hand. Amber took over, matching the cow leap for leap, dodging and ducking. The heifer stuck her tail in the air and made a break. Somehow the turn-back rider was too slow; the maverick ignored the herd and ran off.

Sam raised his hand. The copper mare snaked her head down, jerking the leather reins through his glove.

The cow streaked for the wooden side-gate, rapping it with her hind legs as she leapt it. Amber raced two strides behind. Sam realized she was going over and leaned forward to stay balanced. She jumped the gate clean and followed the cow through the break in the stands. Faces, shouts whipped by.

His face flushed. That turn-back rider blew it on purpose! He'd never be able to prove it. Amber's ears went flat back against her neck as she caught the cow. Teeth bared, she bit the cow hard, shouldered it in a circle and herded it back to the arena. The crowd that followed to watch scattered between the bleachers as the heifer half jumped, half crashed the gate, breaking the top board. Amber cleared the mess and lashed out at the cow. The brown skidded to a stop. Amber spun between it and the herd.

"Time," the announcer called over the loudspeaker. "Too bad one of you fellers over there didn't open the gate."

Sam reached down and patted Amber's neck. She shook herself like a dog and sauntered out of the cutting area. The crowd argued loudly about his performance.

"No score; you can't leave the arena."

"The horse can't attack the cattle, either."

"Yeah, but you ever seen anything like that mare before?"

"Billie Joe's bay would've done the same."

"Naw; I wouldn't bet on it."

"That's one crazy A-rab."

Matt met Sam with a huge grin. "No matter what, nobody here will ever forget Amber!" Bud placed his paws on the rail. "Good thing I grabbed hold of your dog; he slipped his collar and wanted to run after you."

Sam's temples throbbed. He clenched his jaw. "Which rider was it? He missed my cow on purpose."

Matt reached up, grasped Sam's elbow, smile gone. "Now Sam, get a grip. Punching the guy out won't solve a thing. Folks hate a bad sport."

Sam glared at the turn-back rider.

"Think about it," Matt told him. "I'll bet everyone here admires your guts and your mare. Of course, they'd never admit it."

Matt was right but it still irked Sam. His friend squeezed his elbow and let go. Sam slowed his breathing. They wouldn't pull that stunt on him again. What would it be next time?

The timer cleared his throat. Everyone quieted down. "Uh, score for Sam West is zero."

Sam swung from the saddle and led Amber through the gate.

Matt shook his head. "Any fool could've seen what happened. In all fairness, they should give you another go."

"Not here." Sam rubbed the copper mare's forehead. "Anyway, I'm proud of her. She's no quitter."

TWENTY-SEVEN

Late Sunday evening, Sam lounged on the old leather couch, reading farm and cattle publications. Bud lay next to his feet, panting slightly in the heat of the woodstove, which was used sparingly as the spring weather warmed. Sipping coffee, Sam tossed the magazines aside and thumbed through the Sunday paper.

In the community section, a large quarter-page photo showed him on Amber jumping the gate back into the arena with the cow. The photographer caught Amber mid-air, her mane streaming into his lap. The caption read "Not Your Usual Cow Horse."

He remembered the first time he'd seen Amber. He'd laid in the dirt, that ornery bull charging and how the copper mare saved his life. The memory of the way she winked at him through her forelock caused him to smile.

The phone rang, interrupted his thoughts. The voice belonged to Matt. "Hey, did you see your picture in the paper? Everyone missed you this morning, especially Jessie."

Sam wondered if maybe Matt liked her, too. "Why tell me about Jessie?"

"Why not?" Matt paused. "You think I'm interested in her?"

Sam set his coffee mug on the rustic coffee table. "Aren't you?"

"Nope; Dawn Stillwater is the girl of my dreams. You met her at Easter."

Sam took the phone from his ear, shook it and put it back. "You're kidding!"

Matt laughed. "Someday I hope she'll be my wife."

"You hate Indians! You used to pick fights with them at the rodeos." Sam pulled himself upright, the leather squeaking.

"Yeah, I did," Matt admitted. "That was B.C."

"B.C.?" The moment Sam uttered it, he knew what was coming.

"Before Christ in my life. I changed my mind and then the Lord changed my heart. The Bible says 'if anyone be in Christ, he is a new creation: old things are passed away; all things become new.'"

"You've changed, alright. What'd Jessie say?" Sam bent over and pulled off his boots. Bud vacuumed his socks with his nose.

"She wanted to tell you about the gallery in Sisters. She's opening an exclusive show there starting Friday."

After Matt's call, Sam pulled his harmonica from the leather keeper on his belt and played a melancholy tune as the moonlight cast shadows on the tall junipers outside the living room window. Matt and Dawn . . . who would've ever guessed? His silver wrist cuff gleamed dully. Jessie wanted him to know about her show. She wanted to see him. He wanted to see her, too. But for it working out between them? He sighed.

Except for a few photos and antique pieces of cowboy equipment, the walls stood bare. He wanted one of Jessie's paintings. Maybe he'd find one at the gallery of a Cascade sunrise. In the meantime, he clipped Amber's photo from the newspaper. He'd frame it and hang it in the office along with Tucker's Endurance photos.

Sam drove to Sisters by way of Lower Bridge along the river. The flat ranch land gradually rolled and filled with tall pines. A magnet for tourists with the nearby wilderness full of lakes and rivers to fish and ski resorts, Sisters nested at the eastern foot of the Cascades. He parked the flatbed on a side street under a shady tree and left Buddy with a bone.

Barn wood siding and a covered boardwalk decorated the gallery, fitting in with the western style town. The crowd mixed with tourists filled the room with Jessica's paintings. He shuffled through the folks from wall to wall, looking for Jessie and for the right painting.

There it was. The tips of the snow covered peaks bright with the first rays of dawn, a cloud filled sky and the sagebrush that same warm color he'd painted his walls.

"Isn't it lovely?" A thin woman with gray-blond hair in fancy western clothes stood beside him, a 'Sisters Gallery' tag pinned to her vest.

"I want to buy it." Sam even liked the subtle wood frame and the way the matting complemented the colors in the scene.

"An excellent choice," the woman said as she reached for the painting.

"Wait! That one isn't for sale!" Jessie rushed to the woman's side, her back toward him. "It's there for display only. It's a gift for someone special." She wore the same angel dress from Easter, filmy cream with lace. She turned. He stared at her ocean eyes and peach-flushed cheeks. "I was saving it for you," she told him.

The gallery lady smiled and slipped away to another customer.

"It's beautiful. You're beautiful." Sam didn't know what else to say. He edged closer, bent and kissed her cheek. "How can I ever thank you? This show is awesome! I'm so happy for you. Will you be able to get away for a while?"

Jessie nodded, took his hand and led him next door to an ice cream shop. "You got me hooked on Expresso Madness," she said as they ordered and settled to enjoy their cones at an umbrella shaded table on a brick patio off the side of the building.

"The show is almost sold out," Jessie shook her head. "I'm taking orders. Can you believe it?" She laughed.

"Congratulations," Sam saluted her cone with his. "You deserve it. I've never seen any paintings as great as yours." He touched her cheek. "How can I ever thank you for my painting? You somehow knew exactly how I described the scene."

"My pleasure to give it to you for your 'new' home. Promise you'll invite me over to see it there above your couch." She licked her ice cream where it dripped down her cone. "Now tell me all about the cutting show. Matt told me he went with you. Take me with you next time!"

Sam grinned. Between licks of ice cream he told her how Amber locked onto the cow. "I couldn't stop her." He ate the last of his cone. "She would have to be an Arabian. But she's special anyway. The ranch is coming along. If only . . ." He bit his words, not wanting to dump all his troubles on her.

Jessie kept prodding so he finally told her about the attacks, making light of it all so it wouldn't spoil her day.

Jessie wiped her hands on a napkin. "A dark blue pick-up with yellow clearance lights?"

He nodded.

She wrinkled her brow. "Russell Miller drives a truck like that."

Sam clenched his fist. "You're sure? Russ never liked me. I guess the feeling has always been mutual, but why would he do all that?"

"Oh, Lord." Jessie crossed her arms and shut her eyes. "I just thought of something." She paused. "It might be because of me that you're having all these troubles, Sam."

"No way!" Sam grabbed her hand. "Enough of Russ. This is your special day. Let's not spoil it. What time does the gallery close? Want to celebrate afterwards? Dinner?"

Sam fed Bud a couple of plain burgers from a nearby fast food stand and gave him a drink from a small water bucket in the truck while waiting for Jessie to arrange for his painting to be delivered and payment for her paintings that sold.

Jessie stepped from the gallery. Sam rushed to her side and hugged her, pleased that she hugged him back as he pressed his face into her lavender scented hair. He reluctantly let her go as she stepped back.

"I forgot to tell you that Matt and Dawn were by and want to meet us for dinner. I was distracted by what we talked about earlier." She made a face. "Do you mind?"

"Not much," he admitted. "It'll give me a chance to get to know Dawn and watch Matt trip over himself."

Jessica laughed. "Yeah; he's usually so comfortable with everyone but it's obvious he's interested in her." She pointed to her Land Cruiser parked nearby. "I'll drive over, I know where the restaurant is and can go straight home afterward."

TWENTY-EIGHT

Jessie's painting looked great hung above the leather couch. Sam could see it from the table where he sat eating his dinner of Hungry Man beef pot-pies. Bud sat beside him, front paws lightly resting on his thigh. "You beggar. You're gonna get fat." Sam caved and gave the golden a piece of meat anyway.

Sam savored the afternoon spent with Jessica, the way she smiled and the sound of her voice. How right and easy it felt to be a couple with Matt and Dawn as they ate spaghetti at the Gallery Restaurant after the art show. How amazing that she wanted anything to do with him. She'd even walked with him as he gave Buddy a break out of the truck, holding his hand. Sam looked forward to seeing her again.

She said Russell owned a blue truck. Well, he could find out easy enough; just go visit the elderly Millers and check on the old mares that he'd given them.

Sam grew up beside the Miller's Dairy with Mr. Miller's youngest son, Russell. As wild as Sam and Matt had been, they'd never done anything really mean. Russell ran with a different bunch.

While washing his plate, he wondered who hung out with Russ. There'd been several guys at the bar. Why pick on him? He turned off the lights and headed to the bathroom, Bud at his heels. After pulling off his clothes, he stepped over his dog to stand at the sink and shave. He stepped over him again to get in the shower. When Sam slid between the sheets, Bud bumped against the bed as he flopped on his bed on the throw rug. Sam reached over the side and rubbed Bud's ears.

Miller's dairy had changed since the last time Sam had been there. A new triple-wide modular home perched on the knoll overlooking the barns contrasting with a dilapidated single-wide mobile tucked under the milk barn overhang. The old farmhouse still looked the same as Sam parked in front of the porch and left Bud to nap in the truck.

Mr. Miller opened the door. "Hey, Sam. Betcha want to see the mares. You're just in time. Ma's cooling a peach pie right now. You gotta stay; we've got fresh whipped cream."

Sam followed the old man around the corner of the porch, past a small greenhouse and garden to a new three-sided shed and corral that opened to a large pasture. The two mares grazed knee-deep in the lush grass, their coats slick and shiny. They raised their heads and nickered. Sam grinned. "Sure looks like horse heaven to me."

Mr. Miller hooked his thumbs in the straps of his overalls. "I shut them in at night so they won't overeat. The Mrs. watches them for hours. Gives her something to do now that the kids are all on their own. That's Larry's place." He gestured to the home on the hill. "He married Marilee, remember her? They got three kids now. Larry has lots of ideas for the operation here since graduating college. Our daughters are all married off and happy."

"What about Russell?" Sam leaned against the fence.

"Aw, he'll never amount to much. He feeds on trouble. Don't know what ails him. Gonna have to learn the hard way, like you. Your Pa used to worry about you but you turned out okay. I hear you're fixing up the ranch. Saw your picture in the paper. Boy, Tucker would've loved to have seen that!"

"Does Russ still live here?" Sam pulled away from the fence as Mr. Miller started back to the house.

"That sorry looking place by the barn is his. It didn't look that bad until he lived in it. I gave him free rent for milkin' the cows. He's not dependable so I kicked him out. He traded in a perfectly good truck for a piece of junk. Go figure. Don't know how he'll get by."

"His truck wouldn't happen to be dark blue with running lights above the cab, would it?" Sam tried his best to sound nonchalant.

"Yeah, did you see it?" Miller opened the door to his house. "Look who's here, Ma! Good thing you baked that pie."

Sunday morning Sam decided to go by the cemetery. He hadn't been there since the funeral. He should've gone before now to check the headstone. By the time he returned, the day would warm to eighty degrees, perfect for cutting hay. The older fields stood ready. After checking the horses, tractor and mower, he and Bud headed to town.

A tall iron fence surrounded the cemetery. Sam drove through the gates and parked near his father's grave. "Wait here," he told Bud. He wandered through the headstones a couple of minutes before he found it. Sam sat on his heels to read the marker. "Tucker West; born 1928, died 2015." Plain and simple. A fresh bouquet of day lilies lay at the base. Jessica?

Sam rubbed the silver cuff on his wrist. His father had always worn it, now he wore it to hold him close. Dad, what would you do about Russell? Regret filled his heart. He wiped his eyes with the back of his hand. Why did his father have to die right then? Why hadn't he talked to his father more? Why hadn't Tucker reached out to him like he did his horses? Why did he do such a stupid stunt like poisoning Tucker's stud? And what was Russell's problem?

Dad, I'm so sorry. I wish you were here, that I could talk to you.

He stood. Maybe this wasn't such a good idea. He trudged back to his truck. Bud rose, slowly wagging his tail and settled as Sam climbed behind the wheel. What now? The day was still too cool to hay. The Brown Bear would be opening. He'd stop in and ask about Russell. Besides, Griz still owed him a beer.

Sam took his time driving to town. Church wouldn't be out yet. No one would probably see him at the bar from there. Should he care? Should he feel guilty for having a beer? He wasn't going to get drunk for crying out loud. Deliberately, he parked in front of the bar. "One more stop, then we'll go home," he said as Bud lifted an eyebrow.

Inside, he paused to adjust his eyes and made his way to a stool at the counter. The air still smelled like stale smoke. The two other customers down at the other end ignored him.

Griz set a cold one before him. "Now we're even."

"Thanks." Sam took a swig. "Hey, you ever see much of Russell Miller?"

"No way! Threw him out over a year ago for bustin' up the place for no reason. He's not welcome here, uh-uh." Griz grunted. "That boy has a screw loose. Take my advice: stay away from him."

Sam nodded as Griz turned to answer the phone. He sat a few minutes more, enjoying the brew. He'd get home and drive the tractor out to the forty acres on high ground that needed to be cut first. Afterwards, he'd look over the irrigation pipes and pump to make sure they'd be ready to go soon as the hay got baled.

He finished his beer and stood. Outside he blinked his eyes from the glare off his windshield. Opened the door. Where was Buddy?

TWENTY-NINE

Sam peered up and down the highway. Not much activity on a Sunday. No sign of his dog. Buddy never wandered. Sam whistled. Waited. As he leaned against the open door of the flatbed, a sour churning built in his stomach. Finally, he lugged himself behind the wheel and slowly drove down the road, searching every side street.

Most businesses were closed. He stopped at a gas station and a mini-market asking if anyone had seen a Golden Retriever. Sam reached the end of town and started slowly back, looking over fences, checking fields and driveways.

Bud, where are you? We've got alfalfa to cut. Sam flexed his hands. His thoughts went back to the snowy day when he almost ran over that butter-colored bit of fluff puppy, the day that his father died. How the pup with the sad eyes stood with his front paws on his running board. Did someone see him alongside the road and take him? He stopped on the edge of the pavement. Lifting his Stetson, he wiped the sweat from his brow. Buddy's collar had his address and phone number. Still, Sam couldn't imagine the dog leaving the truck on his own.

He drove back to the Brown Bear. No dog waited at the door. He pushed inside and asked Griz to call if a Golden Retriever showed up. Back to his truck. Maybe Bud got too hot and decided to go home. Sam doubted it, but headed that way just in case.

A chill hit him along with a thought he tried to avoid, raising the hairs on the back of his neck. Someone took Bud from his truck. Russ? He'd probably never find out. How could someone take a pet that'd become family from somebody else? How mean hearted. Cruel. Low-down rotten scum. His eyes blurred.

He'd always treated animals as tools to make ranch life easier. Cow dogs saved steps; that was their job.

The empty highway stretched before him. No dog.

His mind flashed to his father astride his dark bay stallion, Ranger. How Tucker smiled as the horse strutted, tossing his head. Sam's heart withered with the memory of what Tucker had said when he cut a hunk of the horse's mane before they buried him. "You just don't understand, son."

For the first time, Sam really did understand. HE was the mean hearted scum. Because HE took Ranger from his father. Sam choked and his chest heaved. "Dad, I'm sorry," he whispered. "I can't blame you for not forgiving me 'cause I won't forgive whoever took Bud. Ever."

He couldn't face going home to a ranch without Bud. Even if the dog was a fluffy Golden Retriever; he didn't care anymore about the jeers. He made a U-turn and drove aimlessly with thoughts of Ranger and Tucker. Amberwind and Bud.

As much as he wanted to improve the ranch and make it a success, without family and friends it was all meaningless. Yeah, animals, too. Bud was his family now.

Sam parked behind the now empty church. He slammed the door and stumbled to the built-on shed that Matt called home.

His friend opened the door before Sam could knock. "You don't look so good."

Sam eyed Matt's old tee shirt and jeans, thinking Matt should talk except he didn't feel like joking. Instead, he pulled out a pine chair and sat at the table where Matt's Bible lay open.

"Someone stole Bud," Sam blurted. Matt sat across from him as Sam told how he'd found out about Russell's truck from Jessie, snooped at the dairy, gone to the cemetery and the Brown Bear. "Why is all this happening to me? Just when I think I can have a life, someone takes it out on Buddy."

Matt ran both hands through his mop of hair and leaned his forearms on the table. "You've been through it, that's for sure. Sorry about Bud. I love that hairy dog, too. Can I pray for him? For you?"

Sam hooked his hat on the back of the chair. "Is that supposed to make me feel better?"

Clasping his hands, Matt shook his head. "Prayer changes things. It works. Not always the way we think, though. Sometimes, instead of situations, we're the ones that get changed."

"I have changed," Sam studied the silver cuff as he gripped his hands on the table edge. "Losing Bud . . . I understand now what I did to Dad and Ranger."

Matt laid a hand on Sam's shoulder. "Tucker hoped you'd love animals like he did someday. Do you know that God sees each bird that falls? He sees Bud."

Sam scraped back his chair. "If you're gonna give another sermon, I'm out of here."

Matt poked Sam's heart with his forefinger. "Listen, Sam. God's thoughts toward you are of peace, and not for evil, to give you a future and a hope."

Sam pulled away. "What makes you so sure?"

"Because of what He's done for me." Matt patted his chest. "Jesus died for us all so we could be forgiven. He can turn what was meant for evil to good. He knows everything about you, how much you care about Bud."

"What about Bud?" Sam grabbed his hat.

"I'll call the prayer chain and ask folks to keep an eye out for him. Someone will hear or see something." Matt followed Sam outside. "Let's check in with each other later, okay?"

Sam nodded as he started his flatbed, flexing his shoulders as he put the truck into gear, a heavy yoke pressing him down. He wanted to make sure Amber was all right so he hurried home, scanning the roadsides for his dog. Maybe like the dogs in movies, Bud found his way home.

At the turn off to Tersis, Sam stopped to unlock the sixteen-foot wide metal pipe gate. He paused and looked around before driving to the barns.

Amberwind's coat glistened like a new penny in the late afternoon sun. As he walked out in the pasture, she ambled over to meet him, swishing her tail and biting flies from her chest. He scratched her jowls and braced himself as she rubbed her face against his shirt. She stomped a foreleg and shook her head. Her mane whipped back and forth; the flies on her neck lifted and settled back.

He'd separate the horses from the cows tomorrow. Most of the flies would stay with the cows. The horses could go in Ranger's old pasture where he could watch them from the house.

There was still time to cut at least one field except Sam couldn't do it. The sun dropped closer to the Cascades off in the distance. Amber grazed, tearing bites of grass. Sam missed his floppy excuse for a ranch dog. What else could he do? Please, let Bud be okay. Please bring him home.

THIRTY

The sky darkened to deep sapphire blue. A bright star shone above the silhouetted Cascades. Sam sat on his heels while Amber grazed a circle around him. The other horses wandered nearby, blowing their noses now and then. He could hear his own heartbeat in the still cool evening.

If Bud were there, he'd be spent from exploring the pasture and would lie at Sam's feet and probably snore. Sam crossed his arms, a blade of grass stuck in his teeth. How could some dumb animal get to him?

Something about the way Bud looked at him, lifting his eyebrows and tweaking his hairy ears forward was so engaging, Sam couldn't believe he even thought of the dog that way. Just rubbing that soft fur made him feel good. One thing for sure: he couldn't keep his mind on the ranch until this thing was finished. Bud depended on him and he let the dog down.

He slowly straightened, wincing as his cramped muscles protested. Perhaps Matt knew something by now. Sam decided to call and ask. He climbed the fence. Halfway through the space between the barn and house a horn honked out on the highway in the distance. Someone whooping and hollering. Faint, but that's what it was. What fool would be racing around on a Sunday night? Russell.

Sam pounded for his truck, yanking the keys from his pocket. He had to catch them. Gravel spun from his duallies as he punched the accelerator. The mile to the road stretched longer than ever. He skidded the flatbed to a stop at the gate, turned off the lights and engine and waited several minutes for them to come by again.

Impatient, he stepped from the cab and strode to the middle of the pavement. Listened. So quiet. His heart beat erratically. Could he be imagining things? Did he hear a whimper? C'mon, Russell, don't chicken out now. Sam paced in front of the truck. He'd just decided to start the diesel so he'd be ready when he heard a soft whine.

Sam pulled his flashlight from the toolbox and aimed the beam along the fence and road. Nothing. The drainage ditches bordering the highway were deep.

"Buddy?" His voice shook.

A weak cry came from the dark. Sam leapt toward the sound and shone his light in the ditch.

Bud lay still on his side, a gash above one ear, his coat matted with gravel and thistles, blinking in the light.

"Bud-boy! My Buddy," Sam cried as he eased into the ditch and bent over his dog. Carefully, he worked his arms around his friend and lifted him. Bud yelped once and licked Sam's face.

Sam scrambled up the bank, hurried to the truck and gently laid Bud on the front seat, covering him with the spare saddle blanket he kept in the cab. Tucker always said Doc Fisher was the best. Sam threw the truck into gear and flew down the highway toward Redmond. As he drove, he kept a hand on Bud.

The sign for the veterinary clinic stood in front of an older well-cared for farmhouse. Sam jumped from the cab and pounded the door.

The porch light blinked on, and a stocky man with mutton-chop sideburns opened the door. "Sam? Sam West?"

"Yeah, Doc; my dog's been hurt. You've got to help him."

The vet peered toward Sam's truck. "My clinic's in the barn. Meet me there."

Sam bolted for the truck, drove it to the barn and parked as the doctor hurried from the house under the yard light. Doc Fisher opened a side door and flipped on lights as Sam carried Bud inside. He laid his dog on a stainless steel table. Doc washed his hands. Bud raised an eyebrow and weakly thumped his tail.

As Sam lifted the blanket, he trembled at the sight of blood smeared in Bud's hair. The dog's side was scraped raw. The gash above his ear still bled. Sam had seen worse accidents with animals. This was different, like he'd been kicked in the ribs.

Doc examined Bud, running his hands over his legs and joints, probing gently. "What happened?"

Sam told how his dog disappeared and what he suspected as the vet gave Bud a couple of shots, clipped the gash area and stitched the wound.

"Hold his head." The vet took a stitch, tied it, cut the suture and took another stitch. "From the way he looks, I'd say he got dumped from a moving vehicle and possibly knocked out. He's hurting but because of possible concussion, I don't want to medicate him."

Sam nodded as Doc finished the stitches. Buddy licked his lips and relaxed with his head cradled in Sam's hands. Next, the vet filled a pan with a benadine solution and cleaned the abrasions. Using tweezers, he picked bits of gravel and thistle from raw flesh, adjusting the overhead light to check his progress.

Doc Fisher glanced at Sam. "Don't worry; he'll be alright, a bit sore for a week or so. He'll heal fast. Keep him clean and quiet."

Bud winced a few times, his eyebrows raising one at a time as he looked from Sam to the vet. Sam stroked Bud's head, shoving down images of what those guys might have done to his dog all that time, choking on the bile that rose in his throat.

Sam reached for his wallet as Doc finished.

"Never mind for now; I'll send you the bill." Doc handed him a small tub of wound dressing. "By the way, I saw your photo in the newspaper. I remember that mare, always thought she'd be special."

"Thanks, Doc. Sorry for bothering you so late." Sam tucked the dressing in his shirt pocket, gathered Bud in his arms and carried him to the truck.

Doc waved as he headed back to his house.

Sam sighed and started the flatbed. What a day. His energy depleted, all he wanted was to get Bud home, comfortable and crawl into bed. Now that he had his dog back, he'd be extra careful. Good thing he heard the noise at the road or Bud would've spent all night in the cold ditch. He could've died. "I'm so sorry Buddy-boy," he said. "I'll never leave you like that again." He stroked the golden's head.

While driving back to Tersis, Sam stewed over reporting the incident to BJ. The dognapping might seem petty to the Deputy, although it'd be another complaint stacked against Russell. B.J. said to keep him advised. Who else could've done any of this? Sam had promised to call Matt. He groaned, thinking how long it'd be before he got to bed.

At the turn off to Tersis, Sam realized he'd left the gate open. He better check the horses. About a quarter mile from the barns, his headlights swept across a pick-up half hidden, parked in the sagebrush. Nerves jittery, he quickly doused his lights, set the brake and ran to the strange truck. The hood felt warm. He strained to hear noises. Nothing. He tried the door; it opened.

Hmm. A cell phone. He punched in Matt's number. Matt must've been asleep. He finally answered. "Listen, Matt. I'm at Tersis. I've got Bud with me. Call the Sheriff. Russell's trapped and I can't wait to pound him good." He wondered how many he'd be up against. By having Matt call nine-one-one, he'd bought a bit more time.

Pulling the latch, he lifted the hood on the big gas engine and popped the plug wires. He grinned as he removed the distributor cap. He gathered the parts and ran to his truck, backing it to a curve where he hid it in a stand of junipers. He locked the cab and headed across the open range with Bud in his arms.

First off, he wanted to find those boys. He should hide Bud in a safe place like a horse stall. Sam shifted Bud in his arms as his dog raised his head and squirmed. "Easy, boy. I'll set you down soon," he whispered.

Sam went to the barns first. No sign of anyone. The horse gate was secure. Bud thrashed; Sam let him down. He held onto Bud's collar and crept around the corrals approaching the house from the rear.

Three figures squatted near his bedroom window. He could barely make them out in the light of the half moon. Bud growled, a deep rumble. Sam covered his dog's nose, trying to figure out what damage the guys planned. A match flared, a torch blazed. They're going to burn down his house!

Bud growled again, straining against his collar. Sam pulled him back. Why didn't he put him away first? Bud jerked his head and backed out of the collar. Roaring, he leapt toward the men.

THIRTY-ONE

As Bud charged the men, Sam grabbed the first thing handy – a softball sized rock and sprinted after his dog. Sam's stomach clenched as a short stocky man turned, cigarette dangling from his lips. Shorty! Of course, Russell's side-kick from high school. He couldn't believe it when Shorty slung a gas can at Bud.

Sam pitched the rock as hard as he could, striking Shorty in the forehead. He crumpled to the ground. The can flew, hitting a heavy man in the chest who swore loudly while gas splashed his shirt and jeans as he stumbled over the can.

Like a slow-motion nightmare in the light of the torches, Sam raced forward. Bud gripped the third man's long sleeved arm, savagely shaking his head as the man tried to pull away.

Someone kicked the can, landing it on the fire.

"Bud, watch it!" Sam yelled and ducked.

A loud blast blew a blinding orange fireball over the heavy man. He whirled, beat himself with his arms and screamed as flames wrapped around his body. The side of the house flickered like a stage set against the dark night.

Sam yelled, "Don't run," and tackled the man as he burnt like a torch. Sam rolled him in the dirt, slapping flames out. As he rose from the smoking body, sirens sounded nearby. He gagged at the sight and smell of charred flesh and singed hair.

Shorty moaned where he lay.

Bud stood nearby, his head high, tail like a plume, staring into the brush.

"Good boy, Bud. Let him be; he won't get far." Although Sam didn't see the third man's face, it had to be Russell in the long sleeves and black vest. The torches intended for his home still blazed on the ground. Sam's hands throbbed with pain.

Buddy gazed at him a moment. He barked and raced toward the vehicles with flashing lights that arrived at the house. Seconds later, he returned followed by BJ, another deputy and Matt.

"Send for an ambulance," BJ ordered. His partner reached for his radio as BJ checked the burnt man. "Douse those torches and get a blanket."

Shorty stirred.

"Sit there and don't move." BJ ordered as Shorty rubbed his head and blinked his eyes. "Okay, Sam. Tell me about it."

Matt covered the burnt man with the blanket the other deputy brought. He turned to Sam. "Your hands!"

Sam knelt beside Bud. His dog's tail wagged as he slurped Sam's face while Sam replayed the day for BJ and rubbed Bud with the back of his hand. Buddy's stitches held. Matt's hand on Sam's shoulder calmed him enough to answer BJ's questions.

BJ's partner cuffed Shorty as the ambulance sped to the scene. EMT's hooked the burnt man to IV's and loaded him into the ambulance. When Sam refused to ride with them to the hospital, one of them dressed and wrapped his hands before driving away.

"BJ, can we finish inside? I need to make Bud comfortable and sit in my chair with a beer." Sam studied Bud's muzzle. "You should check the emergency room to see if anyone comes in needing stitches. That blood on Bud's mouth isn't his."

Thirty-Two

Sam wished for something stronger than beer as he opened the refrigerator with gauze-mittened hands. He gingerly lifted a beer, hoping he had aspirin in the medicine cabinet.

"Got any coffee?" Matt poked around in the cupboards and found a ceramic mug.

"Over there." Sam gestured to a row of canisters on the tiled countertop. Bud followed him to the leather couch and flopped as Sam propped his feet on the coffee table.

BJ stood in the doorway, barking orders as the back-up arrived. "Take Shorty in and have his head looked at on the way to jail. Get a tow truck out to impound that pick-up. Call Larry; I want his dogs here now. Call the hospitals in case someone arrives with a dog bite. Are those torches out yet?"

Sam gulped his beer. Groaning, he laid his head back against the cushion. This would be a long night. Bud raised his head and nudged Sam's hand. Sam automatically rose, filled his dog's water bowl and set it between Bud's paws. The golden dog lapped it dry while lying down.

Matt walked in with a steaming mug of coffee and settled next to Sam. "Before I leave, I'll bring your flatbed over to the barn and check your horses."

Sam sniffed. That coffee smelled so good. "Thanks. For everything."

BJ turned a page in his notebook. "Okay. Here's what I've got. You tell me if I left anything out."

Sam leaned forward, listening to the report while stroking Bud, who quickly feel asleep and snored. If he was lucky, he might get a few hours of sleep himself.

Bullfrogs sang a chorus of "huh, huh, huh" in the irrigation pond at the bottom end of the hay field. Sam wiped sweat from his eyes, swung the mower conditioner in line behind the tractor and set the pin. His hands stung. He wanted to get the grass mowed before unwrapping the gauze. Hopefully, he wouldn't pop his blisters.

He took a horse blanket from the truck and laid it in the shade of a nearby juniper. Sam wanted Bud's scrapes to stay clean. He set a bowl of water beside it. "Okay, Bud. You stay here and keep an eye on me while I cut hay." His dog obeyed, panting heavily, his eyes half closed.

Sam climbed onto the tractor seat and engaged the power take off by pulling the PTO lever. As the machine slowly followed the edge of the field, he twisted to watch the mowed swath of bright green pass through the rollers to come out the chute, forming a perfect fluffy line behind him. Another hot day tomorrow, he'd turn the hay with a tractor-drawn rake in the morning and bale it that evening, anxious to make up for lost time.

While he cut the field, working his way to the center, Sam recounted the recent events. The pick-up he disabled the night before belonged to Shorty, who refused to talk to BJ. Matt called Sam a hero for rescuing the burnt man who lay unconscious in the hospital. Sam shrugged. He'd just reacted to the situation. Russell was missing. Sam couldn't positively identify him as the third man. Who else could it be?

The newly cut grass smelled green and sweet. Sam kept the tractor at a steady pace. What a relief his house wasn't torched. Sam drew a ragged breath. If it had burned, the insurance would barely cover it. The thought of another investigation gave him a chill. No doubt the insurance company would try to pin the arson on him. If he hadn't caught those guys in the act, he could've been thrown back in jail. Leave it to Russell to plan something like that.

Sam glanced toward the juniper to check on Bud. Jessie stood with his dog, waving her hand. He stopped the tractor, disengaged the PTO and hopped down; his blue tee shirt blotched with sweat.

"I brought lunch," she yelled. Even in a sleeveless denim shirt and white shorts, she reminded him of an angel with her curls pinned on top of her head. As he strode closer, he stared at her neck, at the stray ringlets that stuck damply to her skin.

"Lunch?" He sat on the edge of the blanket.

Jessie nodded. "Yep. Hungry?"

Sam smiled. Bud's nose twitched as he rested his head on Sam's thigh.

"First we have to do something about your hands. That gauze is filthy." She knelt before him and pulled her basket close.

Sam raised his hands. They looked ugly enough to kill an appetite. "Sorry; my gloves wouldn't fit over the bandages."

Jessica wrinkled her nose as she used a pair of scissors to cut the wrappings. Her basket held sterile gauze and all kinds of stuff. He felt as helpless as a little kid while she cleaned his blisters, applying more cream, pads and gauze.

His pain eased. "Where'd you learn to do this?"

166

"Carlos. Remember him from church? He plays guitar and he's the EMT that responded to your place last night." She dug out a pair of cotton gloves from her basket. "Wear these for now. They're stretchy. You've got to keep your hands clean."

"Did Carlos tell you what happened? Or Matt?" Sam eased his hands into the gloves.

Jessie put her doctor stuff away and threw the old wraps into a plastic bag. "Don't you listen to the local radio? You're in the news. Soon as I heard, I called Carlos. The story will probably be in today's paper." She opened a small cooler. "Plus, Matt had called me earlier to start the prayer chain after you stopped by his house about Bud." Jessie held out a wrapped sandwich. "Ham okay?"

"Anything you bring is more than okay." Sam took the offered food. "Thanks, Jess. I'm really glad you came." Bud settled against his leg, eyeing the sandwiches. "Matt was here last night. Russ and his gang kidnapped Buddy, threw him out of their truck, and tried to burn down my house."

She gently stroked Bud's face. "Is that how you got beat up? I want to hear all about it."

Sam filled her in on the story between bites of sandwich.

Jessie reached across and rubbed his shoulder. "I'm glad you're both okay now. The Lord answered our prayers; Bud is back."

Sam hung his head, unable to look her in the eyes. "I guess I got what I deserve." He lifted his hands. "But not Buddy. It's all my fault, leaving him in the truck at the bar." The golden wriggled his head into Sam's lap, eyeing their sandwiches. "Jess, I understand now what I did to Dad . . . killing Ranger, his favorite horse. I'll never forgive myself or blame him if he didn't either." He shut his eyes, keeping back tears.

Jessie's voice was a whisper. "Remember? I know your Dad forgave you. The Lord forgives you, if you'd only believe." She paused. "Sam, thank you for sharing your heart with me."

He looked up. Her eyes glistened. He had to be the luckiest cowboy in the state having Jessica care for him.

Thirty-Three

Sam rose before dawn and as the sun's rays crept over the land he rode Amber with Bud racing beside the copper mare, the two animals flashing gold in the light. He enjoyed the easy rhythm of her lope, the lightness of her hoof beats and the way she arched her neck. He doubted he'd ever get used to the cowboys staring at his Arab. But with the next big cutting show only a month away, Amber needed another practice in public.

If only his Dad were here, to see Amber, to see how well they bonded. Bet he would've got a kick out of Buddy. If only they'd had more time . . . if only he hadn't wasted so much of his life. Sam rubbed the silver cuff.

He slowed the copper mare to a jog at the far pasture and looked over his pregnant cows. Soon he'd have twice as many cattle. He reminded himself to run another ad for the few Arabs left. Bud's stitches could come out anytime. Peach-fuzz hairs already filled the scrapes on his shoulder and ribs.

By the time Sam reached the barn, the dew dried. He drove the tractor and raked the hay fields. Buddy lay in his spot under the juniper tree and watched. The side delivery rake with its wheels of metal fingers flipped rows of hay to dry.

Jessie had been so gentle when she bandaged his scorched hands. Soon as his haying was done, he wanted to spend more time with her. He flexed his gloved fingers. They'd healed fast. The wound dressing he used on Bud worked well on him, too.

He finished raking the first field and stripped off his plaid western shirt. Soon his tee was blotched with sweat. Buddy moved with him from field to field, yawning in the shade or snapping at flies.

Sam's stomach rumbled as he finished the last field. He stopped the tractor, disengaged the rake and called Bud. The golden leapt onto the tractor and sat between Sam's legs for the ride back to the barn. Sam rubbed the golden's ribs. He'd stopped by the vet's on the way back from town a while back so Doc could take out the stitches. Sam couldn't feel any traces of where they'd been now.

Inside his home, he filled Bud's water bowl and fixed a left-over beef sandwich. He'd just grabbed a cold beer as the phone rang.

"Hi Sam, Sierra here. We've been thinking of you; how's everything?"

"Hey, it's all working out. Thank you for all the buyers you sent my way for the Arabs. All but a few have sold." He twisted the cap and took a swig.

"Great! Did the old mares sell?"

Sam pictured Sierra with her long red braid. "Nope . . . turns out my neighbors had always admired them, knew Dad wanted to retire them, so I gave them what Dad wanted: lush pasture and care for the rest of their lives."

"Oh, how perfect. I'm sure Tucker would be glad." She paused. "What about Amberwind? Have you changed your mind about her yet?"

"No way. That copper mare is phenomenal, even if she is an Arab. I never thought I'd say it, but I wish I'd paid more attention to Dad's way of training. Amber is training me, it seems." Sam remembered how his father and Sierra would stand together in the round pen, working horses, Sierra hanging on every word his father spoke, every move he made.

It hit him: he'd been jealous of her. He wanted to impress her back then, wanted her to go out with him so he could be seen with such an exotic woman with her wild hair, and . . . she was just different. Half horse in the best sense.

"That's how it is with Arabs. They do train you. But, if you ever do want to sell, we're first, right?" Sierra's voice sounded bubbly. "Sam?" She said as he hesitated.

"Right." He shifted his weight, set his beer on the counter. "Sierra, I ah, I've never told you how sorry I am for what I did. I've been such a jerk. Besides hurting Dad, you could've been seriously hurt." He cleared his throat. "I'd like us to be friends. I'd like to keep Dad's memory good." Sam waited several heartbeats.

"Yes, that's what Tucker would want. We all need forgiveness. It's a good thing." She sighed. "I've been meaning to thank you for the photo you left in our truck. Every time I see it, I remember something else special about Tucker and Ranger. Thank you."

Sam hung up the phone, picked up his beer, and sat in the office with Bud's head laying on his boot, staring at the photos he'd put up of his father, reminiscing all the endurance rides he'd crewed for Tucker until he graduated high school. He'd gradually made excuses until he quit. Tucker always took time to help out any of the riders, even during competition, answering questions on training and sharing his ways with horses. Sam rubbed his face. If only he could ask his Dad's advice now.

Sam waited until the sun settled low enough to put the fields in shadow before running the baler. The 'L' shaped contraption pulled behind the tractor combed and lifted the hay into a box where a rod packed the bales with a rhythmic clack-thump and spit them out the rear all tied with wire.

Sam drove the tractor at a slow steady pace, entertained by Bud chasing mice from row to row of hay. He lifted his straw hat to let the breeze cool his brow and breathed in the scent of hot grass. He knew the best way to see Jessie again would be in church. Sam wasn't sure what he believed, but he wasn't comfortable there. Could spend time talking to her on the phone except he often baled past midnight.

His thoughts turned to his last conversation with B.J.. An uneasy knot of apprehension coiled itself in his stomach. Larry's hounds had lost the trail at the highway where Russell probably thumbed a ride. Knowing Russell, Sam knew he hadn't seen the last of him.

THIRTY-FOUR

Sam wet his bandana with water from the jug in his truck. He wiped off a mixture of sweat, grime and bits of hay plastered to his face and neck. His long-sleeve western shirt stuck to his shoulders and loose hay from the bales itched his chest. How it ended up all the way down inside his jeans, he never could figure. He heaved another bale onto the flatbed, climbed after it and wrestled it onto the top of the stack.

"What's keeping you?" Matt yelled out the cab window. "The rate you're going, we'll miss the cutting practice."

Sam glanced at the sun still high in the sky. "Quit your whining and drive. I'll get those five bales in the corner and save the rest for tomorrow." He jumped off the truck as it began to move, angled over to the next bale and stabbed it with his hay-hook. When the flatbed crept near, he swung it onto the load.

"You plan to hire some help?" Matt looked ridiculous wearing his baseball cap backward on his head. The cap sported a burgundy Maranatha logo embroidered on tan twill.

Sam knew it had something to do with Matt's faith, but couldn't help asking what the word meant. Matt said it was in the Bible and the translation was, 'our Lord come.'

"You're going to have hundreds of tons of hay. You can't handle each bale yourself," Matt yelled.

"I know already," Sam panted. "Let's get this load to the hay barn. C'mon, Bud." He yanked his pearl-snap shirt open and slapped his straw cowboy hat on his thigh.

Bud crawled out from under the tractor and jogged to the truck, his tongue hanging out the side of his mouth. Poor dog stuck with a fur coat. Sam opened the passenger side door and they both climbed inside.

Matt adjusted the AC on high. "You going to have any energy left to ride?"

"Yeah. A shower will work wonders." Sam shut his mouth and eyes tight as Bud licked the salt from his face. "That's enough, Buddy." He'd loaded near a hundred bales on the flatbed and trailer, and barely dented the field. Bales dotted the field in neat rows and in the field next to that one and in the next several fields. Whatever it cost to have someone with one of those automatic bale loading rigs work his fields would be worth it. Bud nosed his hand. He rubbed the Retriever's ears while trying to avoid dog-breath.

Matt backed the truck to the barn. Tons of fresh smelling green hay already filled the far end. Sam used the tractor with the 'cherry-picker' in place of the loader. With it, he unloaded layer by layer of hay in just a few minutes.

"Why don't you use the shower first." Sam slapped Matt's shoulder as they headed for the house. "I'll start the bar-b-que. You can cook the steaks while I shower."

"Works for me. What time did Jessie say she'd be here?" Matt grabbed a change of clothes from his truck as they strode by it.

"Half-hour. We'll have plenty of time to eat before going with Amber." Sam peeled off his shirt as he strode into the back porch and tossed it into the washer. He lifted a bag of charcoal and tramped back to the front porch. A few minutes later coals burned in the black iron box Tucker built for bar-b-que long ago. Bud sat nearby, nose twitching.

Sam rubbed his silver wrist-cuff, pulled out his harmonica and played a lonesome melody. He wondered if Tucker could see him, would he laugh at him turning farmer. No, his father wouldn't do that. He'd probably say something like, 'be patient; don't give up.'

"Hey, we need you in the church band. That sounds good. When did you learn to play like that?" Matt strolled out the door, hair wet, wearing clean wranglers and a tee. He held a platter of steaks in his hands.

"Prison." Sam tapped his 'mouth organ' and slid it back into its case on his belt.

"Want to talk about it?" Matt set the platter on the grid attached to the bar-b-que.

"Not much to say," Sam said, adjusting the vent on the coals.

"Did they have church there?" Matt sat on the railing. Bud settled at his feet.

Sam laid the meat on the grill. "Yeah, they tried to make me go. Don't get started now, okay? I mean, we all have our own way. Yours isn't the only truth. You've been my best friend all my life, Matt. This church stuff spoils it."

Matt combed his hair with his fingers. "If we all have our own way that seems right, what feels good, then a person could justify anything that he does. Like Russell. For him, terrorizing and destroying are good and acceptable."

Sam smirked. "Get real. Everybody knows right and wrong, good and evil."

Matt rose and placed the lid over the meat. "Exactly. And WHO do you think put that knowledge into everyone's heart?"

Sam headed inside. "Why should I go to church when I've got you around? I've got to shower."

He emerged from the shower a short while later, fresh and cool. As Sam dressed in a banded collar white shirt and clean jeans, he heard Jessie's Land Cruiser. He padded barefoot to the kitchen.

Jessie laughed at something Matt said while arranging plates on the table. She filled out her form-fitting jeans perfectly and bits of lace and ribbon decorated her sleeveless blouse. He could quit worrying about anyone noticing his Arab mare; they'd all be gawking at Jessie. She caught him looking and they stood, just staring at each other.

"I'll go check the steaks," Matt said.

"How do you do that? I've never felt it from anyone before." Jess blushed and reached for the glasses in the cupboard.

"Do what?" Sam leaned against the doorframe.

"It's like you hug me with your eyes." She laid out the silverware as Matt brought the meat, followed closely by Bud.

Jessie set the salad and garlic bread she brought on the table, Sam filled their glasses with lemonade, his with beer.

As they all sat, Matt held out his hands. "Let's thank the Lord for our food, okay?"

Jessie placed her hand in Matt's and grabbed Sam's before he could even blink.

Matt closed his eyes. "Thank you, Jesus for blessing us with great crops and a productive day. Thank you for this food and for my friends. We ask for you to be with us tonight at the cutting practice."

"Amen," Jessie said as she let go of their hands. "Sam, could you pass the salad?"

He handed her the salad bowl. Why would Matt want Jesus to be with them? Go figure. He shrugged it off and enjoyed the way it felt to have friends at his house for a meal . . . they were like family, laughing and ribbing one another; talking about their day.

Shadows lengthened as Sam backed Amber out of the trailer at the arena. Amber's coat reflected the sun like a highly polished copper penny, muscles rippling under her satiny hide.

"She's so beautiful. I've never been close to her before." Jessica touched the mare's face. "Let me help."

Sam handed Jess a brush. She worked over the long mane as Matt lifted the saddle onto the horse's back. "Guess you two have everything under control. I'll go sign in." Sam patted the bed of the truck. Bud leapt onto the platform. "Stay here."

On his way to the covered arena, more rigs arrived. A few horses and riders rode around the ring, warming up. All Quarter Horses except Amber. He made his way to the timer's table, signed on the list and paid the cattle fee.

Back at his rig, Matt bridled Amber and stood holding the reins. Jessie brushed every hair in the copper mare's tail, which touched the ground. The mare pricked her ears forward, almost touching each other at the tips, her large doe-eyes bright and her nostrils flared from her tiny muzzle.

Sam took the reins from Matt and stuck his boot in the stirrup. Suddenly Bud stood at attention, tail and hackles raised. A low snarling growl rumbled from his chest as he gazed at the far end of the arena.

THIRTY-FIVE

Sam handed the reins back to Matt, who refused to take them.

"Don't miss your turn. I'll go check it out," Matt said. "Jessie, why don't you take Bud to the arena. Sit near the doorway so you can keep an eye on the rig and keep Bud out of sight under your seat. That okay with you guys?"

Jess snapped Bud's leash to his collar. "Makes sense to me. I'll grab my camera and head on over there."

Sam slowly stuck his foot in the stirrup and swung onto the copper mare. He longed to get his hands on Russell and from Amber's back he strained to see past the trucks and trailers parked in the lot.

"Go on," Matt told Sam. "I can handle this."

Amber half-reared and shook her head. Sam loosened his hold on the reins. Taking a deep breath, he forced himself to relax and lighten his touch. Focusing on the practice, he rode Amber into the arena and joined the group jogging circles. He carried on an unspoken conversation with his horse through the reins, seat and legs. She asked to hurry and gallop; he answered with wait, take it easy.

"Still tryin' to cut with that A-rab, huh? They can go through the motions but never have it bred in them like the Quarter Horse."

Startled from his concentration, Sam jumped, causing Amber to shy sideways. He recognized the cowboy riding the gruella from his last practice.

The cowboy smirked. "See what I mean? Dingie A-rab'll spook at their own shadows."

Sam fought to keep his voice even and quiet. "Amberwind has more 'cow' than you'll see in a lifetime. One thing about Arabs is that they're too smart for most. You show them something once and they never forget. You don't have to bully them into it, either."

"Sounds like a mule to me!" Cowboy snorted. "How 'bout a wager? You willing to prove your mare?"

"How? By seeing which of us has the better 'go?'" Sam studied the gruella. The gelding looked well-bred and all business.

Cowboy rubbed his mustache. "Naw, how would that show if she had the instinct? You could win by pure luck. A hundred dollars says she couldn't do it without a bridle."

Sam didn't hesitate. "What's your name, cowboy?"

"Conner."

"Well, Conner," Sam stuck out his hand. "Wager's on."

Grinning, Conner clasped Sam's hand.

While Sam jogged the copper mare, he watched Conner circulate through the other riders and realized bets were being made. He knew Amber could do it. Would she understand what he wanted? He'd never ridden her without a bit or hackamore.

When the timer called Sam, Conner rode over. "You have a steer picked out?"

"You didn't say anything about having to choose before my go." Sam stepped down and unbuckled the bridle's throatlatch.

"We're willing to raise the bet; say two hundred?" Conner hooked his right leg over his saddle horn. Every rider reined his horse into a row across the arena to watch.

Sam ran his hand down Amber's neck. She rubbed her face against his chest. What to do? He gazed into her wide-set eyes. Tucker always bragged about his intuitive Arabs. Sam decided to trust her and pulled the bridle off, hanging it on the railing. Amber tossed her head, her long forelock falling like a veil over her eyes. Sam straightened it and she winked.

"Alright, girl. Let's show them." Sam mounted. Amber headed toward the herd of cattle. He twisted in the saddle toward Conner. "The white-face is the one."

Sam sat quietly in the saddle, paying attention to the motion of the copper mare beneath him, keeping his eye on the steer he'd chosen. Amber responded to the subtle changes of his seat bones as she edged deep into the herd.

The cows milled around them; the white-face turned their way. Sam touched Amber's neck. Her ears swiveled back to him and forward to the steer. Sam squeezed her. The copper mare locked on.

Bolting, the white-face tried to circle around to rejoin the herd. Amber blocked every move. Dancing lightly on her hooves, she crouched low, spinning back and forth off her haunches. Sam gripped the saddle horn to keep his balance. She never moved so fast. He kept his eyes on the steer. Amber mirrored every move of the whiteface. Sam and Amber became one; fused together with purpose.

The white-face hadn't been worked before him and being fresh showed determination to find a way back to the herd. Amberwind leapt sideways and cut him off, staying with him all the way.

"Time." The announcement rang over the loudspeakers.

Sam sat back. Amber slid to a halt. The white-face bawled as he rejoined the herd. Sam slid off and scratched Amber's favorite spot under her jowls. "You're awesome, Amber," he whispered.

He walked back to Conner with the copper mare right beside him.

Conner held out a wad of bills. "You made me lose a lot of money. Have to admit it was worth it. I still wouldn't trade a good

Quarter Horse for an Arabian; not many of them could do what your mare just did."

Sam tugged off his gloves and folded the bills into his shirt pocket and snapped the flap. "Not all Quarter Horses can cut, either." He lifted his bridle off the rail and hung it over the saddle horn.

Many of the riders reined their horses close to shake Sam's hand and offer congratulations. Amberwind made believers out of the crowd that night.

For the first time, pride welled within as he gazed at his horse, seeing her no longer as the wrong breed but as his partner. From the get-go, she'd chosen him, when she cut the bull that would've run him down. She'd winked at him then as she did this evening. Awed that she understood him, he kept a hand on her crest as they slowly left the arena.

Another thing Tucker used to say all the time came back to mind: 'you don't sell your friends.' "Amber," he whispered, "I'll never get rid of you. You've been a better friend to me than I've been to you. I'll make it up, I promise." His eyes misted and he roughly rubbed them. How could these non-cowboy animals, Bud and Amber fill his heart with such emotion? They'd changed him, opened to him a new understanding of his father.

Bud and Jess met him as he neared the exit. Bud strained at the end of the leash, grinning and wagging his tail. Sam ruffed Bud's neck. Jess beamed, threw her arms around Sam's neck and hugged him close. The only thing that could make this moment better would be if his father were there.

Matt pounded his back. "Way to go! Let's get out of here. Those 'no-see-ums' are hard on the eyes."

Sam unsaddled Amber at his rig and stepped her into the trailer. He'd rub her down good back at the Tersis.

Jessica fed the mare a carrot through the slats of the trailer. "She's fantastic! I shot over a hundred pictures! I should have something really special for you."

Matt climbed into the driver's seat. "I better drive. Your adrenaline's spiking and I want to make it home in one piece."

Jessie slid to the middle of the seat. Sam put his feet close to the door so Bud could sit on the floorboards and rest his muzzle on Sam's thigh. Sam draped his arm on the back of the seat behind Jess.

Matt waited until turning onto the highway before speaking. "In case you're wondering, I caught a glimpse of Russell leaving the fairgrounds right before your go."

Sam leaned forward, meeting Matt's glance. He'd forgotten in all the excitement. "You're sure?"

Matt shifted gears as they left town. "Yep. He didn't see me. I got a good look at him. I didn't recognize the truck he drove. It's a real beater. Blue, with running lights."

Had Russell followed them there? He checked the side mirror. Sam didn't see anyone behind in the dusk. Russell had plans, no doubt. He tried to sound nonchalant. "So Jess, what's your next project?"

She rummaged through the camera bag on her lap. "Oh, I got a brilliant inspiration tonight. I'm going to photograph cowboys at work on their spreads. Should get interesting shots of silhouettes in the dust, stuff like that. Might see some funky rustic barns and such."

Matt chuckled. "Funky rustic?"

"Yeah." Jessie zipped her bag, leaned forward and patted Bud.

Sam looked over her head at Matt. "You have a cell phone, don't you? Does it work in the in the middle or nowhere?"

Matt lifted an eyebrow. "Uh-huh. It depends on the phone, though. Why?"

"I'm thinking of getting one. Never know when I might get stuck on the back forty. Or hundred." Sam dangled his hand over Jessie's shoulder. "You should have one, too, Jess. Driving like you do way out in the mountains alone."

Matt stared at Sam. "You know what? That makes a lot of sense. I'll write down what kind I use; you two could go cell phone shopping together.

"Well, you're going to make points with my folks. They've been after me to have one," Jessie said. "Let me know when you have the time and we'll make it happen."

"Okay." Sam relaxed, determined not to let thoughts of Russell spoil this evening. Having a connection with Jessie and Matt in case of trouble was smart. If Russell would pick on his trucks, his dog, his house . . . Hey what about not spoiling this time together?

THIRTY-SIX

Sam brushed calf-deep through his alfalfa field trying to balance a forty-foot section of aluminum irrigation pipe. A standpipe with a rainbird made one end heavier than the other as he held the pipe in the middle, both ends flexing up and down with each step. He needed to move sixty sections, hook them together, and turn on the pump to get the water going on the next field.

Buddy followed at Sam's heels, back and forth across the lush green fields. Sam gazed down at the dog's soft brown eyes. "I know you're trying to help; believe me, I wish you could."

The moon hung low on the horizon, a transparent disc fading as the first rays of dawn touched the tips of the Cascades. Sam paused to wipe his face with his bandana. He needed to spread the word for a live-in laborer.

Since Sierra left, the singlewide mobile sat empty. Tucker could've used some help while he'd been in prison. Didn't Tucker want any or couldn't he get it? Sam shrugged. Didn't matter now.

He'd advertise for a solid family man with a couple of strong teen-age sons.

The purse for the championship at the cutting show could be as much as a hundred thousand dollars. That would help upgrade the irrigation system to wheel-lines that automatically crept across the field. And increase his herd of cattle. Sam knew he shouldn't count on it.

His new cell-phone chirped from its clip on his belt; he and Jessica had met in town and bought phones just like Matt's the day after the cutting practice. Buddy sat with his head cocked to the side. Sam flipped the phone open and scratched his dog's ears.

"Want an adventure?" Jessica's voice. "I'm on my way to your place. What're you doing?"

"Moving pipe on the bottom land." Sam sat on his heels so he could rub Bud's belly as the dog rolled onto his back. Jessica's newest photo-op required a horse and another wrangler for a cattle drive. Was he interested? Right now, today?

You bet. Sam replaced the phone and hurried to hook the sections together. Bud's ears flopped up and down as he ran ahead to the pump set at the river. Satisfied that the birds all 'clicked,' spraying water in circles over the alfalfa, Sam jogged to his flatbed and with Bud beside him and drove past the arched sprays of water sparkling in the morning sun.

At the barns, he backed under the fifth-wheel stock trailer and secured the hitch. Jessie arrived and parked her Land Cruiser. She looked great with her jeans tucked into cowboy boots, yellow tee and straw cowboy hat.

He handed her a halter and lead rope. Together they walked to Ranger's pasture where he kept the horses. Amber loped to the gate with the others trailing behind her.

"Which one can I ride?" Jessie rubbed the Quarter Horse mares' neck.

"Not that one; she's pregnant. Not my gelding; he bucks." He squeezed through the rails of the fence and studied the Arabs. "The flea-bitten gray, that's the one. Dad rode her when he wasn't on Ranger."

Jessica slid through the rails and quietly approached the gray. The mare lowered her head to snuff Jessie's hands and halter. "I like her, Sam. She so beautiful, like a white porcelain statue that has a bad case of freckles. And she's shorter, easier to get on and off."

Sam haltered Amber. "Wait here," he said to Jessica. He flipped the halter rope around the gray mare's neck. "Let's see what kind of horse you are." He grabbed a hunk of mane and leapt onto her back. She willingly jogged and cantered with Sam's cues. He swung off beside Jessie. "Freckles is well trained. You're going to enjoy riding her."

They led the horses to the trailer, stepped them in and tied them to the side. Sam went to the tack room, hesitating as he looked over the saddles. He chose Tucker's endurance rig for Jessie. Besides looking comfortable with a sheepskin seat pad, the dee-rings on the saddle would secure her camera gear along with packs to carry snacks. He placed the saddle on a rack below his in the trailer's tack compartment. Jessie loaded her small cooler and other gear.

When he started the diesel, Bud's tail swatted his face. The dog pressed against Jessie's shoulder, begging for an ear rub.

Jessie laughed and patted her lap. "Down, Bud."

Sam drove south on Ninety-Nine to Redmond and turned east on One-Twenty-Six. Almost immediately, open farmlands stretched over gently rolling hills.

"Is the show next week in Burns?" Jessie uncapped her water bottle. "You wouldn't dream of going without me and Matt, right?" She took a swallow and passed it to him.

He sipped the water. Having his friends along would be fun. Being a loner was just that: lonely. Jessie roamed through most of his thoughts these days. How often did she think of him?

"Well? Need more time to decide?" She reached over Bud to slap his arm.

"No! I mean, I want you to come. It's two weeks away." Sam divided his attention between Jess and the road. "I'm trying to figure out how to spend more time with you. We're both so busy."

She smiled, cheeks glowing. "We'd be together a lot more if you joined the church band. We'd have church and lots of practices together."

Sam's gut rolled. "You know how I feel about church." He rubbed his hand on his jeans.

Jessica leaned toward him to lay her hand over his. "Just ask Jesus to show you that He's real." She lifted his hand and traced the scars left by the fire. "His hands are scarred, too."

They blinked past the intersection of Powell Butte. Sam drove in silence. He didn't want to spoil the day with an argument. Jessie lightly stroked his hand and forearm. He loved her touch. His guts stirred again, but in a different way. Reluctantly, he pulled away to shift when they dropped into the throat of a huge crevice where the city of Prineville sat swallowed at the bottom.

Sam clenched his jaw. He didn't want to change anything about his life except having Jessie. He liked being in control of his world. After all, he'd done well pulling the ranch out of debt, getting himself together and being a pretty good guy. He'd even quit chewing.

Something Matt quoted popped into mind. "For what shall it profit a man, if he gain the whole world and lose his soul?" That's heavy. Sam braked for a traffic light.

A horn beeped behind him. The signal changed. Sam eased into gear and glanced at Jess. She rubbed Buddy's ear as the dog sat between them. Did he dare ask if Jesus was real? Did he really want to know?

Thirty-Seven

Sam guided his rig on the main highway past a golf course and down the main street of Prineville, a clean old-fashioned town with diagonal parking at the curb. Large new houses dotted the hillsides on the other end of town. A few miles later, Jessie pointed the turn-off near Ochoco Lake.

Small clouds dotted the sky above the canyon land. Sam checked his mirrors as he geared down to make the turn. Since Matt saw Russell at the arena, Sam stayed alert. Which was another reason why he needed to rent out the mobile home. Someone would always be around to watch the ranch.

"Jessie, I've been thinking about renting out the mobile on the ranch, get some help haying and keeping watch." He glanced at her. "Know anyone? Someone with teenage boys that'll work for rent?"

"I don't, but I bet Matt would. You should call him. I'll let you know if I hear of anyone." She checked the directions she'd written down and pointed at a cattle guard in the fence line.

He drove his rig over a bumpy metal grate and followed the gravel road to the ranch headquarters.

Several barns clustered together and behind them, cattle stirred dust clouds in the holding pens. Sam parked his rig beside a crew-cab pick-up and stock trailer.

Jessie climbed out. "I'll go find the boss."

Sam nodded as he headed to the rear of the trailer. Bud leapt to the flatbed to keep watch. Sam unloaded the mares and tied them to the outside of the trailer. He groomed and saddled the horses as the sun's rays reached the barn roofs. Bud barked as he buckled on his chinks.

Jessie walked toward him accompanied by a silver haired cowboy with black bushy eyebrows. "This is Mr. Lawton; owner of this spread."

Sam clasped the man's hand. "Sam West."

Mr. Lawton rubbed the side of his nose. "Call me Leon. Glad to have the extra help; we have roughly three hundred head to drive into the Ochocos." He did a double take as he glanced toward the horses. "What's that with the spots? Looks like a poor excuse for a pony Appaloosa."

Jessica winked at Sam. "They're Arabians, Leon. These aren't the silly kind, though. That copper mare is a cutter."

Leon slowly shook his head. "Yeah. Right. You two realize that you're on your own. There's no nine-one-one where we're headed."

Sam draped his arm over Jessie's shoulders. "No problem."

Jessie giggled as Leon strode away. "Tucker bred these horses for endurance. I remember him talking about his rides after church. From what he said, our horses will out-last theirs."

Sam turned to the horses. "This ought to be interesting, anyway." As they bridled the mares, Sam's thoughts drifted back, ticking off all the fifty and hundred mile rides Tucker had completed;

winning more than half of them. Sam had grudgingly admired Sierra taking his place to help crew for his Dad. He rubbed the silver cuff.

"Sam? Could you help me?" Jessie struggled with the saddlebags he'd brought for her gear. He buckled them to the dee-rings of the saddle, checked her cinch and helped her mount.

"Bud, you stick close." Sam grabbed the dog's ruff and gently shook Buddy's head. He swung onto Amber and they guided their horses toward the action.

A half-dozen horses and riders stood off to one side of the green metal panels that formed the sorting corrals. A short stocky man hung onto his pinto with one rein while the crazed gelding spun around him, the saddle slipping under its belly. The man cursed as the horse stepped on his hat that fell to the ground.

The riders laughed. One called out, "Hey Shorty, forget to check your cinch?"

Another yelled, "Must be a green-horn! Where'd Leon find him?"

Sam's pulse hammered in his ears.

Jessica nudged Freckles close to Amber. "What is it, Sam?"

He glared at Shorty. "That's one of the losers that tried to torch my home!"

Thirty-Eight

Sam clenched his jaw. What was Shorty doing here? Somehow, sometime today, he'd get the scum alone; beat answers out of Shorty if necessary.

Shorty finally got his horse to stand still. The pinto received a kick in the belly for cooperating as Shorty shoved the saddle back into place, tightened the cinch and climbed onto the gelding.

Sam scowled at the stocky rider. Shorty looked his way, surprise crossing his face before he jerked the pinto around to follow the riders.

Startled by the click-whir of Jessie's motor-wind, Sam turned as she lowered her camera.

"Such an intense macho-cowboy look. I wanted to capture it." She smiled slightly. "You alright?"

"Sure. Shorty's the one with the problem today."

Jessie reached across and touched his arm. "Just be careful, okay? That man gives me the creeps." She straightened. "Guess I'm off, taking pictures. No posing allowed." Freckles responded to her squeeze and jogged toward a low hill nearby.

Sam watched her stop at the top. The sun glinted off her telescopic lens. He moved Amber along with the other hands to get his position assigned, Bud heeling beside the copper mare. Leon stood on the chow wagon and explained the route they'd take and gave orders. Sam would ride the left flank. He felt sorry for those riding drag except Shorty, who grumbled loudly about eating dust all day.

Leon mounted his sorrel stallion. A cowboy opened the stock gate and the drive to the mountains began as the cattle spilled out into the yard, mooing to each other as cowhands flapped their ropes and hats to get them moving in the right direction. Several cows wore leather collars around their necks with large clanging bells.

Tucker had done the same thing when Sam was a kid. They ran a large herd, leased BLM land and drove the cattle on it for summer. The bells helped locate the different groups when they went to check the herd and deliver salt blocks. Later, come round-up time in the fall, they'd bring them all back down to the ranch. Someday, Tersis would have its own drive once again, this time with quality stock.

The ranch fences made the first part of the drive easy; the cattle followed the gravel road. Sam rose in his stirrups, looking for Jessie. He barely made her out at the very end, shooting her camera at the dust-shrouded butts of the herd.

Sam kept his eye on Shorty. The guy could barely keep out of his own way. His rope almost tangled in his pinto's legs and Shorty took it out on the poor animal, which was already lathered. If the pinto made it to the mountains, Sam would reckon with Shorty there.

Bud jogged alongside Amber, keeping one eye on Sam and the other on the herd. "Good dog," Sam told him. The cowboys focused on their work and ignored Sam's Arabian and Retriever, if they noticed them at all.

Leon loped his sorrel out front. His foreman galloped past to open the gate at the ranch's boundary. Out on open range the cattle spread out and the real work began as cowboys kept the herd bunched and headed in the right direction. The herd wanted to stop and graze the dry grass and needed constant urging.

Some wandered off through scrubby junipers. Sam and Amber cut off several before they got too far. Bud got the idea. Although not as efficient as the Border Collies, he tried hard.

Sam saw Jessie all around, changing lens off to one side, later taking photos in front. She dropped back and let the herd surround her, shooting right and left, Freckles doing a great job at staying calm and steady.

They stopped at the river for lunch, allowing the cattle to drink and graze. Sam halted Amber in the shallow water. She lowered her head to drink next to Bud as he laid down in shallow water and lapped noisily. At the chow wagon, Sam helped himself to a sandwich and a drink.

Jessie sat on a log off to the side, talking to a cowgirl, their horses grazing behind them. He didn't notice the girl earlier; she'd blended in with the guys. He intended to join them and changed his mind when Jessie put her hand on the girl's shoulder and they both bowed their heads.

He slid off Amber, sat on his heels and let her graze. Bud shared his sandwich as Sam watched Jessica. The cowgirl looked nice enough. He couldn't get over how Jess shone with that angelic quality of hers. She gave the cowgirl her whole attention. He admired and respected her, for she truly lived her faith, showing kindness to everyone. Jessie wasn't afraid to let her faith show either, for she wore a silver ring with a dove; the symbol of the Holy Spirit she told him.

Guess he had to admit Matt was the same. No one else reached out to him like Matt since he'd returned home. Sam still couldn't get over the change in his friend. No one had been wilder. Dare him and he'd do it. Sam shook his head.

Bud stuck his nose under Sam's hand. He automatically scratched the Retriever's ears and fed him his last bite of sandwich.

Sam rose, stretched and tightened Amber's girth, which he had loosened at lunch. Mounting, he joined the other hands pushing the cattle in the water to splash belly deep through the river, Bud swimming off to the side.

The trail climbed. They all kept after the herd and chased runaways.

By the time they reached the higher elevations, the sun cast long shadows through tall ponderosa pines that ringed meadow after meadow of lush green grass with patches of purple and yellow wildflowers. All the elk and deer that roamed the mountains couldn't put a dent in the feed.

Sam halted Amber along with the other riders as the herd buried their noses in the rich smorgasbord of grasses, their tails swishing, softly lowing in contentment. He searched for Jessica and found her standing next to Leon, holding Freckle's reins in one hand, talking on her new cell phone. Where was Shorty?

Panting, Bud laid next to the copper mare as she grazed. Sam figured it was a good time to go water a tree and walked a discreet distance into some dense ponderosas. He'd barely finished when a heavy pine limb crashed into his shoulders, knocking him down. He rolled, caught Shorty's boot as he raised it to stomp on him and pulled the man off balance. They rose and faced off, glaring at one another. Anger that smoldered flared.

"What are you doing out of jail?" Sam didn't wait for an answer. He swung and his fist connected to Shorty's jaw. Shorty landed one in Sam's ribs. Sam broke Shorty's nose. They grappled, breathing heavily. Sam punched another blow to Shorty's jaw. Shorty stumbled backwards, blood smeared over his face.

Sam gladly imagined how Shorty's nose would look later. He grabbed Shorty's shirt front, jerked him forward and spun him around, shoving him toward the group of cowboys. His shoulders ached as he rotated them.

Leon stood examining the pinto. He turned as Shorty snarled at Sam, "Git your hands off me!"

"You're nothing but trouble. Don't ever set foot on my ranch again." Leon's black brows drew together as he poked a finger hard into Shorty's chest. "Look at this horse. He's pretty near done in. You're going to walk him the last five miles on foot and pay for his vet bill."

The pinto stood on quivering legs with lowered head, dull eyes too tired to graze. What really angered Sam was the fly covered crusted blood on the gelding's flanks where he'd been spurred. The pinto was past caring to swat them with his tail. If Sam had seen the horse before his fight, he would've broken more than Shorty's nose. In his past, he'd used animals as tools. Animals or tools, you took care of them.

"Sam! Sam, are you alright?" Jessie gently touched Sam's shoulder. "What happened?"

No, I'm not alright . . . Ranger had eagerly munched the apples he fed him. Poison apples. What right did he have to judge?

The cowboys shuffled closer. "Just minding my own business when Shorty jumped me." Sam hoped his expression would hold off her questions 'til later as he turned her toward the pinto.

Jessie gasped and shot several pictures.

One of the hands called out. "Mr. Leon, I'll ride behind and make sure Shorty walks that pinto. If he gives any more trouble, I'll truss him with my rope and drag him a while."

"Call the vet; give Shorty the bill," another cowboy hollered.

Sam was sick to his stomach. The dark bay stallion, Ranger, had been his father's favorite, his hope for winning Endurance. And now, Amber was Sam's hope for cutting.

Leon smiled as the cowboys laughed. "That's good, Henry. You do that." He turned to the crowd. "Okay, the herd is settled; time to head home. Ride due west to the forest service road. Follow it to

Highway Twenty-Six. You'll arrive at the Bandit Springs turn off. Our rigs have been shuttled there."

The crowd drifted apart, some grabbing sandwiches from the chuck wagon to eat on the last leg. Cowboys stiffly climbed their saddles for the last leg and slowly rode off in pairs and small groups.

Jessie led Freckles beside Sam as he stumbled toward Amber and Bud.

She grabbed his arm. "What's wrong?"

He couldn't face her, but she needed to realize what he was. "I'm no better than Shorty. I poisoned Ranger."

"Oh Sam," she pulled him around. "There's a difference. You're sorry; he's not."

Sam couldn't speak until he reached his golden dog. His voice sounded ragged. "You really out-did yourself, huh, Bud-boy. Maybe Amber will pack you, too." He gathered the dusty-yellow pile of hair and laid the dog across the saddle. Amber raised her head to sniff Bud. She snorted and finished chewing the grass she held in her mouth.

Jessie rubbed Bud's head. "Sam, I hope you won't be upset. I called BJ a while back."

Sam glanced her way. "Why? What will he do?"

She pulled off her hat and shook out her curls. "There'll be a State cop waiting at the rigs. Shorty's out on bail. He wasn't supposed to leave Deschutes County. This here is Crook County."

She stepped close to him. She'd worked hard, ridden thirty miles and still managed to look great. As she leaned nearer, the color of her eyes deepened. Their lips touched and melted together. His hands circled her waist as her arms slid around his neck. Jessie snuggled against his chest for a moment. Slowly, he drew apart. He didn't deserve her.

She smiled as she swung aboard Freckles.

Sam stepped in the stirrup and settled into the saddle, lifting Bud across his lap.

They let the horses amble as evening stole over the mountains. The gravel road was a bit lighter shade than dark by the time they reached it. The pines spiked a black silhouette against the evening sky and the milky way spun overhead, along with countless other stars.

Jessie sang. He'd missed hearing her voice. She started softly and built the melody, evoking emotions that made him glad for the cover of night. Her song spoke of how the Lord created the heavens and the earth, knew each star by name, knew the number of grains of sand on the shores, knew her and Sam and all of their days before they'd even been born, soothing his aching heart.

Like waking from a pleasant dream, he blinked as they approached the glaring headlights of the rigs parked near the highway. Bud lifted his head and squirmed; Sam stopped Amber and let him down.

Jessie led the horses to Sam's rig while the Trooper asked questions about Shorty and the incident. The stocky man leaned against the patrol car, cuffed, shoulders hunched like a bulldog. When the Trooper asked if Sam wanted to press charges for assault, Shorty spat. "Wait 'til Russell hears about this."

Denise Sager

THIRTY-NINE

By the time Sam parked in front of the barns back at Tersis, Jessie fell asleep with her head on his shoulder and Bud's head in her lap. He hated to disturb either one of them. When he shut off the engine, they both woke.

"Are you okay to drive home?" He asked her.

"Sure. No problem; let me help with the horses first." She followed Bud out the passenger side, the barn area illuminated by the yard light.

Sam met her at the back of the trailer. Together they rubbed down the mares and turned them loose in the pasture. Amber lowered herself and rolled in the moonlight. Bud yawned at their feet. Sam linked hands with Jessie back to the trailer, unloaded her packs and walked her to her Land Cruiser.

"Wait for me to unhitch the trailer, okay? I'll feel better following you home." Sam helped her store her packs in the rear compartment of her Toyota.

"I'm really okay; you don't need to." She opened her door.

"I know," he wrapped her hands in his. "But Shorty's threats make me jumpy."

She squeezed his hands. "Alright."

He opened her door and as she stepped in, he jogged to the trailer and quickly unhitched it. Bud leapt inside the cab as he opened the door and slid behind the wheel. "Good boy. Bet you're tired. We'll be back soon." He fired up his truck and followed Jessie back down the drive, keeping her in his headlights.

Along the way he relived the day. Bud laid his head on his lap. He was so proud of Amber and Bud. The time riding in the dark with Jessie would stay with him forever. It would've been perfect except for Shorty. The dash clock neared eleven. Matt wouldn't mind him calling.

He parked next to Jessica at her cabin, followed her to her door. She unlocked it and turned on lights.

"Everything alright here?" Sam stepped inside the door and looked around.

"Yes. What a great day it was." She rubbed his back. "I know you're concerned about Shorty. But he's only got one phone call from jail and I doubt if it'd be to Russ."

Sam turned and hugged her. "You're right. Let's end with good thoughts. Thank you for today." He kissed her gently.

Jessie kissed him back. "Call me soon. I'll have photos to share with you."

Back at Tersis, Sam fed Buddy and lifted a beer from the fridge. Settled on his couch and tapped Matt's number.

"This better be good," Matt picked up.

Sam relayed the day with Jess and the Shorty episode, drinking his beer while Matt asked questions. Answering most. "So Matt, the reason I'm calling is I want to rent out the mobile here at the ranch to someone with teenage sons who can help with the haying and stock and keep an eye on the ranch. You know anyone that might be interested?"

Matt spoke fast. "Well now. I ran into someone from the church today that might fit what you need. He's a heavy equipment mechanic, military trained; his wife teaches grade school. They have a teenage son who wants to be a cowboy. The home they were renting got sold out from under them, so they need a place quick. Something reasonable so they can save up enough to buy a home."

"When can I meet them?" Sam rubbed his eyes.

"Okay with you if I tell them a bit about you?" Matt hesitated.

"Better they hear it from you than somewhere else," Sam said while tugging off his boots.

"They'll be at church tomorrow," Matt told him.

Sam woke several times through the night. Bud snored, curled up on his bed on the floor. The golden drug his bed everywhere in the house to lay on. Sam reached over and touched his dog. Of all the ways he'd thought to spend more time with Jessica, church was the best option. He felt like a hypocrite. But he knew it'd make both Jessica and Matt happy, so he rose before dawn and checked the irrigation on the hay field, horses, cows and filled water troughs. Back inside he drank coffee and shared donuts with Bud. On the way to church he stopped and locked the driveway gate.

There were more vehicles than ever in the church parking lot. Sam found a spot near the front door in the shade near Jessica's rig. "Wait here, Bud-boy," he said as he shut the door on his truck, leaving the windows open. He found Jessica inside talking to Carlos, the EMT that had dressed his hands at the fire.

"Good to see you," Carlos shook his hand. "Jessie said you play the harmonica; sure hope you'll join the worship team."

"Uh, thanks," Sam said.

Jessie smiled, beautiful in her flower print dress. "You're here," she whispered. "I'm so glad; I wasn't sure when I'd see you again. Come sit up front with me and my folks." She tugged him up the middle aisle.

Her mother leaned toward him. "Thanks to you, she has a cell phone finally. I've wanted her to get one since she's alone so much."

"Yes, mam," he said as Jessie joined Matt on the platform with Carlos.

She picked up her violin as the guys strummed their guitars and sang, the congregation lifted their voices with them. "God is our refuge and strength, a very present help in troubled days." The melody and words washed over him like a soft breeze. The song sounded familiar; like a scripture, a comforting thought although he didn't understand how God would want to help any of them.

Normally, he loved hearing Jessie sing as one song flowed into another, her voice harmonizing with Matt's and Carlos, but Sam worried about Bud waiting in the truck. He wished he'd sat near the back door so he could check on him. Since Bud was taken, he'd been careful not to leave him alone for long. Shorty's threat caused him more anxiety than ever. He wished he'd asked Matt to have this family meet him at the ranch. He shifted his position.

The worship ended and Jessie stepped down to sit between him and her mother.

Matt and Carlos set their guitars in stands; Carlos walked to his seat as Matt stood at his podium and opened his Bible. He looked straight at Sam and then something caught his attention and he grinned.

A ripple of laughter flowed from the back of the church. Sam twisted in his seat along with Jessica to see Buddy smiling at everyone as he entered through the open door and wandered up the center aisle, tail wagging gently.

"Well hello, Bud," Matt said.

Sam stood. Bud's tail wagged so hard it hit his sides as he bounded up front to him. Sam reached for his collar to take him back outside, but Bud laid under the pew and refused to come out.

"I don't think anyone would mind if he stays quiet," Matt said.

"Let him stay," someone called out.

Sam sat down, his neck hot. Slowly he relaxed with Bud nearby.

Jessica reached down and petted the golden. "You two are inseparable," she whispered.

Matt cleared his throat. "We've been studying God's promises through the Bible. Let's take a look at Isaiah sixty-one, verse three. 'To give them beauty for ashes, the oil of joy for mourning, the garment of praise for the spirit of heaviness . . .'"

Sam glanced at Jessica. As Matt spoke, she read the verses in her Bible and wrote notes on the back of the bulletin. He wondered if Tucker had brought his Bible to church. Bud rested his paw on Sam's boot. Sam thought about all the work waiting him at home and wanted to ask Jess about seeing her again.

Matt closed his Bible. "Comfort one another. Rejoice always, in everything give thanks and pray without ceasing."

Everyone stood as Matt strummed his guitar and joined him as he sang, "Great is Thy faithfulness, great is Thy faithfulness, morning by morning . . ."

Sam whispered to Jessica. "I've got to meet someone here that might help out at the ranch in exchange for the mobile. Can I call you later? Maybe we can get together?"

"I'd like that," she said as the service ended. She followed her parents as folks drifted outside to visit in the parking lot.

Matt ambled over. "Hey, the family I told you about is outside."

"I'll be right there as soon as I put Bud back in the truck," Sam said. "Thanks for letting him stay. Let's go, Buddy." He slipped out the side door and after settling his dog back in the cab, found Matt with a strong looking man with dark hair, his petite wife and teen aged son, a younger version of his father.

Matt clapped Sam on the back. "Travis, this is my friend, Sam. He owns the Tersis Ranch I told you about."

"Glad to meet you," Travis said, shaking Sam's hand. "Rachel, my wife and this is Brad, my son. Matt says you're looking to rent a place on your spread."

Matt checked his watch. "Hate to run, but I have an appointment. Sam, let's get in touch later, okay? Hope this works out for you all." He strode toward a young man waiting for him.

"I'll call you," Sam told Matt, then focused on Travis. "Matt's right; I've decided that I could use some help. What kind of work do you do? What kind of time can you give?"

"I work at the heavy equipment repair shop in Redmond," Travis put his arm around Rachel. "But my hours are flexible. I can run and fix anything you have there on your ranch. I had all kinds of experience working farms and ranches before my time in the service." He paused. "Rachel teaches. She's home by early afternoon; Brad is a junior in high school and if anything involves animals, he'll be the first to volunteer."

Sam rested his hands on his hips. "Do you have a horse, Brad?"

"No, sir," Brad glanced at his Dad. "But I can ride with the best and I work hard."

Sam grinned. He liked the young man's attitude. "Well now, sounds good to me but you all had better see the mobile before you get too excited. It's not fancy. Want to come check it out?"

"Sure," Travis said. "Would now be a good time for you?"

"Let's go," Sam pointed to his truck, Bud's head out the window. "That's my flatbed; you can follow me."

"That's the dog in the church," Rachel shaded her eyes with her hand.

"Nice," Brad said as he followed his folks to a nearby pickup.

Sam rubbed Bud's ears and headed out the lot. "Well now, shall we give these folks a try?"

FORTY

When Sam stopped at the gate to unlock it, Travis joined him.

"Do you keep your gate locked all the time?" He eyed the heavy chain.

"How much has Matt told you?" Sam asked. "I only lock it when no one is here. I've had trouble with vandalism. Somebody has me on their don't like list."

Travis nodded. "I've been there. If you're gone in the afternoons, both Rachel and I will need a key; maybe Brad."

Sam rubbed his chin. "I'll have a couple more made; maybe find a place to hide one by the gate. Frankly, it's a pain in the butt having to lock it. Hopefully things will change and we won't need to lock it later," he said as he stepped back inside his truck.

Sam parked at the barns. Travis stopped nearby and they gathered together.

"Before I show you the ranch, let's go look at the mobile. That by itself might make up your mind," Sam told them. He pointed at it, sitting within sight of the house and barns up a short drive. Long ago, he and Tucker had built a metal shed roof over it with a covered porch on the front, back when they could afford ranch hands. Sierra was last to live there; he hadn't been inside for years. He led the way.

"How many horses and cattle do you have?" Brad walked by Sam's side.

"Well, right now I have ten horses and a dozen cattle, although six of the horses are for sale." Sam made a mental note to give Sierra another call about the remaining Arabs.

"Matt said that right now you needed help haying. What kind of equipment do you have, and how much hay are you putting up?" Travis asked as he and Rachel walked behind.

"I have a tractor, mower-conditioner and baler. I'm hoping to find a pull type bale wagon. Right now I'm hand picking with my flatbed." Sam paused. "I'm about a quarter of the way done haying a hundred acres. It's a lot of work."

"Well now; at the machine shop I'm working on one of those wagons; I think the owner is fed up with it. But it'll be in good working order when I'm done with it," Travis said.

"Really? Could you find out how much he'd take for it?" Sam hoped he could afford it. They reached the mobile and stepped onto the porch.

Rachel looked around. "I love this view of the mountains."

Sam opened the front door, stepped inside in shock. Sierra must've repainted the whole thing. Did Tucker know? The walls and ceilings were fresh and clean. She'd removed the carpets and installed pergo flooring. When? He never noticed anything going on when she lived there. The appliances were clean although a layer of dust covered everything. The minimal furnishings were old.

"Well now," Rachel wandered through the dwelling. "We have our own furniture; everything else looks better than I hoped."

"Feel free to use anything here; what you don't want I have a place to donate it," Sam told her.

Brad and Travis checked out the two bedrooms and baths. "Let's see the rest of your ranch and barns, what work you've got here," Travis led the way outside.

Bud and Brad sat behind the cab on flatbed while Sam pointed out the hay fields, river and ranchland to Travis and Rachel.

Back at the barns, Brad leaned on the pasture fence as the horses moseyed over to check him out, the golden sitting nearby.

Sam joined him as Travis and Rachel talked quietly together. "Ever ride a horse that bucks?" He asked Brad. The boy's dark hair was cropped short, like his father's.

"Been on a few," Brad gazed at the horses.

"If your folks decide to move here, that buckskin will be yours to ride when we check on the cattle," Sam told him.

By Brad's grin, Sam knew he'd made some points.

Travis and Rachel joined them. "We've decided this is a great opportunity and we appreciate your offer. But you haven't said anything about the rent," Travis said.

Sam shook his head. "Sorry; I thought it was understood. Rent for work. You help me and live here free." He held out his hand.

Travis shook it. "Done deal, then."

"Thank you." Rachel leaned against her husband. "When can we move in?"

"Whenever you want." Sam hesitated. "How much time do you need to settle? Do you need help moving? I'll be baling hay this week."

After dinner, Sam left a message on Sierra's phone, letting her know he still had a half dozen horses for sale, hoping he could use the money for a pull behind bale loader or a self-driven one would be even better.

He'd offered to help Travis move into the mobile, but ended up watching that afternoon in amazement as members of Matt's church drove up in flatbeds and pick-ups with the families' belongings and in one day had them moved in. The women had the mobile cleaned and prepared by the time the furniture arrived. All Sam had to do was show where to store the old furniture they didn't need from the mobile.

Sam rubbed the golden's ears as he sat on his couch. "What do you think, Bud? More change for us here." Buddy's tail wagged. "Yeah, it'll be good all around."

Bud's ears lifted and he barked as a knock sounded on the kitchen door.

Sam rose and opened it; Travis. "Come on in," he stepped aside. "Want some coffee?"

"Thanks; we're settling in," Travis joined Sam at the table. "I called work; I can get the morning off if you need help picking up hay."

"You sure? I thought you'd need a few days at least before starting," Sam poured Travis a cup.

Travis wrapped his hands around the coffee mug. "Oh yeah. You have no idea what this means to us. We've been looking for a rental for the last several months and were right down to the wire."

He sipped his coffee. "I'll go to work after lunch, then Brad will help when he gets home from school."

"I appreciate it." Sam watched the golden sniff Travis' work boots. "Don't be a pest, Bud."

Travis patted Bud's head. "No problem. We love dogs; lost ours a couple months ago." He stood. "What time do you start in the morning?"

The sun's rays lit the snowy tips of the Cascades, where snow stayed year round. Sam inhaled the cool sagebrush morning scent as he checked the water tank in the horse pasture. Amber stood out from the other horses with her copper coat as she grazed.

Bud barked. Sam followed the golden toward the truck as Travis waved on his way to meet them. They settled in the truck and Sam headed to the hay fields down by the river.

"What's the plan?" Travis rolled down his window.

"You drive, I'll pick up hay; at the barn I'll toss it down as you stack. Then next load, I'll drive as you pick up hay . . . sound okay to you?" Sam shifted gears downhill, the fields below dotted with hay bales bordered by the river still shaded in the wide canyon. For a load or two, Sam figured.

Travis gazed at him. "All the hay in the barn; you did that all by yourself?"

"Pretty much," Sam patted Bud sitting between them. "Matt drove the truck for me a few times." He pointed at a row of bales on the grass. "Here's where I left off. I'm anxious to get this field done so I can set irrigation lines this evening."

He set the brake and jumped out of the cab, Bud right behind him, and grabbing a pair of hay hooks from the back of the truck, stabbed the nearest bale of hay and swung it onto the flatbed. The golden ran around while he stalked to the other side of the truck and lifted another bale up.

Travis dutifully eased the truck forward as Sam worked. When he had enough bales on the truck, he climbed up and arranged them tightly together up against the cab. Lift, arrange; repeat. When the hay stacked six bales high, he slapped the cab of the truck.

"Come on, Bud," Sam called as he slid inside. His dog leapt in climbed over his lap and sat in the middle. "Let's go unload at the barn."

Travis drove back and backed up to the stacked hay. Sam climbed up on the truck and tossed the hay over to Travis, who stacked the hay onto the existing pile. Sam appreciated how efficiently together they worked, words spoken as needed.

Shortly before eleven, they made three trips. The sun rose high in the sky, their shirts damp with sweat as Travis checked his watch.

"Time for you to get some lunch and ready for work?" Sam slapped dust and bits of hay from his shirt and jeans.

Travis wiped his face with a bandana. "Yep; although work at the machine shop will seem easy after this." He paused. "Brad says he'll be here by three."

"Thanks," Sam told him. "I'll check with you later this evening."

FORTY-ONE

Sam wolfed down a bacon sandwich and drank a beer for lunch. Buddy lapped water from his bowl, and lay panting at Sam's booted foot. "You need to take it easy while I set up the irrigation lines," he fed the golden a bite of sandwich. "Cool off in the river; maybe I'll join you."

He leaned back in his chair, smiling at the memory of his Dad talking to Amber as he combed out the knots in her mane with his fingers. At the time, Sam scoffed at such silliness but he 'got it' now. "Dad, I hope you know how much I miss you," he said and ruffed the golden's ears.

By mid-afternoon, Sam had finished setting up irrigation and turned on the water, spraying huge arches over the field empty of hay to grow another crop. He lingered at the barns afterward about the time he thought Brad would be coming from school; there he was a younger version of his father, carrying his book pack walking the driveway from the road.

"You need to stop by the house and change clothes or eat?" Sam yelled.

"No, I'm ready right now," Brad answered as he angled toward him.

"Okay then, lets head on out." Sam opened the truck door and Bud launched himself inside as Brad climbed in the passenger side, let the golden lick his face then tugged a pair of leather gloves from his pack.

"You ever buck hay before?" Sam asked.

"Yeah, a couple summers ago," Brad said, his head turned toward the horse pasture.

Sam knew the feeling; he'd rather work stock than hay any day. Down at the hay fields, he repeated the hay bucking routine with Brad that he had with Travis earlier. The teen worked equally as hard as his father, impressing Sam with no complaints, few questions and he worked hard.

After moving two loads of hay to the barn, Sam called it good. He'd never get that much done in a day on his own. He parked the truck and caught Brad as he shouldered his pack. "Want to set that down in the barn for now and ride with me to check the water tank in cow pasture?"

"On horseback?" Brad's voice was hopeful.

"That's the plan," Sam said with a wink.

"You bet."

Brad tagged alongside as Sam handed him a halter from the barn and strode to the horse pasture in front of the house that had been Ranger's. What's with today? Sam glanced toward the spot where Tucker's bay stallion was buried. His Dad and horse both coming to mind.

Bud barked at the gate and the horses lifted their heads from grazing. Amber loped to the gate with the rest following behind. Sam slid the halter on the copper mare.

"The buckskin might not want to be caught," he cautioned Brad as the teen quietly approached the biscuit colored gelding with the black mane and tail. Maybe it was curiosity on the buckskin's part, but he allowed Brad to halter him without any trouble.

Sam hoped the horse would behave as he saddled Amber and snuck glances to see how Brad was doing with the gelding. The teen knew what he was doing, his moves quiet and confident as he saddled the horse.

"You know how a humped back feels?" Sam asked as he mounted. "If that horse starts acting up, use one rein and yank him around in a tight circle and repeat if he doesn't settle. Otherwise hold on 'cause he'll buck."

"Okay." Brad stuck his foot in the stirrup and swung into the saddle. The buckskin's ears flipped back.

Amber walked off and the gelding's ears pricked forward as he walked beside her.

"I think he likes you," Sam said. "You should've seen him buck with Matt."

"Really?" Brad patted the buckskin's neck. "Well, I think we'll get along fine."

Sam led the way, avoiding the ranch roads, jogging a trail looping around the long way to the pasture as Bud chased quail off to the side. At the pasture, they filled the large tank, then rode through the bypass gate alongside a cattle guard and found the cattle grazing at the far end of the two hundred acre fence line.

On the way back to the barns, they loped the ranch road, the golden leading the way, Amber tossing her head, their shadows lengthening before them in the early evening sky.

"Now you know two ways to check the cows," Sam told Brad. "Depending on what we're doing, I'll probably send you out on your own."

"Yes, sir," Brad said, sitting easily in the saddle.

Sam looked away; thinking of himself at that age, how he loved working the ranch with Tucker.

Sam and Brad slowed the horses to a walk as they approached the barns. Travis stood beside his truck, a pull behind hay loader hitched behind it.

"Hey, Dad, what's going on?" Brad stepped down.

Sam halted Amber beside the buckskin. Bud sniffed the contraption.

Travis gestured at the loader. "I've got this rig all fixed up and running good so I suggested to my boss that maybe we should try it out and make sure it's going to hold up for whoever buys it." He paused and grinned. "I'd like to see how it works tomorrow."

Sam shook his head. "No kidding?"

FORTY-TWO

Sam stood in the hay barn alongside Travis and Brad, gazing at the baled hay stacked over their heads filling over half the barn. "I can't believe we got it done." He slapped bits of hay from his western long sleeve shirt.

"Are we done now?" Brad asked, lifting his straw cowboy hat and wiping his brow with his sleeve.

"For now. Those fields we're watering? They'll be ready to hay again in a few weeks." He laughed at Brad's expression. "Travis, that hay loader was a life saver; thank you. Think your boss would sell it to me on payments?"

Travis nodded. "I think that was the plan."

Bud rose from his watch post by the barn door and barked as Matt drove up in his truck and greeted him with a wagging tail.

"How's it going?" Matt eyed the stored hay.

"Thanks to Travis and Brad, I'm caught up," Sam told him.

"Everything is working out well," Travis shook hands with Matt. "Rachel likes living on the ranch, says she feels peaceful here."

"And I rode Sam's horse," Brad shook Matt's hand as well.

"How about going inside for a cold drink," Sam ruffed Bud's ear as the golden sat beside him. "I actually have something other than beer or water."

"Thanks for the offer, but Rachel's probably got dinner ready for us." Travis headed for the door with Brad. "See you tomorrow, Sam."

Sam paused in the doorway with Matt and watched father and son walk the road to the mobile, admiring their closeness, regret sitting as a hard cold rock in his soul. Bud nosed his hand.

"Looks like everything is working out for everyone," Matt punched Sam's arm.

"Yeah; better than I imagined." Sam slugged him back. "I wasn't sure how I'd feel with Travis and his family living on the ranch, but we're getting along and they're really helping."

"I'm pretty thirsty," Matt said.

"Let's go inside and talk; that's why you came isn't it?" Sam walked to the house.

Bud edged inside ahead of them and plopped on his bed under the table.

Sam set out a pitcher of lemonade and glasses on the table and looked at the paper Matt unfolded from his pocket. "What's that?"

"Cutting show schedule for this weekend in Madras. What do you think? A warm up for the big show in Burns?" Matt held the flyer out to him.

Sam took it and read the details. "Yeah; saw that." He sat and poured himself a drink.

"Amber could use the practice," Matt held out his glass for Sam to fill.

"And you'd want to come along?" Sam rose, opened the fridge and smiled as Bud's ears lifted. "Hungry?"

"Yes to both questions." Matt ruffed his hair. "Jessica will want to come, too."

Sam slid his cutting saddle on the rack inside the stock trailer and latched the door.

"Got everything you need?" Matt leaned against the trailer.

Sam checked his old friend, who looked like his old self: plaid western shirt, wranglers and cowboy boots. Identical pretty much to Sam's outfit.

Jessica brushed out Amber's thick long tail, humming a song on the other side of Matt. She caught his gaze and smiled. She shone along with his mare with her mane of pale golden curls, jeans and a white blouse in the early morning sun rays. Hoped she didn't expect to keep it clean. He'd already stowed her camera gear. They were ready.

Sam stole a glance at Brad lingering off to the side. The teen had that wistful look on his face that Sam recognized from his own years aching for a chance to ride at the rodeo. "Hey Brad, you'll be the first to know how we did, okay? Meanwhile, you have the most important job of being in charge of the ranch and stock while we're gone."

Brad nodded. "I can do it."

Sam untied Amber from the side of the trailer and led her inside, tied her and shut the rear door. "You have my cell number, right? Any questions you have, give me a call."

"Yes, sir," Brad said, standing tall, a lock of his dark hair falling over his forehead, sweat dampening his tee from moving irrigation pipe at daybreak.

Jessica slid into the driver's side of the flatbed as Sam opened the door. Matt climbed in the passenger side where Bud laid halfway in his lap. Sam waved at Brad as he drove off.

"One of these times, I'm gonna have to cut that kid a break and let him come along," Sam muttered.

"You'll have to trade this rig in for a crew cab." Matt adjusted the golden's position as Jessica laughed. "We all barely fit as it is."

Sam grinned as he glanced at his friends, soaking it all in, anticipating the day ahead. The drive north on Ninety-Seven with the now familiar route over the bridge crossing the deep Crooked River canyon to the low hills surrounding Madras passed quickly, catching each other up on recent events in their lives: Sam having Travis and his family move into the mobile, Jessica's photography book on ranching in Oregon going to the publisher, Matt asking Dawn to marry him.

"What'd she say?" Sam and Jessica asked together.

"Yes!" Matt patted the golden laying over his lap. "We haven't set a date yet."

"Congratulations," Jessica told Matt. "I was wondering when you'd ask. It's been obvious you two were meant for each other."

Sam glanced from the road to Jess. He wanted to ask her to marry him, but didn't feel worthy or ready yet. She caught his gaze and he looked back to the road.

FORTY-THREE

As he entered Madras, Sam forced himself to loosen his grip on the wheel. Riding Amber would always bring stares, but he'd never get over the rush of competition on her.

"Remember the last time we rodeoed together?" Matt reached behind Jessica and nudged Sam.

"How could I forget? We both won our championship buckles. It was awesome." Sam turned onto the ranch road to the arena. "Cutting is another goal come true. Don't you miss rodeo, Matt?"

"A part of me does," Matt replied. "But I'm hoping to win souls now for a different kind of glory."

Sam glanced at Matt. He didn't doubt what his friend said was true. He shook his head, sure that Jessica felt the same way.

He parked his rig outside the arena along with twenty-some others. Time to get his head back on cutting.

Sam saddled Amber as she gazed head up, ears forward toward the arena. Jessie gave her mane and tail a quick brushing as Matt checked the parking area for Russ's blue truck.

Shorty hung out in jail and their side kick that'd been burned lingered in rehab, according to BJ. Small consolation knowing Russ wouldn't let go of a grudge, whatever it was.

"I promise to make it up to you," Sam told Bud as the golden balked being shut in the slant load livestock trailer. It was the safest place for him as he locked the back door.

He mounted Amber, meeting up with Matt and Jessica at the huge covered now familiar arena.

"I've got you signed in," Matt said. Your class will begin after they changed cattle; you're fourth in the open class."

"Good luck; we'll be right here," Jessie added as she climbed the bleacher seats.

Sam nodded as Matt opened the gate for him into the arena's far end where horses were jogging and loping. Amber's ears swiveled back to him and forward as she pranced.

Riding Amber, Sam joined the other contestants warming up their Quarter Horses. Many glanced his way and nodded. He tipped his Stetson and rode relaxed, confident this show would be fair but tough.

Glancing toward the stands, he sighted Matt and Jessica; Matt gave a thumbs up. The first rider was called and Sam paid close attention to which cattle were chosen until his turn.

"Sam West," the announcer called.

He quietly walked Amber past the time line and eased deep into the herd. A bald face cow was the one he wanted; Amber locked on as he cut it from the herd into the middle of the arena and lowered his rein hand.

His copper mare jumped into her dance, mirroring every move of the cow as it tried to return to the herd. Except it only tried twice, gave up and stood there.

Sam lifted his hand and guided Amber back into the herd to cut another cow. The white one; no one had worked it yet so he cut it close to center and dropped his hand as Amber locked on.

The cow was quick; Amber was quicker. Sam gripped his saddle horn and braced his boots in the stirrups as she sprang side to side. The buzzer sounded. He lifted his hand and turned the copper mare back across the time line. A smattering of applause erupted from the crowd.

Sam rubbed Amber's damp neck as he guided her toward the rail near Jessica and Matt and dismounted to watch the rest of the riders have their two and a half minutes.

After the last rider, he mounted his copper mare and joined the other horse and rider pairs to hear the results. His name was called for second place, which he knew was fair since the one cow quit.

The cowboy on the blue roan first place horse picked up his ribbon and rode back to Sam. "You would've gotten first except for the luck of the draw; you have a great horse there. Do us a favor, huh? Go play with your own crowd."

"Uh, thanks," Sam replied. What was he talking about?

Matt slapped him on his back as he dismounted. Jessica hugged him, a wide smile on her face.

Once they turned onto the highway south, Jessica said, "Guess what I found out? There's cutting shows just for Arabians!"

"Huh?" Sam and Matt said together.

Jessica laughed. "Duh; we need to look up the Arabian Cutting Horse Association. The woman sitting next to me in the arena said she's heard of it."

Sam shook his head. "Are you kidding me?"

"Do you know what this means?" Matt raised his voice. "You can breed Amber and raise Arabian cutting horses as well."

"I'll have to look into that." The notion of splitting off his plans into both breeds overwhelmed him at this point.

Forty-Four

Sam tied Amberwind to the side of the stock trailer, lifted the hose and squirted her with water. She pulled back on the rope, turned a wild eye his way and pinned her ears back. Her pinched nostrils showed Sam what she thought of her bath.

The copper mare swatted Sam's Stetson off his head with her wet tail as he bent for the shampoo. He glared at her. "Look; I know this is a bit la-te-da but I don't want to be embarrassed by a dirty horse in that slick show crowd."

Bud pulled on the hose. "You're next," Sam tugged the hose back and laughed as his dog hid in the trailer. All Sam could think about besides the cutting show was kissing Jessica at Bandit Springs. In spite of all his mistakes, she still wanted to be with him.

Amber shook gobs of soap all over him. Oh brother, how much of that stuff did he use? "Sorry girl," he muttered as he held the hose on her and wiped the suds with the flat of his hand. The soapy water cascaded over her body, ran down her legs and dripped off her belly. Her tail smacked his backside as he sprayed water over her head.

He turned the faucet off as Matt drove to the barns and parked. Matt stepped from his truck almost identical to Sam in his polo shirt and wranglers. Matt always had good taste.

"Good thing you laid all that gravel this spring." Matt pulled his duffel bag from the bed of his pick-up and stashed it in the tack compartment of the stock trailer. "We'd be up to our knees in mud otherwise. Washed the flatbed and trailer, too? I'm impressed."

Sam used a metal sweat scraper to swipe the excess water off Amber's body, starting behind her head, working down her neck, back and hind end. "Yeah; well no backing out now; sent the entry fee last month."

Matt grabbed a towel and wiped Amber's face. "Bet your stomach is crow-hopping big time thinking of competing against the best in the Northwest."

Sam grunted. "It'll be even worse if we do well. I plan to take her to Red Bluff."

"Just focus on Burns this weekend first." Matt tossed the towel. "You'll do great. Then we'll both have nerves at Red Bluff with Amber cutting against the best on the West Coast."

"Yeah; just like the old rodeo days, right? Grab Buddy; he's next." After wetting the Retriever, Sam carefully applied just a small amount of the shampoo. Bud looked two sizes smaller with all his hair plastered down. After the final rinse, Bud shook himself from head to tail, spraying Sam and Matt. Set free, he ran wildly back and forth, narrowly missing Sam.

Matt wiped his hands on a dry towel. "Have you looked up the Arabian cutting horse info yet?"

"No, first things first. I'm interested, though," Sam gazed toward the road. Hurry up, Jessica.

"You ever hear from BJ what happened to Shorty?" Matt coiled the water hose.

"He's in jail on charges of assault and cruelty to animals." Sam checked the tack compartment, making sure he hadn't forgotten anything for the show. "BJ's sure Shorty knows where Russell is hiding out."

Matt took the rope sitting on the flatbed, made a hitch, and threw it over the hay bales stacked against the back of the cab. "That threat Shorty made bother you?" Matt walked around the truck to tie the other end of the rope.

Sam checked his watch. He'd asked Jessie to be there by eight. "Sure it does. Don't know what crazy stunt Russell will try next." He checked the gravel road leading to the highway again. No dust.

Matt rubbed Bud with the towel. "Only the Lord knows."

Amber's side facing the sun was warm and dry. Sam untied her and turned her the other way. "If only this thing could've been settled before the show. I'd feel a whole lot better. Makes it hard to concentrate." Amber pawed. The sun warmed Sam's back. Eight-thirty. "Did you talk to Jessica this morning?"

Matt checked his watch. "Nope. She wasn't at morning worship. Give her a few more minutes; it's probably a girl-thing."

Sam led Amber into the trailer. He'd bedded it deep with fresh shavings. On long trips, horses will pee in a trailer if they won't get splashed. She shook herself as he tied her. He shut the door and peered at her through the slats. The copper mare pulled some hay from the hay-net hanging in front of her.

He leaned against the flatbed beside Matt. "It isn't like Jess to be late. Especially today with us all heading to the show."

Matt shrugged. "Call her."

Sam reached for his cell phone and punched the buttons. His guts crashed as he recognized Russell's voice.

"About time you called. Your lady-friend here was getting worried you'd forgotten all about her."

Forty-Five

Sam clenched the phone. Matt tapped his shoulder, motioning to the speaker button on the phone. Sam punched it and ground out, "Jessica has nothing to do with us. Let her go."

Russell shouted. "That's right; get riled good. Too bad; you gotta play the game. Unless you want poor Jessie exploring the bottom of the lake."

Sam yelled, "Come fight me, you coward, fair and square!" He cursed, not caring that Matt heard. His pulse thudded in his ears.

Russell's voice went flat. "You have 'til sundown."

Sam stared at the phone as the connection broke. He rubbed his face as Matt laid a hand on his shoulder.

"Russell mentioned a lake and a game. That has to mean something; he's leading you. Think, Sam! We've both known him all his life."

Sam met Matt's gaze, trying to remember everything he'd ever known about Russell. He ticked off their run-ins. No doubt that Russell was behind it all. Why?

Russell's reputation for meanness went way back. Sam paced. Years ago, when they camped as kids during elk season with their dads, Russell would hide and shoot Sam, Matt and their friends with his BB gun. They always stayed at Waldo Lake.

"Waldo Lake!" Sam tried Jessie's number as he hurried to his rig. No answer.

Matt and Bud leaped in the passenger side. "You're right! Remember how mad Mr. Miller was when Russell lost his BB gun? Well, he didn't lose it; I chucked it into the lake one night after he'd fallen asleep."

Sam grinned as he put the flatbed into gear. "Really? You never said a word." He sobered. Jessie must be so scared. He pictured her hog-tied. Where at Waldo? The lake was huge. His guts twisted as bile rose in his throat. If Russell hurt her . . .. "Get a hold of BJ, Matt. Have him meet us there."

While Matt phoned BJ with the details and explanation, Sam kicked away thoughts of how this day was to be so perfect, the three of them off to the show. On Ninety-Seven, he turned south. You have 'til sundown. The road stretched straight before him as he pressed beyond the speed limit.

In Redmond, the traffic lights slowed him. Past city center where the divided road came together again, he sped the ten miles to Bend.

Moments spent with Jess tumbled through his mind like sagebrush in the wind. That night he'd run out of gas, crept to the doors of the church and heard her singing; the connection he'd experienced as she asked, "How do you do that? Hug me with your eyes?" The day she'd surprised him with lunch and bandaged his hands; the way the sun backlit her hair like a halo as they kissed in the Ochoco Mountains . . ..

Matt's voice startled him. "BJ's headed for the horse camp. I called the prayer chain. You gonna turn at Century?"

Sam nodded. Morning traffic slowed to a crawl. He drummed his fingers on the wheel. Hurry! The back way through the mountains required slower driving off pavement, but it would take far too long to take the highway clear down to the Oakridge turn-off on Highway Fifty-eight over the Willamette Pass.

He turned west winding up the two-lane highway into the towering Cascades. The traffic thinned. Conifers thickened. He slowed on the curves, mindful of Amber riding in the stock trailer behind. Near Sunriver, he angled west, climbing higher. On top, the road became gravel as he skirted Crane Prairie Reservoir. Sam turned onto a forest service road with clouds of dust rising behind them.

As far as he knew, this was the only road that cut across the lower part of the Three Sisters Wilderness. Finding Jess seemed so impossible. Somehow, with BJ's resources, they had to locate her.

Sam checked his watch. He slowed in places where cat-work left a washboard surface. Should he have gone the other way? Bud licked his lips and crinkled his brow.

Matt gazed out the window. Sam figured his friend was praying. Too bad Russell hadn't kidnapped Matt instead. Matt could take care of himself. Sam suppressed a grin thinking how Matt would preach to his captor: "the wages of sin is death!" Sam was the one Russell terrorized. If only Russell would've taken him!

Sweat trickled down his ribcage. Would Russell really drown Jessie? The forest opened to a small clearing with wooden corrals. A pond surrounded by rhododendrons lay behind them.

Sam eased through potholes. "Think I'll check the campgrounds first."

Matt stirred. "I had the same thought. Maybe Russell is stupid enough to leave his truck somewhere."

Sam pulled onto pavement. Out in the open, the sun overhead cooked the air. Bud sat and panted. Five miles south, Sam turned at the Shadow Bay boat ramp.

Tall pines and firs gave way to a large parking area where several trucks were parked with their empty boat trailers like metal skeletons lying prone with arms lifted to heaven.

Sam set the parking brake near the dock. He slid out. Bud jumped past and ran to the water's edge to wade and quench his thirst.

Sam strode out on the dock with Matt. They stood at the lower end of the lake which stretched before them like an arrowhead, deep navy blue in the center with turquoise edges, the water so clear each little pebble stood out as if under glass.

From times past, he knew the forest info sign read that the lake's waters went four hundred and fifty feet deep. He shivered at the thought of Jessica lying on the bottom and squinted his eyes. The sun glinted off the water, sending diamonds skipping across the ripples. A few boats floated as indistinguishable dots. A canoe glided along the shore.

"I don't think any of these rigs are Russell's." Matt turned as a State Patrol car stopped near them.

Sam followed Matt to the Trooper.

"Are you Sam West?"

He nodded.

"We have command set at the North Waldo campground; would you proceed there right away?"

Sam leaned an arm against the roof of the car. "Have they found anything yet?"

The Trooper's face shielded by sunglasses revealed nothing. "You'll have to speak to the person in charge."

"Sure." Sam pulled away and whistled for Bud.

A few minutes later, he swung the rig into another similar boat ramp area. The shallow bay held an anchored sailboat. A State Patrol truck backed a boat into the water near the dock.

BJ stood next to his vehicle, radio in hand. Sam stopped his flatbed next to BJ and leaned out the window. "What've you got?"

"We're starting by launching this boat. We'll be questioning all the folks out on the water as well as the campers." He lifted his hand for a moment as he spoke into the radio and removed his sunglasses. "The dog team is on its way; they'll take the lake trail. My helo will be here any minute."

Matt spoke. "That trail is over twenty miles long! It'll take forever for the dogs and men on foot to cover it."

Sam put his rig in gear. "I've got my horse. I can saddle up and check out this end."

BJ put his hand on the hood. "I can't allow that. One person out there to rescue is enough; I don't need two."

Sam's guts coiled. "BJ, Russell said, 'you have 'til sundown.' Can you guarantee you'll find her by then? What are we supposed to do? Just sit here on our rear ends?"

Matt grabbed Sam's arm. "Over there! That old truck with the fog lights! It's the one Russell drove, I'm sure of it! See the trailer? He took out a boat!"

FORTY-SIX

Sam set the brake as Matt jumped from the cab. "You sure that's Russell's truck?"

"Yeah; I got a good look at it." Matt started toward the rig.

BJ grabbed his arm. "Whoa, son. I'll run the plates; have my team check it out." He reached for his radio. "Sam, park your rig over there under the trees. Stay out of the way. I'll keep you informed."

Matt stepped onto the running board and bowed his head. Sam maneuvered his flatbed and trailer. He unloaded Amber and tied her to the shaded side of the trailer. Matt filled a bucket for her from a nearby faucet. Sam didn't have much hope for Matt's prayers. Did BJ really think he'd just sit and wait? How could he? Where would Russell hide Jess?

Bud laid in the shade, nose on his paws. Sam sat next to Matt on the ledge over the tandem wheels of the trailer. BJ and a trooper with a couple of bloodhounds searched Russell's rig.

Matt nudged Sam. "Look there." He nodded toward the boat that'd been launched. The engine idled, tugging the lines that held the

230

boat alongside the dock. A Trooper handed an air tank to a man in the boat wearing a dry suit, the front half of the neoprene folded down at his waist. Another man on the dock in a similar suit checked a pile of gear. "They're ready for anything," Matt said.

A chill snaked down Sam's spine, raising hairs on his arms. "That's good except how many boats are out there? Six or seven? How long will it take to check them? They're all over the lake, we're talking a huge area here."

Matt rubbed his chin. "Way too long. Would Russell make it that easy, though? Just sit out there?"

"Uh-uh. It's got to be a decoy." Sam stood and searched the sky. The muted whop, whop, whop of a helicopter drawing near inspired him. "While they're busy with BJ and the chopper, I'll slip away on Amber. Do me a favor, Matt? Act like I'm still here and keep Bud with you."

Sam didn't wait for an answer. He rushed to the tack compartment for his saddle. Amber pawed as he plopped it on her back and tightened the cinch.

Matt slid Amber's bridle on over her halter and handed Sam the reins. "God is our refuge and strength, a very present help in trouble."

Sam expected something like that. He stepped into the stirrup, swung onto the saddle and held out his hand. Bud's tail thumped Matt's legs as Matt held the Retriever's collar with one hand and grasped Sam's hand with the other.

The helicopter slowly lowered onto the parking lot, blasting air and noise. Dirt and pinecones swirled as Amber spun. Sam let her go. She galloped into the dappled shadows of the forest.

Near the lake's edge, he slowed her to a ground covering trot, rising with the motion like a piston in his saddle. He recognized the lake trail and turned her on it. The copper mare swung her head, glancing behind. Sam twisted. Bud ran at Amber's heels, eyes bright, tail flagged and tongue waving out the side of his muzzle.

Sam stopped Amber, dismounted and felt for Bud's collar. Gone. The dog would slow him down. He couldn't take him back. Too bad he forgot to tighten the collar. After what happened when Russell tried to torch his house, he might've learned.

The helicopter flew across the lake. No one missed him yet. Now what? Russell launched a boat. Most likely, he'd gone across and stashed it along the water's edge. He'd never find it. Sam gently shook Bud by his ruff. "You better mind me and stay out of trouble." He mounted and urged Amber onward at a slow trot, winding through the trees.

Through the years, he'd been over all the trails along the lake. So had Russell. They always camped at the Moss Ridge Cabin when hunting, built in the eighteen hundreds by Sam's great-grandfather. Would Russell take Jessie there?

He checked the time. He could make it around the lake in three hours if he didn't go off on side tracks. You have 'til sundown. Too many trails and too many decisions!

Amber loped the long smooth stretches of path, brushing past ferns and rhododendrons that lined the small ponds to their right. On the left, through the firs and pines, Waldo Lake shimmered. Where the trail climbed, the copper mare took care, stepping over tangled roots and large boulders.

Minute by minute Sam's gut wound tighter than a watch spring. Was he going the right way? If anything happened to Jessica, he'd never forgive himself. The list of things never to be forgiven kept growing. Anger piled heavy in his heart. Why did he always have to feel so helpless? Every time he turned around, something else happened. Why did Russell pick Jessie?

Amber gathered beneath him as she half stepped, half slid down some switchbacks to an old burn. An old forest fire had devoured acres to the water's edge. Naked snags towered over them as heat radiated off barren ground. The faint track of the trail led off through the site. So empty.

BREAKING SAM

Sam lifted his Stetson and wiped sweat with his forearm. He'd tried to fill his life with goals: save the ranch, make it into something fine; win a cutting championship. His heart weighed like an anvil sharp and hard against his ribs.

Amber stopped at a narrow stream to drink, Bud lay in the water, lapping right beside her. Along the edge of the bank, fine hairs of green grass sprouted. New life. With each heartbeat, Jessie's song tapped his heart. "He has healed the broken hearted, opened wide the prison doors . . ."

The copper mare splashed across and lifted her hooves over a log in the trail. Behind, Bud shook water from his coat and ran to catch up.

Sam gazed at the mountains surrounding him. In a prison of a different kind, trapped in circumstances beyond his control, Sam needed hope. A sharp pain filled his heart, as if it'd cracked apart, exposing raw flesh.

Tears sprung to his eyes as he bowed his head. "Okay, I thought I could manage on my own. I didn't need any help from anyone, not even You."

Amberwind halted and flipped her ear back. Bud sat panting with his tail gently wagging, sweeping a clean spot on the path.

"If You're real, Jesus, help me. Come into my heart. I need You. I'm sorry for all the times I failed and hurt the ones I loved . . . for all the times I turned my back on You. Please, Lord, save Jessica." The crack in his heart widened. He broke into sobs with the pain. He surrendered everything, letting it spill out; anger toward Stevens, Russell and himself; disappointments, regrets about his father, Ranger and lost dreams. After what seemed a long time, Sam took a shuddering breath and waited on the One whose scarred hands had stretched out on a cross for him.

For the first time, he didn't worry about what would become of his life. It was out of his hands now. A breath of air lifted Amber's mane as the mare lifted her head and snuffed along with Bud, his muzzle dripping water.

Sam turned his face into the breeze, surprised by the cool sweetness reminding him of spring, a sense of newness beyond understanding, a glimpse of the love his Savior had for him as he sat still on Amber.

In awe of the invisible Presence he felt wrapping arms of comfort and acceptance around him, filling the emptiness within Sam, a comfortable weight calming his heart with peace like a salve.

"Is that really You?" Sam questioned in his mind.

"I have loved you with an everlasting love: therefore with lovingkindness have I drawn you."

Sam shut his eyes. His heart constricted. "What about Jessie? Where is she?"

Bud barked. Amber jumped forward. In spite of his fears of the moment, for the first time he decided to trust the Lord. His thoughts bounced around like tumbleweeds, bittersweet with joy and sorrow combined.

He rode Amber back into the live forest on a loose rein, hands resting on his saddle horn as he talked to the Lord about his dreams of marrying Jessica, having the ranch be a success and having a champion cutting horse. He confessed his faults, how disappointed he was in himself for being so cruel to his father and Ranger and for not being worthy of forgiveness or Jessica.

Everything spilled over now, his thankfulness for forgiveness, for Jessie's patience, Bud's devotion, awesome Amber and a friend like Matt. He pondered over what had just happened and sought guidance for finding Jessica. Sam laughed with the new freedom he experienced within; he was forgiven! He understood now how his father could forgive him. Sam forgave himself; free at last.

The smell of sun warmed cedar brought him to his senses. Before him in the shadow of a mountain ridge of moss covered granite sat the old cedar bark sided cabin. Lichens grew on the shake roof and posts of the covered porch. Sam rode to the step. Bud flopped on the porch as Sam tied Amber to the rail. Inside, everything looked tidy, bare mattresses on the bunks, sink clean, cupboards filled with canned goods and utensils. The woodstove held no ashes.

Sam paused on the porch. He'd been pretty sure that Russell would've come here. He looked over the ground for signs, seeing nothing except Bud's paw prints and Amber's iron shoe prints. He lifted his boot to step off the porch when something glimmered in the duff below.

Sam reached down and picked up a small silver ring with a silhouette of a dove cut from the band. Jessica's ring.

FORTY-SEVEN

Sam squeezed Jessica's ring tight in his fist. Would he ever see her again? "I don't know how to pray," he whispered. "Jesus, please let her be alright. Help me find her." He shoved the ring deep in his jean pocket.

Leading Amber, he slowly searched the edge of the clearing, paying attention to bare spots on ground covered by pine needles. There. He found large boot prints and small treads. Bud sniffed the ground, nosing about and ran down the trail. Sam yelled, "Wait, Bud!" He leaped onto the saddle and Amber sprinted into a gallop. Where'd Bud go? Sam hoped his dog stayed on the trail. He didn't dare call Bud again if he hoped to surprise Russell.

The trail made an abrupt turn. Amber cut tight around a tree trunk and Sam's knee thumped against it. That hurt; he tightened the reins, slowing her down. She pulled against the bit, snorting with each stride.

Sam could hear the creek before he reached it. Under a gloomy canopy of fir boughs, the trail split. Boulders jabbed through the rushing stream like teeth in a trap. Which way did Buddy go? Upstream or down? Thick forest duff cushioned any tracks.

He rubbed his silver cuff. He knew what his father would say. Don't give up. By now, Matt was probably in trouble for helping him sneak away. No doubt, Matt would be praying. Sam would thank him for it later.

A breeze through the trees sighed in harmony with the water splashing over the rocks. The forest held a thousand shades of green. Sam inhaled the scent of mint growing along the bank. Jessie needed help and here he dawdled in this new aliveness. He didn't deserve God's presence.

Amber rubbed her face on her knee. Matt's words from his sermon flowed to mind. "It's a free gift; we can't earn it."

The copper mare lifted her head high, working her nostrils. Her ears cupped forward as she turned upstream. He knew the trail; knew it climbed the rocky mountain at the north end of the lake. He worried about Bud. Where was he?

Amber turned her head and bumped his boot with her muzzle. "Okay; let's go!" Sam patted her withers as she moved out at a trot.

The trail climbed out of the ravine and cut across the shoulder of the mountain. Shadows crept over half the lake below him. You have 'til sundown.

Sam dismounted and wove his horse through some large boulders. The track narrowed as it got steeper. They both scrambled upward.

Bud's barking echoed. "Lord, please protect Bud from Russell. Keep Jessica safe." Back in a dark ravine, Sam mounted Amber and rode her across the stream urging her to jog the switchbacks.

The copper mare dripped sweat by the time they reached the top. The path cut through a rock cliff and leveled out.

Too late, he glimpsed Russell leaping on him from above with the flash of a blade. Amber shied as Sam was slammed from the saddle. He hit the ground hard, grappling with Russell, gritting his teeth as the knife nicked his forearm.

Forty-Eight

Sam rolled with Russell, struggling to get on top. He grunted, "Where's Jessie?"

Russell smirked. "You'll never find her."

Sam gripped harder as Russell twisted his wrist, trying to free his knife hand. "Why? Why pick on us?" His arm burned as blood oozed from his wound.

Russell straddled Sam. "You both gotta pay."

Sam kept his grip on Russell's wrist. "Pay for WHAT?"

Russell clawed Sam's throat. "Miss Goody Two-shoes was too holy to go out with me. I asked real nice, lots of times," he panted. "Made me feel like a jerk in front of my friends. Then you come back and she hangs out with you, jail-bait!"

That was it? Russell's feelings were hurt? Sam's fury lashed out. He flung himself over, pulling Russell with him. He smashed his fist into Russell's gut. His attacker gasped for air. Sam bashed the hand holding the knife against a rock. The blade clattered among the boulders.

239

They scrambled to their feet. Sam swung hard, crunching Russell's nose with his knuckles. Blood spurted. Russell stumbled backward, cracking a dead limb from a pine. Sam moved in as Russell recovered, tripped Sam and delivered two quick punches. Ignoring the pain, Sam pounded back in a blur of anger, the thought of Russell touching Jess spurring him on.

When Russell fell, Sam stood over him, fists poised. Russell moaned and raised his arms for protection. Sam slowly lowered his hands. Russell was a sorry sight with his bloody face, torn shirt and missing buttons from his vest. A wad of leather lacing hung from Russell's pocket. Sam had waited for this moment to tear his old enemy to pieces. Somehow, it didn't feel as good as he'd imagined.

"You're a poor excuse for a human," Sam yelled, kicking dirt at Russell. "What you need is –you need help! You need Jesus!" The words just sprung out; Sam couldn't believe he'd said them.

Russell sat, shaking his head. "You've got to be kidding!"

The roar of the helicopter distracted Sam as it hovered high above them. Russell sprang to his feet, sprinting along the rock wall down the trail for cover.

Amberwind cut him off, teeth bared, her ears flat back. Russell dodged back; the copper mare spun and caught him in one leap. He lunged for the reins. Sam sprang toward the pair. He couldn't let Russell get away on his horse!

Before Russell could catch the rein, Amber struck him on the thigh with her hoof. Russell cursed and howled, clutching his leg.

Sam rubbed Amber's neck. "Good girl." She blew softly in Sam's face, swung her head and snapped at Russell.

Russell leaned against the rock wall, his face ashen. "Your horse broke my leg!"

"Where's Jessie?" She just had to be all right! She couldn't be far. Where's Bud?

Russell rubbed his jaw. "Forget you. If I can't have her, no one will."

Breaking Sam

The helicopter made a tight circle overhead. Sam figured they must be looking for a landing spot. Bud bounded through fir boughs and stood beside Sam, facing Russell with a low rumbling snarl.

"Turn around and put your hands behind your back." Sam braced himself as Amber rubbed her sweaty face on his back.

Russell flinched as Bud snarled. He slowly turned, watching the dog over his shoulder. Sam pulled the leather lace from Russell's pocket and bound his hands. While Russell sputtered about Sam tying the lace too tight and hurting him, Sam pulled Russell's belt loose. "Sit with your back to that tree."

Bud lowered his head, exposing his teeth as he growled, and stepped forward. Russell did as he was told. Using the belt, Sam quickly shoved the end of the leather through Russell's bonds and around the trunk of a young fir, tugging hard to get the end through the buckle.

"Hey Bud-boy," Sam held Bud by his ruff. "Did you find Jessie?" The Golden Retriever barked once, his tail waving. "Where's Jessie? Let's go find her!" Sam released Bud and mounted Amber.

"Don't leave me here," Russell screamed.

Sam ignored him as he rode the copper mare behind the Retriever. Bud's and Amber's coats glowed like honey in the last rays of the sun as they moved out of the forest and climbed the rocky slope. He wouldn't trade either one for any amount of gold.

His skin prickled as a Presence surrounded him. *"See how Bud loves you with unconditional love?"* The Voice spoke within. *"Know how you want the best for him? That's a picture of My love for you."*

Tears blurred Sam's vision as love burst in Sam's heart like fireworks. Not the selfish love of his past. This was strong as steel, permanent and real. He couldn't wait to find Jess and tell her about it. To tell her that he loved her. If anything happened, if she was lost forever, could he stand it? To come this close . . ..

Amber tossed her head. Bud stood near the edge of the cliff. He barked, looked at Sam over his shoulder, then focused on a crevice in the rock. Sam leapt from the saddle. "Jessica?"

FORTY-NINE

Sam crouched over the crevice. Twelve feet down, wedged away from the edge on a narrow ledge, Jessie sat gagged and bound, her tear streaked face turned upwards. Beyond the edge, a hundred feet below, the dark surface of Waldo Lake rippled.

"Jess! I'll get you out; I'll be right there." He sprinted for Amber, grabbed his rope from the saddle, shook it out and tightened the lasso end over the saddle horn. His hands shook as he led Amber closer to the edge. Sam tugged on his gloves and gripped the rope. "I'm coming, Jess." He braced his back against one side, feet on the other and worked halfway down, jumping the rest to land next to Jessie as Bud watched from above.

Sam drew his pocketknife from his jeans and cut her gag. "Jess." Her ocean eyes pooled and he gently kissed them.

"Russell! He's around here somewhere." She pressed her face to his chest.

"Don't worry. He's tied to a tree down the trail. Did he hurt you? Are you alright?" Sam cut the leather laces that bound her wrists and ankles.

"Oh, it hurts; my legs fell asleep." She rubbed her limbs. "You sure he can't get loose?"

"I'm sure." Sam lifted her and hugged her close. "Easy; you're going to be okay now." He combed his fingers through her hair, caressing her curls. Gradually her trembling subsided.

Jessie took a shuddering breath. "Wow; you look like you've been run over by a stampede."

"I'm sure I'll feel trampled later. How's your legs? You ready to get out of here?"

She nodded.

Sam knotted the rope around her waist. "Amber will pull and I'll lift you while you try to climb." He cupped his hands around his mouth and yelled. "Back, Amber! Back up!"

The rope tightened. Sam boosted Jessie as far as he could reach. Slowly she was hauled out as Sam kept encouraging Amber. Bud whined at the top.

Jessie disappeared for a second. She returned to the edge, feeding the rope down to him. He pulled it over his shoulders and climbed with Amber's help.

Bud jumped, resting his paws on Jessica's waist, going crazy licking her face as she bent over him. Sam grinned. He sagged against Amber with relief and coiled his rope. Although the sunlight blinked away behind the mountain they'd be able to ride back to the campground before dark.

Jessie scratched Amber's shoulder. She cried and laughed as the mare stretched out her neck and wiggled her upper lip. "You're all heroes; Bud, Amber and you, Sam. You saved my life."

He reached across the saddle to touch her face. "Let's go." He stepped into the stirrup and settled on the saddle. Jessie grabbed his hand, used the stirrup on her side and with his help sat behind him. She wrapped her arms around him and Sam covered her hands with his.

Bud gave a low woof and jogged down the trail with Amber following. Jessie laid her head on Sam's back. He liked the way it felt as they followed Buddy quietly on the faint trail. *Thank You, Jesus. Jessica is safe. We're all here now.*

Minutes later they reached the place where Sam left Russell. BJ and several troopers were there helping Russell to his feet as he whined. "Some lunatic attacked me and left me here to die."

Sam pointed. "He's a liar. That's Russell Miller. He kidnapped Jessica Rivers, vandalized my ranch and assaulted me." Sam guided Amber close to the group.

"That horse broke my leg; watch out for that mean dog!" Russell turned and spat at Sam. "Hypocrite pole-cat! Got religion for the girl, huh?"

"What's he talking about?" Jessie whispered in Sam's ear. Sam looked over his shoulder. "I told him that as a poor excuse for a human, he needed Jesus."

"You did?"

"Yeah." He squeezed her hands.

"Let's see some ID, mister." One of the deputies checked Russell's pockets. "That fluffy dog couldn't have a mean bone in its body."

Another deputy radioed the helicopter as it returned and hovered nearby.

BJ stood beside Amber. "So much for staying put. I'll be waiting for you back at base for a full report." He reached out to Jessica. "Miss, soon as the helo lands, we can get you out of here and have the medics check you."

"Thank you, but I'll ride down with Sam. I don't ever want to see Russell again. All I need right now is something hot to drink; I'm getting cold," Jessica replied.

"We have coffee." BJ called out, "Jim, grab that thermos and bring it over here."

Sam rubbed Jessie's hands as Russell was handcuffed and listened to radio traffic discussing the pick-up point.

BJ handed Sam the thermos. "Get on out of here."

Overhead the helicopter headed for a landing spot. BJ and the uniformed men followed after it with Russell held firmly between them. Sam stroked Amber's neck as she danced in the rotor-wash. Bud jumped out of her way.

"There's going to be a lot more commotion down at the lake," Sam said guiding the copper mare down the trail.

Jessie clutched the thermos. "I know. I was just thinking about it. I need this ride to calm myself before facing everyone. Mom, Dad, probably TV, too."

"Matt's there. I'll be looking forward to seeing him. I've got some apologizing to do." Sam missed Bud. Where'd he go? He whistled.

Jessie tugged on his shirt. "Look."

Bud bounded through the boulders with Sam's Stetson in his mouth that had been knocked off when Russell jumped him. "Good dog! You're going to sleep well tonight, aren't you?" He reached from the saddle for his hat as Bud stood on his hind legs.

Jessie wrapped her arms around Sam again as Amber picked her way down the steep switchbacks. "Matt will be having a prayer meeting; that'll bring more people."

Sam enjoyed feeling her close and warm against his back as the mountain air cooled, relieved and comforted she felt safe riding back with him.

Bud stood nose twitching in front of Amber. A bull elk raised its head, tilting his massive rack over his back. The power of the animal snapped limbs of trees as he thrust his way through the woods.

"Where's a camera when I need one?" Jessie whispered.

"We'll come back someday." Sam squeezed Jessie's hands clasped around his waist.

The forest settled for the evening. Aside from the squeak of saddle leather, all was quiet. Bud trotted ahead, nose to the ground.

At the fork in the trail by the creek, Sam halted. "Need a break? I'm sure Amber would like a drink. We could have some of that coffee."

"Sounds good." Jessie slid off Amber.

Sam swung down and led the copper mare to the stream. She and Bud drank from the symphony of water cascading over boulders.

Jessie untied her bandana and dipped it into the water, washing her face. Sam crouched and splashed his face and neck, wincing at the puffiness in one cheek. He cleaned the blood from his arm.

Jess dipped her bandana again, wrung it out, and wrapped it around his wound. "That may need a few stitches." She sat on a log with the thermos.

Sam joined her, giving Amber rein so she could graze the grass. Bud lay at their feet. "Are you okay? Want to talk about it?"

Jessie poured coffee into the cap, took a sip and handed the cup to Sam. "Russell grabbed me as I left my house. He threatened me with a knife." She shuddered while rubbing her wrists. "He tied me and shoved me in his truck –he'd hidden it behind the shed. I never heard him."

She glanced at him. "I knew you'd come, after the phone call. I tried to leave you a sign. The worst part, besides all the hiking and being left on the ledge was thinking that you'd blame God if anything happened." She shook her head. "Really, I'm to blame. A while back Russell kept asking me to go out with him. I wasn't very kind; I said some mean things . . . and it's all led to this!"

"No one's to blame. Russell didn't need much of an excuse." Sam set the coffee aside and clasped her hand. "I was so scared of losing you. I did what you said, Jess. I asked Jesus into my heart."

Jess squeezed his hand. "Tell me!"

Amber grazed, flicking her ears in his direction.

"Time was running out. I didn't know where to look for you. Amber and Bud were drinking water in a burned off area." He paused. "It was hard to give in and ask Him for help. I can't begin to describe how it felt to be free . . . forgiven."

Jessie looked angelic; her halo of hair and white-fringed tee glowed with her face against the shadows. "Hallelujah," she whispered.

"I asked Him to help me find you. Russell jumped me as Bud located you."

She reached down, rubbed the Golden's head. "When I saw this face looking down at me, it was such a relief."

Sam leaned over and scratched Bud all over his body as his dog rolled over for more. "Bud, you're awesome. What would I do without you? Good dog." Sam straightened and poured the last of the coffee. They sipped it slowly, sitting side by side.

Jessie snuggled closer as Sam draped an arm around her shoulders and rubbed her arm. Bud rested his chin on Sam's knee. He scratched Bud's ear. His wrist cuff gleamed. "If only my father was still alive. There's so much I want to tell him." Like how I understand now.

Jessie hugged him. "You'll see Tucker again someday. Imagine what a great reunion we'll have."

Sam nodded, unable to speak for the lump in his throat. He imagined Tucker smiling when told about the copper mare's successes.

He rubbed his hand on his Levis, felt the lump in his pocket. Sam stood and dug out Jessie's ring.

"You found it," she cried as he handed it to her.

Yes he had, indeed. He tugged her to her feet. Time to move on. "What would you say if I gave you a ring to wear?"

Her kiss was full of promise. "I'd say yes."

Sam grinned. Bud's tail wagged as the copper mare lifted her head, tugged the rein he held and winked.

2

FIFTY

"**R**eady to go home?" Sam capped the thermos.

Jessie nodded. "My folks must be going crazy." She rose. "The cutting show; we missed it."

"Are you kidding, Jess? There'll be plenty of shows; there's only one you." Sam gathered up the reins, mounted Amber and held out his hand to help Jessie swing up behind him.

Bud wagged his tail, leading the way as shadows deepened under the dense canopy of forest. The trail leveled out through dense Rhododendron. Sam kept a firm hand over Jessie's. She'd been silent for a while. Poor girl must be exhausted; he knew he was past tired.

He glanced upwards, the sky darkened above the towering forest. The end of his old life; tomorrow beginning the new. Thank You, Lord. Thank You for answering my prayers.

A light shone ahead of them on the trail. Bud barked and dashed ahead. Jessie stirred behind Sam.

"Sam! Jessie!" A voice hollered.

"Matt!" Sam yelled. "We're here." Amber jogged toward the light.

Bud stood beside Matt, who shone the flashlight downward at their approach. "Are you alright?"

Sam held onto Jessie as she swung down first. He dismounted and grabbed Matt together with Jessica into a group hug. "We're fine now," he said.

"Thank the Lord," Matt answered. "I know you'll have to repeat the story a dozen times with all the law enforcement and media ahead, but could you cue me in first? I about ran after Buddy when he slipped his collar."

"We'll give you the 'saved' version," Jessie slid her arm around Sam's waist.

Matt grasped Sam's shoulder. "You've found peace?"

Sam nodded, unable to speak for a moment.

Matt wrapped him in a giant bear hug. "Praise the Lord. Welcome to the family!"

Sam thumped Matt on his back. "Thanks . . . thanks for not giving up on me, for praying for me."

He gently wrapped his arm around Jessie's shoulders while she told Matt how Russell grabbed her as she was leaving to meet them; how Russell forced her onto the ledge at the lake.

"Meanwhile, the sun was setting." Sam choked. "I've never felt so desperate and helpless in all my life. I couldn't think." He rubbed his eyes.

Matt nodded, squeezing Sam's shoulder.

"I surrendered. I asked Jesus to forgive me. To help me. He did." Sam paused, scratched Buddy's ears. "Buddy found Jessica while Amber and me dealt with Russell. I think Amber broke Russell's leg."

"Was that before or after Russell cut your arm?" Matt let go of Sam's shoulder to inspect his bandana wrapped wound.

"After," Sam said. "I was pounding him, had him down and beat when for some reason, I just stopped."

Jessie nudged Sam. "He told Russell that he needed Jesus!"

Matt interrupted. "You did?"

Sam looked down. "Yeah; anyway, Amber helped pull Jessie to safety. By the time we rode back to where I left Russell, BJ and LE's from the helo had Russell cuffed."

Matt whistled. "Wow. The helicopter has come and gone; Russell's been arrested and driven to jail. Let's pray before facing the crowd waiting to see you." He knelt down with Jessica and Sam, giving thanks and praise.

Sam wove his fingers with Jessica's as he led the copper mare and walked with Matt toward the campground, Buddy leading the way to generator powered lights.

At the edge of the parking lot, Sam took a deep breath in the shadow of forest, then stepped forward with his friends. Flashbulbs popped from the media. Bud grinned and greeted everyone in sight, wagging his tail and nosing hands. Amber pricked her ears and stood quietly at his side.

Jessica's parents swept forward and hugged her, tears in their eyes.

BJ stepped between the reporters and Jessie. "Okay, folks, you've got your photos. You can get in touch later for interviews." He rested his hands on his hips. "As you can imagine these folks have been through a lot, they're exhausted and we have yet to debrief. An official statement will be announced in the morning."

A low murmer rose from the crowd as they gathered equipment and packed to leave as BJ asked for Sam, Jessie and Matt to meet over at the command trailer.

Jess's folks slowly walked arm and arm with her in the general direction. Sam looked after her for a moment before leading Amber to his rig with Matt and Bud at his side. Sam opened the container of Bud's kibble and filled his bowl, setting it in the cab with his dog. "I bet Bud will sleep all day tomorrow."

Matt unbridled Amber and tied her to the trailer. "I bet we all will sleep long and hard." He unsaddled Amber and stored the gear in the tack compartment. "Although Amber looks like she could do it all over again."

Sam grabbed a rubber curry and quickly groomed his mare, poured grain in her feed bucket and led her inside the trailer to enjoy a much deserved feed.

Matt filled her hay net. "Don't be disappointed if Jessie drives home with her parents, Sam. You know how close her family is."

"Yeah. I know." Sam closed the trailer door after making sure Amber was set for the trip home. "But you're the first to know, Matt. On the way down the mountain, we stopped for coffee. I asked Jessie if she'd wear my ring."

Matt faced him. "Did she say 'yes'?"

Sam grinned.

Matt whacked him on the back. "Congratulations; I'm really happy for you both." He looked upward. "What a day, huh?"

"Yeah. Let's go get it done so we can go home." Sam gestured toward the command trailer where BJ, Jessie and her folks waited for them.

BJ held the door open as they stepped inside. Sam sat next to Jessie at a folding table, Matt on his other side. Jessie's parents, Jim and Jennifer Rivers, sat off to the side against the wall. BJ took a seat across from Sam along with another officer.

"It's getting late. I know you're all anxious to be on your way, but I need to collect your statements." He picked up a pen and a stack of forms. "If you think of anything later, just give me a call. This shouldn't take long. Jessica, let's begin with you."

Sam reached for Jessica's hand under the table, wincing as she once again relived the day, so thankful the Lord allowed him to find her in time.

BJ kept his questions brief as he filled out the forms. "Sam, you're next."

Details from the day replayed as Sam filled BJ in on Russell's threat on Jessica's cell phone that morning, how he and Matt figured out Russell's clues, then using the helicopter landing for cover to ride the trails . . . finding Jessie's ring, Russell's attack and Buddy finding Jessica.

Several minutes later, BJ looked up from the form. "Anything else?"

Sam glanced to his friends by his side to BJ. "I'm so thankful for Jessica and Matt standing with me throughout all this mess with Russell. I'm sure now Russell was responsible for the incident at the Brown Bear, trashing the farm trucks and kidnapping my dog along with everything else." Sam blew out his breath. "I'm really sorry that Matt and especially Jessica got drug into it."

BJ nodded and made note. "Alright. Matt. I understand you're a Pastor?"

Matt answered BJ's questions. Finished, he added, "For the record, we all grew up, went through school together: Sam, Jessica, myself and Russell. We camped together with our parents. Russell's problems go back as far as I can remember."

BJ scooted his chair back. "Russell will have his day in court, but I feel confident that he'll be put away a very long time. Again, feel free to call me anytime for any reason. Drive home safe." He stood by the doorway as one by one, they filed out.

"Sam," BJ held out his hand. "There's something different about you. Whatever it is, it's a good thing."

Sam shook BJ's hand. "I guess you could say I'm a new man. I met the Lord today."

Matt standing behind Sam added, "And the beginning of a new life!"

Jessie and her parents waited for Sam in the parking lot. Jim held out his hand. "Jessica's mother and I can't begin to thank you enough for saving our girl. We're forever indebted to you."

Sam gripped his hand. Folks he'd known most his life. Jim, tall with grey peppering his brown hair.

"Will you join us for dinner soon?" Jennifer touched his arm, an older version of her daughter.

"Just say the day; I'll be there," Sam told her.

Jessica stepped beside Sam. "Mom, Dad, I'll ride home with Sam and Matt. Meet you for breakfast in the morning?"

"Okay, honey," Jennifer hugged Jessie.

"We'll follow you back," Sam clasped Jessica's hand.

Jim curled his arm around Jennifer's waist and walked to their car.

"They'll be watching their mirror," Matt said. "I'll drive; let's get a move on."

Bud burped as Sam opened the cab door. They all laughed and climbed in.

By the time Matt turned left at the Highway, Buddy settled on the floorboards between Sam's boots and Jessica fell asleep with her head on his shoulder with his arm cradling her close.

Matt glanced at Sam. "You feeling okay? I think we're all going to be wiped out tomorrow."

"I'm probably going to slap myself a few times; this whole day already feels like some kind of dream." Sam yawned. "But Matt, when the Lord spoke it was no dream, it was real. You know?"

"I know. It's awesome!" Matt geared down to make the turn north on Hwy. 97, following the car ahead. "One thing you'll find out as you walk with the Lord is that there's certain scriptures that fit us, a life verse. I'm passing this one on to you: 'Not that I have already obtained this or am already perfect, but I press on to make it my own.

Brothers, I do not consider that I have made it my own. But-'" Matt emphasized the words, "'one thing I do: forgetting what lies behind and straining forward to what lies ahead, I press on toward the goal for the prize of the upward call of God in Christ Jesus.'"

"Wait," Sam turned to his friend. "I need to mark that in my father's Bible. Write it down for me, okay?"

"Sure thing," Matt said as he paid attention to the road. "Hope to see you in church this Sunday."

"I'll be there. I have a lot of catching up to do." Sam rubbed his chin lightly on Jessica's head.

FIFTY-ONE

Sam opened his eyes and tried to move his legs to swing out of bed. Something blocked the bedcovers. He rose on his elbow. Buddy stretched and yawned from his comfortable position on the bed before jumping to the floor. "Is this going to become a habit?" Sam slid from the covers. "You deserved it after yesterday, but you have your own bed."

He rubbed his face hard. Smiled. With Bud's tail whacking his legs, Sam started coffee and went outside to check the horses and cattle. Amber nickered and trotted to the pasture fence to touch noses with Buddy. Both golden dog and copper horse looked great after all the miles they'd run as he spent several minutes rubbing their favorite spots.

The sun's rays barely lit the peaks of the Cascades as his cell phone rang. Sam answered it as he walked back to the kitchen. "I haven't even had coffee yet."

"I'm on my second cup," Matt said. "Before you make plans for the day, I wanted to remind you about worship practice this afternoon."

"I'm not comfortable being in front like that. Besides, you don't need me. Worship sounds great." Sam poured a cup of coffee and took a swallow.

"It'll sound better with your harmonica. Besides, don't you want to spend more time with Jessica?" Matt's tone changed.

"Well, you have a point there." Sam opened his fridge and reached for the egg carton. "Not a very worthy reason to join the worship team, though. Thought that should be for the Lord."

"It will be." Matt ended the call.

While frying eggs and toasting bread, Sam decided to call Jessica. Soon reporters would begin calling and they would have to testify in court. Before all that, he wanted a quiet day with her.

He called before eight. "Jessie? Do you have plans for today?"

"No. What's on your mind?" Her voice sounded happy.

Sam imagined her hair curling below her collarbone. "I'd like to take you to Bend for lunch," he paused as Bud's golden nose poked his hand, "and to pick out a ring."

"I'd love that," Jessica said. "I'll need to be back in time for worship practice; can we do that?"

"No sweat 'cause Matt's convinced me join up with you all," Sam touched the harmonica case on his belt.

"You've just made my day." Her voice sang. "I'll be ready after breakfast with Mom and Dad."

"Okay." Sam hunkered down next to Bud and petted him. "Give a call when ready and I'll pick you up."

He slid his breakfast on a plate and sat at the formica table, reliving Jessica's rescue and how the Lord directed his search for her, amazed how Bud and Amber helped.

He compared his home to Jessica's. The siding on his ranch home still needed attention. He gazed out the picture window to the barns and the mobile home where Travis and his family were no doubt having breakfast by now.

Actually, where the mobile sat was the best place for a home: best view of the Cascades, best morning and evening light and a great overlook for the barns.

If Amber and his stock did well maybe he could afford to build a new home and have the old be the ranch hand quarters. The thought inspired him: a new life together with Jessie. No doubt she'd have some great ideas on the planning.

He pictured a two story with dormers with a wrap around covered porch. In the magazines he'd ordered in prison, he'd always admired the floor to ceiling rock walls for the fireplace or woodstove.

Sam shook his head. Get real. One step at a time, learn form his mistakes and never get overwhelmed by debt again.

Sam stood with his arm around Jessica at the best jewelry store in Bend, scrutinizing trays of rings on shelves inside the glass case. "See anything you like?"

The woman at the counter tilted her head. "We have more in back; I'm sure we can find just the right set for you."

Jessica sighed. "With my work as an artist and photographer, I'm not interested in any of these rings with expensive diamonds. I'm afraid I'd lose the stone. Isn't there anything simple that would express our love and faith?"

Pointing her finger toward the back, the woman nodded. "I think I know what you'd like; wait a moment; I'll be right back." She rushed through a doorway.

Sam held her hand. "I want you to be happy with your choice forever."

"Same for you," she squeezed his hand, looking amazing after her ordeal in jeans and a flowery blouse.

The woman returned with two trays and set them in front of Jessica on the counter.

"This one's perfect," Jessie reached for a wide silver band with a gold cross; at the center of the cross a small round ruby was set even in the gold. "May I try it on?"

"That'd be your engagement ring; here's the wedding band that goes with it." She slid a narrow braided gold ring on top of it on Jess's finger. "I think you'll approve of its meaning: it represents the three strand cord in Ecclesiastes of husband, wife and the Lord and how the braided cord is not easily broken."

Jessica held up her hand. "It's beautiful. I love that verse."

"Here's the husband's ring," the woman lifted a masculine dark silver band with the same gold braid circling the center.

"Perfect," Sam and Jessie said together.

Denise Sager

RUNNING WITH HORSES SERIES:

I hope you've enjoyed Sam's story! Read more about Sierra and Casey in the other two novels of the series:

#1 Saving Sierra~

Sierra Rae would sit through a lifetime of Sundays in church if she could have her father, Doug, back. And she would rather ride a horse one hundred miles in one day in the sport of endurance than run her half of Mountain Insurance, the company inherited from her father.

Two Arabian stallions insured through Mountain die: one while Sierra is competing on the horse in endurance for her mentor and boss, horse whisperer Tucker West, and the other, a famous show horse owned by wealthy architect, Ben Brennan.

As Sierra investigates possible connections between the two horses while starting horses under saddle at Ben's farm, her desire leads to love, danger and betrayal on a trail from grief to grace.

#3 Casey's Choice~ Casey McKenna's brother,

Michael, donned his scuba gear and dove off his boat into Hawaiian waters and never surfaced. Seven years later, Casey's perfect life of managing Valley View Farm where she lives training and showing horses is disrupted by a packet from her lawyer containing Michael's death certificate and title to his property followed by a threatening visit by Mr. Yakamoto, who offers her a huge sum for Michael's estate.

Reluctantly leaving southern Oregon for Hawaii, Casey meets and joins her brother's best friend, Navajo Detective Gabriel Wolf and signs up for scuba lessons in order to search for clues left by Michael causing a ripple that builds into waves of danger, adventure and romance . . . where past abuse and present collide.

37754253R00163

Made in the USA
San Bernardino, CA
03 June 2019